On *The Boy in His Winter*

"Brilliant.... *The Boy in His Winter* is a glorious meditation on justice, truth, loyalty, story, and the alchemical effects of love, a reminder of our capacity to be changed by the continuously evolving world 'when it strikes fire against the mind's flint,' and by profoundly moving novels like this."—**NPR**

"[Lock] is one of the most interesting writers out there. This time, he re-imagines Huck Finn's journeys, transporting the iconic character deep into America's past—and future."—***Reader's Digest***

"To call [*The Boy in His Winter*] a work of fiction is to tell only part of the story. This book is as much a treatise on memory and time and the nature of storytelling and our collective national conscience.... Much of it wildly funny and extremely intelligent."—***Star Tribune***

On *American Meteor*

"Sheds brilliant light along the meteoric path of American westward expansion.... [A] pithy, compact beautifully conducted version of the American Dream, from its portrait of the young wounded soldier in the beginning to its powerful rendering of Crazy Horse's prophecy for life on earth at the end."—**NPR**

"[Walt Whitman] hovers over [*American Meteor*], just as Mark Twain's spirit pervaded *The Boy in His Winter*. . . . Like all Mr. Lock's books, this is an ambitious work, where ideas crowd together on the page like desperate men on a battlefield." —**Wall Street Journal**

"*American Meteor* is, at its core, a spiritual treatise that forces its readers to examine their own role in history's unceasing march forward [and] casts new and lyrical light on our nation's violent past."
—*Shelf Awareness for Readers* (**starred review**)

On *The Port-Wine Stain*

"Lock's novel engages not merely with [Edgar Allan Poe and Thomas Dent Mütter] but with decadent fin de siècle art and modernist literature that raised philosophical and moral questions about the metaphysical relations among art, science and human consciousness. The reader is just as spellbound by Lock's story as [his novel's narrator] is by Poe's. . . . Echoes of Wilde's *The Picture of Dorian Gray* and Freud's theory of the uncanny abound in this mesmerizingly twisted, richly layered homage to a pioneer of American Gothic fiction." —**New York Times Book Review**

"As polished as its predecessors, *The Boy in His Winter* and *American Meteor*. . . . An enthralling and believable picture of the descent into madness, told in chillingly beautiful prose that Poe might envy."
—*Library Journal* (**starred review**)

"This chilling and layered story of obsession succeeds both as a moody period piece and as an effective and memorable homage to the works of Edgar Allan Poe."
—*Kirkus Reviews*

On *A Fugitive in Walden Woods*

"*A Fugitive in Walden Woods* manages that special magic of making Thoreau's time in Walden Woods seem fresh and surprising and necessary right now.... This is a patient and perceptive novel, a pleasure to read even as it grapples with issues that affect the United States to this day."
—**Victor LaValle**, author of *The Ballad of Black Tom* and *The Changeling*

"Bold and enlightening.... An important novel that creates a vivid social context for the masterpieces of such writers as Thoreau, Emerson, and Hawthorne and also offers valuable insights about our current conscious and unconscious racism." —**Sena Jeter Naslund**, author of *Ahab's Wife* and *The Fountain of St. James Court; or, Portrait of the Artist as an Old Woman*

"Bursts with intellectual energy, with moral urgency, and with human feeling.... Achieves the alchemy of good fiction through which philosophy takes on all the flaws and ennoblements of real, embodied life." —*Millions*

On *The Wreckage of Eden*

"Perceptive and contemplative.... Bring[s] the 1840–60s to life with shimmering prose."
—*Library Journal* (**starred review**)

"The lively passages of Emily's letters are so evocative of her poetry that it becomes easy to see why Robert finds her so captivating. The book also expands and deepens themes of moral hypocrisy around racism and slavery.... Lyrically written but unafraid of the ugliness of the time, Lock's thought-provoking series continues to impress."
—*Publishers Weekly*

"[A] consistently excellent series.... Lock has an impressive ear for the musicality of language, and his characteristic lush prose brings vitality and poetic authenticity to the dialogue." —*Booklist*

On *Feast Day of the Cannibals*

"Lock does not merely imitate 19th-century prose; he makes it his own, with verbal flourishes worthy of Melville." —*Gay & Lesbian Review*

"This spectacular work will delight and awe readers with Lock's magisterial wordsmithing."
—*Library Journal* (starred review)

"Transfixing.... This historically authentic novel raises potent questions about sexuality during an unsettling era in American history past and is another impressive entry in Lock's dissection of America's past."
—*Publishers Weekly*

AMERICAN
FOLLIES

Other Books in the American Novels Series

Feast Day of the Cannibals

The Wreckage of Eden

A Fugitive in Walden Woods

The Port-Wine Stain

American Meteor

The Boy in His Winter

Also by Norman Lock

Love Among the Particles (stories)

AMERICAN
FOLLIES

Norman Lock

Bellevue Literary Press
New York

First published in the United States in 2020 by
Bellevue Literary Press, New York

For information, contact:
Bellevue Literary Press
90 Broad Street
Suite 2100
New York, NY 10004
www.blpress.org

Library of Congress Cataloging-in-Publication Data
Names: Lock, Norman, 1950– author.
Title: American follies / Norman Lock.
Description: First edition. | New York : Bellevue Literary Press, 2020. | Series: The
American novels
Identifiers: LCCN 2019030396 (print) | LCCN 2019030397 (ebook) | ISBN 9781942658481
(paperback) | ISBN 9781942658498 (ebook)
Subjects: LCSH: United States—Social life and customs—19th century—Fiction. |
United States—History—19th century—Fiction. | GSAFD: Biographical fiction. |
Historical fiction.
Classification: LCC PS3562.O218 A83 2020 (print) | LCC PS3562.O218 (ebook) |
DDC 813/.54—dc23
LC record available at https://lccn.loc.gov/2019030396
LC ebook record available at https://lccn.loc.gov/2019030397

Bellevue Literary Press would like to thank all its generous
donors—individuals and foundations—for their support.

NEW YORK
STATE OF
OPPORTUNITY. | Council on
the Arts   This publication is made possible by the New York
State Council on the Arts with the support of Governor
Andrew M. Cuomo and the New York State Legislature.

NATIONAL
ENDOWMENT for the ARTS
arts.gov   This project is supported in part by an award from
the National Endowment for the Arts.

Book design and composition by Mulberry Tree Press, Inc.

Bellevue Literary Press is committed to ecological stewardship in our book production
practices, working to reduce our impact on the natural environment.

♾ This book is printed on acid-free paper.

Manufactured in the United States of America
First Edition

1 3 5 7 9 8 6 4 2

paperback ISBN: 978-1-942658-48-1

ebook ISBN: 978-1-942658-49-8

To Carol Edwards & Jerome Charyn

Gentlemen, be seated.
We will commence with the overture.

—Mr. Interlocutor to Mr. Tambo and Mr. Bones

Overture

We live in hard and stirring times,
Too sad for mirth, too rough for rhymes.

—Stephen Foster

W<small>HY</small>, D<small>R</small>. G<small>ARMANY</small>, just look at the state of your hands! And you have blood and cigar ash on your coat.

Yellow primroses! Mr. James, you are too kind. And in this rain! For goodness sake, water is dripping from your hat! Put it in the bedpan, please; I have not used it. They say my womb is wandering, but they will not tell me where. Mr. James, please be acquainted with Dr. Garmany, who will be presiding. You have time to buy a ticket, but only just, for he has already called for the overture. Do say you will! I shall be performing a tragic farce on the Sholes & Glidden. My husband, Franklin, you know. He was grateful for the shaving mug you sent him at Christmas—all the way from London, where the queen is in mourning for us all.

The bedsheet is white, the nurse no taller than a girl. Mr. Tambo and Mr. Bones, O, how you shuffle! On, off. Just look at the horses' fancy plumes! Gentlemen, I am dying underneath the heavy odor of chloroform. Black night is falling fast. Franklin, do not let go of my hand!

Cakewalk

. . . how small the sons of Adam are!

—Elizabeth Cady Stanton

Declaration of Sentiments

MRS. LANG'S SECRETARIAL BUREAU had arranged for me
to stay with Susan B. Anthony and Elizabeth Cady Stanton at their boardinghouse in Murray Hill. They were in
New York City to collaborate on the third volume of their
monumental *History of Woman Suffrage*. Miss Anthony had
traveled from her home in Rochester for the purpose, Mrs.
Stanton from hers in Tenafly. They required a stenographer
and typist. I arrived in a hackney driven by an Irishman
with a put-upon expression and a grizzled beard stained by
tobacco juice. As I entered the ladies' sitting room, followed
by the cabman, who had grunted and grumbled up the
stairs with the bulk of my Sholes & Glidden in his arms,
I was struck by its cheerfulness. Aware of their militant
reputation, I had expected to find Spartan quarters devoid
of the follies that often encrust the rooms of elderly ladies.
But my suffragists, as I would come to think of them, did
not scorn a so-called feminine weakness if the indulgence
pleased them. They were as likely to meet an expectation
based on gender as they were to defy it. Had I not been
prejudiced by accounts of their warlike humor published in
the sensational papers of the day, I wouldn't have been surprised by the scent of violets emanating from Mrs. Stanton's

ample bosom or by the Henry Maillard bonbons they nibbled from a plate, as if the two most formidable women of the age were a pair of schoolmistresses whose delight was to needlepoint sentimental mottoes on fine linen for the adornment of walls papered in the color of dried blood. I was glad no such homely artifacts were displayed and that the walls were enlivened by a pattern of tea roses. A Persian carpet lay on the shellacked floor. Strings of glass beads hung from a gasolier, unlighted at that hour, and the walnut cornices were free of the dust that swayed from the ceilings of my own rooms like tiny trapezes. The apartment declared Mrs. Cady Stanton's Dutch ancestry and Miss Anthony's Quaker devotion to cleanliness. (Later, I would be introduced to Miss McGinty, who came on Tuesdays to do the actual cleaning.)

"I presume you're acquainted with our work," said Mrs. Stanton. She was the plump one of the two, whose white hair was dressed in ringlets.

"I am," I said brazenly.

I knew the story, in its outline, of their long, tempestuous life together more than the particulars of their work, which was denounced by clerics as impious and by politicians as contrary to the self-evident truths announced in the Declaration of Independence. At the time, I had no opinion on woman's suffrage. Had I operated a sewing machine in the Garment District instead of a typewriter, I would have been more mindful of the cause to which the two women were devoted. As it was, I considered myself fortunate in having a profession and did not think my situation could be improved by the election of this man or that one, even if I had had a ballot to cast for either. One can find Washington, Jefferson, or Lincoln on a map of the United States, in the names of its towns and streets, but men of their sort are scarce in the seats of government.

"Would you have any reservations about aiding us in our work?" asked Mrs. Stanton.

"I would not—*ahem*." I had let the sentence "hang fire," as Henry James would put it, uncertain as I was of how to address a suffragist who at one time in her long life had worn pants.

"Ellen, would you like a glass of water?" she asked solicitously.

I wondered if I ought to object to the familiarity; she would not have called Mr. James by his Christian name on so short an acquaintance—or, for that matter, a lengthy one.

"Our notoriety does not give you pause?" asked Miss Anthony in a manner I interpreted as a challenge.

The death of my brother-in-law, whose salary earned as one of Herman Melville's underlings in the U.S. Customs Service had been essential to keeping our small household on Maiden Lane afloat, obliged me to overlook the disapproval with which the two women were generally regarded. In truth, I would have kept the accounts for Mrs. Standly's brothel in the Tenderloin until my husband, Franklin, could find employment in the typesetting trade out west, where I planned to join him.

"Not at all, Miss Anthony."

"You may call me Susan," she graciously allowed.

"And you may call me Elizabeth," said the other, inclining her venerable head toward me.

"When would you like me to start?" I was eager to begin; I had a grocer's bill to pay.

"That remains to be seen," said Susan flintily. "You haven't been examined."

"I was given to understand that the matter had already been decided," I said with what I hoped was an air of dignity and not one of indignation, which was slowly mounting in me.

I thought I caught a glint of malice in Susan's eyes as she went on airily. "No doubt you have stenographic and typewriting experience in business correspondence." By the way she had pronounced *business*, I understood that the manufacture of tinware or galoshes could be of little consequence when compared to the "work."

I nodded in the affirmative, suppressing an urge to battery.

Susan continued: "Here, however, the dictation you would be called upon to take—"

"And the manuscripts you would be typewriting," said Elizabeth, "putting in her oar," as Melville might have said.

"From handwritten notes and scribbles on foolscap or the back of butcher paper—"

"Can be daunting."

Having been a long time together, the two were in the habit of collaborating on each other's sentences whenever excitement or agitation caught them up like an outgoing tide.

"Have you had anything to do with— Oh, homilies, for example, or treatises where the style of the prose and the difficulties of the thoughts expressed would've challenged you more than a feather merchant's letter of complaint to the chickens?"

Apropos of her friend's remark, Susan cackled.

"I am sometimes called upon to typewrite manuscripts for Henry James," I said smugly.

"We are suspicious of Mr. James's attitude toward woman's suffrage," retorted Elizabeth.

"We are indeed!" said Susan, her face having become as sharp as her tone.

"However, in that his prose is difficult—"

"At times, tortuous."

"We believe you are qualified."

"But she has not yet given us a demonstration of her skills!" objected Susan.

"That won't be necessary," concluded Elizabeth with the decisiveness of Caesar settling the vexatious question of Gaul.

"Did Mrs. Lang mention that you will be required to stay here?" asked Susan, relaxing her jaw muscles into the faintest of smiles.

"We do not keep regular hours," explained Elizabeth.

"Yes, she did," I replied to the space between the two women, since I was beginning to find it hard to tell them apart in spite of their very different appearances. One was fat and jolly, the other thin and caustic; together, however, they made an impression as disconcerting as the plaster cast of the Siamese twins Chang and Eng in Dr. Mütter's Museum in Philadelphia.

"You will find the situation a pleasant one, I think," said Susan, whose hatchet-shaped face would eventually become endearing. "Elizabeth loves to bake, you know."

"I have an Eccles cake in the oven right now. Do you accept?"

"Yes!" I exclaimed. Now that my heavy machine and I were comfortably installed in a sitting room fragrant with pastry and currants, it would have been a pity to have had to look elsewhere. Besides, I was feeling sleepy; I remember that I yawned in full view of my new employers. Embarrassed, I reaffirmed my joy at finding so happy a situation: "I accept with pleasure!"

Neither woman raised an eyebrow. Consorting for so many years with those in whom ideas produce the greatest excitement would have inured them to the enthusiastic display of a professional typist—or her back teeth.

"Good," they remarked in unison.

"We are pleased," said Elizabeth, who favored the royal *we*. And then she astonished me by asking, "When is the baby expected?"

If I'd been a reader of romance novels or had laced my corset too tightly, I would have required smelling salts. But I was accommodating the baby's need for oxygen by doing without stays. I was slender to begin with, and even then, in the sixth month of my *gravidity* (a word I had recently encountered in one of Mr. James's drafts), only a practiced eye—or a prying one—could have detected the immanent presence of another human being underneath my voluminous skirts.

The two women apparently sensed my surprise and perplexity.

"We've spent our lives mostly among women and have helped many 'unfortunates,'" said Elizabeth meaningfully.

"Are you married, Ellen?" asked Susan bluntly. "It makes no difference to us whether or not you are."

Elizabeth nodded hopefully. "Not in the least!"

What dears! I said to myself. Bless them for their tolerance.

"I am married," I replied. "My husband is in San Francisco, looking for a place on one of the papers."

They received this piece of intelligence glumly.

"Is that so," remarked Susan, disappointment evident on her face and in her voice.

"We can't allow our work to be interrupted," said Elizabeth, having stiffened. The rigor was provided by her own bones and not borrowed from a dead whale's. "You understand, *Mrs.* Finch, that what we do must take priority over other considerations." She had resorted to an ominous formality. "If your husband were to find a position in California and send for you, we would be very much at sixes and sevens."

"Very much so!" said Susan, offering vigorous confirmation of her friend's misgivings.

Sinking into the horsehair sofa, I beheld in my fancy

the scuttling of the household—Franklin's and mine—awash in debt. I watched as our best hope of rescue drifted among the wreckage like a seaborne spar or bobbing hogshead beyond salvage. I had not counted on the women's single-minded ambitiousness. No, the word wrongs them and belittles the devotion with which they pursued the overthrow of a fraternity that deemed women unequal by law and custom and no more deserving of protection than a mule. Their altruism, then.

As if to clarify the importance of their efforts, Elizabeth remarked, "A negro man can be raised to the dignity of a voter if he possess himself of two hundred and fifty dollars; the lunatic can vote in his moments of sanity, and the idiot, too, if he be a male one, and not more than nine-tenths a fool. But women are voiceless and oppressed."

"The Lord will admit a good and virtuous woman into Heaven, although during her life, she was made to wait outside the polling place while her husband cast his vote. By the law of coverture, his vote represented hers regardless of whether or not her opinion was considered in the matter!" said an indignant Susan, who had neither vote nor husband, but had been arrested for violating the sanctity of the polling place.

I knew that the child's welfare and my own could be assured in those delightful rooms kept by a pair of suffragists besotted on the intoxicant of high ideals and, in Elizabeth's case, a pleasing sense of martyrdom. The infant would be nourished, loved, and endued with sympathy for the disadvantaged, whose lot I did not wish to share as I waited for Franklin to send for me.

I began to sob. They leaned forward, not with the pity that conceals self-righteousness or spitefulness, but with genuine compassion.

Elizabeth sat beside me on the sofa and, putting her arm around my shoulder, intoned, "There, there," as if those two words had the power to resolve the disharmonies of the world. I let my head rest against her bosom and sneezed when particles of her violet sachet entered my nostrils.

"Tell us what's troubling you, child," encouraged Susan from across the room.

"I have no husband!" I cried, but the words were muffled by a snowy expanse of muslin.

"What's that you said, Ellen?" asked Susan, whose withered breasts had never felt the greedy mouths of infants or of men.

I turned my head toward her. "I'm not married!"

"Ah, I thought as much!" she gasped.

"Wonderful!" The word had escaped Elizabeth's lips before she could purse them.

"Please don't send me to the Home for Magdalens!"

"We would sooner send you to the Tombs!" vowed Susan.

"Or to the river, along with a stone to tie around your waist!" cried Elizabeth, the more theatrical of the two.

"You're a skillful Sholes and Glidden operator, not a laundress," said Susan, alluding to the fate of unwed Magdalens who did not throw themselves into the river.

"I have no idea how I'll manage," I said ruefully. Oh, I was shameless!

"You will manage perfectly well with us!" replied Elizabeth, and in her resoluteness, I glimpsed the young firebrand who had omitted the words *and obey* from her marriage vow and affirmed our sex's equality in the Declaration of Sentiments proclaimed at the Seneca Falls convention: "We hold these truths to be self-evident: that all men *and women* are created equal . . ."

"When your time comes, you won't find us wanting in either compassion or skill," she said, or maybe it was Susan who did. I'd begun to weep in earnest, picturing myself left to face poverty and shame on my own. On the other side of the continent, Franklin seemed a figment of a dream.

"Elizabeth brought seven children into the world and can be trusted to know what to do!" said Susan as confidently as if she herself had suffered a woman's agony and, according to men, her purpose.

"An excellent midwife in sympathy with our movement lives nearby," said Elizabeth, who at that moment resembled a flour-faced mammy. "Her swine of a husband beats her when he has 'a brick in his hat,' as she calls his sprees. By now, he ought to have enough bricks to build a house of ill repute."

"'A man can't close his eyes to pray without falling into a rum-hole!'" declared Susan, quoting from *The Lily*. "I'm waiting for someone to take a hatchet to the taprooms, bucket shops, spirit vaults, and doggeries that turn men's fuggled brains to mash!"

"You beat that horse to death!" complained Elizabeth.

"Better that I should beat the horse than a drunkard his wife!"

"Ellen, we are happy that you're unmarried and with child," said Elizabeth pleasantly. "We can point to you as an example of the necessity for statutory protection of unwed mothers. Their welfare and that of their children cannot be left to the whim of churches and the discretion of private charities. *Bastardy*—odious word!—must be expunged from the law books, from the minds of those who set themselves up to judge women, and from the hearts of mankind."

"Which are seldom kind," said Susan. "That New York's married women have a legal right to their wages and to their children is due, in part, to our campaigning." As if having read my thoughts, she went on to say, "I could not give up my life to become a man's serving woman. When I was young, if a girl made a poor marriage, she became a housekeeper and drudge; if she made a rich one, a pet and a doll."

I couldn't imagine her as a young woman, much less a man's pet or doll. Her figure was gaunt like an old stick, her face drawn over bone and framed by two taut drapes of gray hair that appeared to have been screwed into place for eternity by her bun. Yet in her girlhood, she was accounted pretty and had been courted. But no man could inspire in her the passion she felt for her mind's pursuits, which must be kept unencumbered. She refused to be anybody's property. She agreed with Elizabeth, whom I once heard say,

"To be wedded to an idea may be, after all, the holiest and happiest of marriages."

"Wait and see, Ellen; all will be well," promised a broadly smiling Elizabeth.

"You will be happy here with us—"

"And a great help to our cause!"

I thought then that I would be helpful and happy.

Sholes & Glidden

The Remington model number 2 was the latest thing in typewriters, but I preferred my old Sholes & Glidden machine, whose operation I had learned at the Young Women's Christian Association on Lexington Avenue.

"Does it bother you that my machine can make only capital letters?" I asked the ladies at the conclusion of the first day's dictation and transcription. The Remington keyboard had both the upper- and lowercase alphabets in its chassis.

"Not at all!" replied Elizabeth. "It will remind Susan to speak emphatically."

I guessed that she needed no reminder.

"Elizabeth forges the thunderbolts, and I fire them!" she said.

"Women should be grateful to Mr. Sholes for having chosen his daughter instead of a man to demonstrate his machine," said Elizabeth. "As a result, the typewriter is considered a woman's tool, and for the first time in the history of our sex, women work as clerk copyists in offices where previously only men had been employed."

"A man would never choose to operate a machine so prettily decorated," observed Susan, tapping, with a gnarled finger, a wreath of painted gillyflowers emblazoned on mine.

"Naturally, Mr. Sholes was not motivated by altruism or sympathy for our cause," said Elizabeth, who gave every appearance of being omniscient. "He saw women as an opportunity to sell his machine to a boodle of new customers. But we would compact with the Devil in aid of woman's rights."

"Speak for yourself, Lizzie!" growled Susan, who wore no stays except those fashioned of an elastic piety. "I will not give the Devil his due, though he gives women charge over the whole world in exchange."

"I would trade my immortal soul for the vote!" replied Elizabeth theatrically.

"Will you never outgrow the need to be thought of as naughty? Heaven knows why you should find preening in blasphemy and provocation so much fun!"

"Oh, fudge! Heaven only knows how I've stood you all these years!"

"Primp!"

"Prude!"

"Poseur!"

"Prig!"

"Humbug!"

"Stickleback!"

"Egotist!" shouted Susan. "Must you always be the biggest toad in the puddle?"

I crossed my arms on top of the machine and, with a pitiable moan, rested my head on them.

"Ellen, what's the matter?" they asked, competing for my recognition of their sympathies.

"I feel faint."

"Is your corset laced too tightly?" asked Susan.

"If you cannot renounce it entirely, you must do so until the baby is born!" admonished Elizabeth.

"Rest yourself, dear girl. We shall not disturb you any more today."

The two women took the manuscript pages I had finished typewriting into the kitchen, where I could hear Elizabeth reading them over slowly and articulately to Susan, who, now and then, would disagree with a word or phrase. They bickered until they remembered themselves—or rather, they remembered the cause that was their common ground and source of amity. Then they would eat a piece of strudel.

Not caring for accounts of other people's lives unless they're made up by a wizard like Mr. James, I found the ladies' *History* dull. Having fixed my gaze on the machine for nearly three hours, my eyes were tired. I closed them and saw the keys in the darkness behind the curtains of the lids, arranged like a constellation whose stars had assembled into nothing legible.

```
2 3 4 5 6 7 8 9 - ,
Q W E . T Y I U O P
Z S D F G H J K L M
A X & C V B N ? ; R
```

I went out for some air. Underneath its freshness, I caught the unsavory odor of the tidal strait released by the unseasonable heat of a September afternoon. I walked along Forty-second Street, my thoughts not yet my own after toiling at the two women's prose, until I found myself beneath towering plane trees in Bryant Park, not far from the site of the Colored Orphan Asylum, which immigrant and nativist hooligans had burned to cinders during the draft riots twenty years before. I chose an ornamental iron bench placed in the shadow cast by the Sixth Avenue elevated railway. The person sitting opposite, half-hidden in the gloom, whom I had taken for a girl of six or seven, turned out to be—on close inspection—a little person unkindly called a "midget."

I observed her discreetly, with sidelong glances, to satisfy my curiosity without causing offense. She was perfectly formed. Her round face was pretty, her dark hair thick and done à la mode. When she turned her head toward the chittering of a squirrel, her movements impressed me with their grace and elegance. Had she been of ordinary height, she would have been the object of a young man's greedy eyes. Anger arose in me at God or—if He was disinterested, as Deists claim—at the mill of destiny, which will grind human beings into dust. By now, my furtive glances had settled into a stare.

"I've been admiring your hat," she called from across the walk that separated us. Later, I would admire the tact with which she had spared me embarrassment by making herself out to be the one who had been staring. "It's becoming to your face."

"Thank you." Inclining my head, the green felt hat waved a garnet and a sage plume at her.

"I don't think I could wear such a hat half as well as you," she said graciously.

"I'm sure that's not so. It would suit you. Am I mistaken, or are your eyes green?" I asked, feeling that we had exhausted the subject of hats. I don't know why I remarked on the color of her eyes. I couldn't rightly make them out, because of the shadow cast by the brim of her straw bonnet. An awkward silence ensued, which I felt obliged to put to an end by crossing over to her bench. After a moment's hesitation, in which I considered whether to sit beside her or a little apart, I decided on the former as being the less likely to embarrass. I did not want her to think that I was shy of her, as one might be in the presence of an anomaly.

She smiled, gave me her little hand, and said, "My name is Margaret Fuller Hardesty. Father was a Transcendentalist until he followed Mother's example and died. I often wonder what became of him and his philosophy. Having no relations, near or distant, at least no one willing to acknowledge the connection, I came to New York to find employment. I suppose it was small wonder that I found none"—she smiled archly—"until Mr. Barnum happened to see me in the Central Park. I was walking on Sheep Meadow, my eyes intent on the ground, in the hope of finding the remains of a picnic lunch, when I was startled by a lumbering shadow on the grass, accompanied by heavy footsteps. I looked up and there, like a maharajah, sat Mr. Barnum astride Jumbo the Elephant, together with the Milo Brothers and, languid within the curve of its trunk, Miss Adelina, the famous high-wire ascensionist and juggler."

"'How do you do, little lady?' I couldn't have guessed that his voice—he had addressed me in the most cordial way—was able to reach the last row of seats in the Hippodrome, over the din of beasts and human beings come to gloat—or so it always seems to me, who has never felt at one with them.

"'I have not had lunch,' I said, hopeful that a banana or a bag of peanuts might be among the paraphernalia carried on the elephant's back.

"'Where do you live?' he asked. 'I don't mean to pry, but if we happen to be traveling in the same direction, I can give you a ride home.'

"'I am presently stopping at a gardener's unused shed.'

"'Very resourceful.'

"Barnum grew thoughtful while Miss Adelina scratched the elephant's huge leathery ear and Mr. Marsh, a renowned trombone soloist, blew spit from the mouthpiece of his instrument. He had been playing circus 'screamers' in the van to advertise an engagement at Madison Square Garden.

"'I think you'd be happier with us,' said Barnum,

smiling radiantly. He let down a silken ladder and, lifting his high hat in welcome, bade me join him."

"And you accepted his invitation?" I asked, fascinated by her tale, as anyone would be.

"I most certainly did!" replied Margaret, who had been alone and, like other pariahs in the world's richest city, destitute.

A multitude beyond a miracle of fish and loaves to feed is packed into tenement houses, choked by stench, freezing or sweating according to the season, and famished for light and air, from the Five Points to Hell Gate. And a great many more of their predecessors lie in paupers' graves on Ward's, Randall's, and Blackwell's islands—infinitely beyond the reach of Barnum's screamers, in an eternity of silent waiting for the promised recompense.

"Was Mr. Barnum kind?" I asked, hoping that he had been.

"He was and still is," replied Margaret, smoothing her skirt. "I've been with him since that afternoon in 1862."

"And are you happy?"

"I am." She regarded me a moment. "It is not for you to be angry." She took note of my perplexity. "Earlier, I saw it in your face. Your anger at whoever or whatever made my friends and me is as unwelcome as your pity."

I bit my lower lip and frowned. I did not tell her that the anger and the pity had been for myself.

"We are not mistakes," she said, modulating her tone into a softer register. "We are, as Mr. Barnum says of us, 'nature's eccentricities.' And I am '*La Belle Excentrique*.'"

I looked at this miniature human being, remarkable in every aspect, and felt a surge of affection and—strange to say—gratitude. I admired her courage, knowing instinctually that she would have considered my admiration demeaning because it implied a sympathy—a pity, even—for the difference between us, a difference she would have vigorously denied. There she sat, her short legs dangling above the pavement, her head reaching only as far as my shoulder, endowed by nature, as though to compensate her for having fashioned her thus, with a ferocity—a strength of will—that carried her proudly past the rude stares, which might be contemptuous or kind, and the constant insult of a world not suited to her needs and dignity. There she sat as if I and not she were to be pitied for having been born "normal."

"I invite you to tea," she said, and for a dreadful moment, I pictured the two of us sitting in a Fifth Avenue tea shop, inviting careless stares in which I would be implicated. Before I could accept her invitation regardless of the tearoom she might choose, she said, "My rooming house is not far."

I watched her clamber down from the bench as unselfconsciously as a child would have done. Not wanting to embarrass her, I did not offer my hand. We left Bryant Park, which had been a potter's field until, in 1840, the nameless graves were opened and the remains unearthed and transplanted in the demotic soil of Ward's Island. We headed for her rooming house, at the seamy edge of Longacre Square, erstwhile center of the city's carriage trade. I matched my stride to Margaret's shorter one, inconspicuously, so as not to slight her.

The Absurdity in the Room

"WON'T YOU SIT DOWN?" asked Margaret.

She had not needed to point me to the chair in which I now found myself sitting, at ease despite the strangeness of the room. Mine was the only chair, indeed the sole furnishing, that could accommodate a person of my size. The maroon horsehair sofa, the armchair, the carved walnut pedestal table, the cupboard, the plates, cups, and saucers were suitable for her diminutive figure. I was the eccentric, the absurdity in a room bright with fripperies and chintz, rose carpets and claret drapes. I felt as if I were sitting in a private box in a theater where a play was about to be performed for my exclusive enjoyment. In my seemingly big chair, I was Gulliver lording it over the Lilliputians or Barnum's Cardiff Giant among the gawkers. Neither by word nor gesture did Margaret acknowledge the topsy-turvy universe in which we two were speaking to each other as if nothing were amiss. For her, nothing was amiss.

"What a charming room!" I may have sniffed (I hope not) as one might do upon entering a circus dressing room and detecting a lingering odor of greasepaint and sweat.

"Thank you, Ellen."

"You must be very comfortable here," I said, instantly

going red in the face. I was afraid she would infer from my remark my belief that she must be uncomfortable outside of her "doll's house." She did not make an issue of it. Relieved, I glanced at a copy of the *New-York Tribune* lying open on the table to the theatrical notices, one of which announced the death on July 15 of Charles Sherwood Stratton, or Tom Thumb, as he was universally known. Margaret had drawn a heart in black ink around the engraved portrait of the little man.

"India or China?" she asked, rising from the sofa as gracefully as any society lady.

"China would be grand."

She smiled and, with a flounce of her pretty curls, went into the kitchen, which I had no doubt was furnished with a miniature sink and stove. I listened to the rush of water surging into the teapot and the clatter of spoons as I perused Tom Thumb's obituary, learning that he had been born in Bridgeport, Connecticut, in 1838, and after six months of ordinary development and having attained a height of twenty-five inches, he stopped growing.

Margaret returned from the kitchen, carrying a child's tea service on a tin tray illustrated with dogs wearing derby hats and holding in their paws glasses of beer—the sole reminder in an otherwise-decorous setting that the events in my small hostess's life would not be reported in the society pages. Setting the *Tribune* aside, she put the tray on the table and poured the fragrant tea into both our cups.

"Do you take sugar?"

"Yes, please."

"Milk?"

"Not for me, Margaret, thank you."

Her preparations complete, we sipped the hot tea awhile in silence.

"Did you read poor Tom's obituary?"

She took me by surprise, and I put down the tiny cup abruptly, causing tea to slosh over its gold rim and into the saucer. "Margaret, I hope you don't mind."

"That you took advantage of my absence to read a newspaper? Heavens no, child! I would have hidden it in a drawer if I'd intended to keep it a secret."

I was taken aback by her having referred to me as a "child," but looking at her face, I was reminded by the lines time had inscribed there that she was older than I, who was twenty-seven. She would have been in her forties—perhaps the same age Tom Thumb was when he passed on to a miniature heaven: forty-five. At some point, according to his obituary, he had begun to grow again, and at the time of his death, he was three feet tall.

"We called him 'General,' you know," said Margaret—wistfully, I thought. "He was a dear man." She stood, crossed the room, and beckoned me to join her by the wall, where, at the level of her gaze, a row of framed photographs hung. "This is Tom and Lavinia. It was taken on their wedding day, February 10, 1863. I was the maid of honor. Do you see me here?"

She pointed to a young woman wearing a dress trimmed in satin and silk rosebuds, her dimpled arms visible beneath puffed sleeves, the circumference of her ample skirt kept rigid by an old-fashioned farthingale. Long curls framed her chubby face, which wore a frown. One could easily mistake the bridal party for three people of common stature, if it were not for the Episcopal minister seen towering above them.

"Ten thousand people attended the reception at the Metropolitan Hotel. We greeted them, standing on top of a grand piano, as the Band of Caledonian Pipers played. Afterward, we went to Washington to meet President Lincoln. He was so tall, he had to stoop to shake our hands. He said the fault was his for having stretched the truth more than was good for him. General Tom became a wealthy man. He owned a steam yacht, a wardrobe of elegantly tailored clothes, and a summer house built to suit him on one of Connecticut's Thimble Islands. Ten thousand mourners attended his funeral."

Margaret sighed, and a shadow stole across her face.

"Tom used to say that he had willed himself not to grow," she said after a pause.

"Whatever do you mean, Margaret?" I asked in astonishment.

"He liked to say that, having briefly lived among your kind—"

"My kind?"

"I beg your pardon, Ellen, but Tom always used to put it that way. He could be awfully proud."

I thought Tom's pride and his claim preposterous. How on earth could a body will itself to stop growing, and why would it?

"He said that six months as a normally developing

infant had been time enough for him to conclude that 'your kind,' Ellen, were mean and shallow, and he decided to have no part of it."

"What about you, Margaret?" I asked pettishly. "Did you will yourself to stop growing?"

"I really don't recall. Tom had a remarkable memory. Besides, I was not half so smart as he. He was a deep thinker, you know. Very philosophical. He always said that the small people constituted a race of its own and that of the two races—yours and ours—ours was superior."

I could not help feeling resentful toward Tom Thumb and, for a brief moment, Margaret and *her* kind. I swallowed my indignation and conceded that General Tom might have been correct in his dark view of the majority of men and women, which the world considers normal.

The subject was in need of changing, and I did so by inquiring about another photograph hanging on the wall.

"Is that Ralph Waldo Emerson?"

"Yes. He often came to visit Father to discuss Transcendentalism. Sometimes Henry Thoreau would come to Worcester, as well."

The photograph showed a young Margaret sitting on Emerson's lap. I could have laughed aloud at how the scene resembled a ventriloquist's act on the stage of a music hall.

"Mr. Emerson was a very great man and an even deeper thinker than General Tom," she said, her eyes transfixed by a hypnotic light flaring on the pane of glass. "We all loved him."

I coughed twice to remind her of my presence.

"I do recall Father's asking him once if the reason for my stunted growth could be filial disobedience. 'She is a good child,' said Father, 'but inclined to be headstrong.'

"Mr. Emerson smiled and said, 'I believe Nature to be unfinished and that it will forever be tinkering with its creations, in order to ensure that no single form or design becomes fixed and absolute and, therefore, by immutability, proves unable to respond to a universe whose being is one of ceaseless change.'

"Tom loved to hear me tell that story. 'We are Nature's chosen scouts in the vanguard of humanity, searching for perfection,' he would say. Tom became a Transcendentalist in honor of Mr. Emerson."

All of a sudden, Margaret laughed hard enough to make her curls shake. "When Father asked Mr. Thoreau whether he thought I was being cussed, he shouted in answer, 'She is indeed, and I adore her for her contrariety! Hers is an act of civil disobedience that puts mine to shame! Three cheers for little Miss Margaret!'

"It was so much fun, those childhood days in Worcester. Now they're all dead—Henry David, Waldo, Margaret Fuller, my father and mother—all those kind souls have gone off to Glory, or to annihilation, if we are to believe gloomy old Herman Melville."

We returned to the sofa and allowed our minds to drift in the currents of nostalgia and regret. I thought of my own dead, especially my poor brother-in-law, Martin. He and Melville—and Mrs. Stanton's husband, Henry, as I would learn—the three of them had worked in the city for the U.S. Customs Service. Is history a game played by God in which humans are pawns? Or does time whipstitch together people and events, haphazardly catching up this piece or that one in its rumpled cloth?

My thoughts returned to Elizabeth, of whom I'd been thinking during the walk from Bryant Park. Of my two suffragists, she was the elder and worldlier. She had married Henry Brewster Stanton, a former abolitionist, whom I never once laid eyes on, and she had brought children into the turbulent world by "voluntary motherhood." In this, as in all else pertaining to the dignity of women, she would not allow herself to be "forced" or her belief in her own worth set aside. She and Susan rarely spoke of Mr. Stanton; when they did, it was in low voices and never to me. I was unable to satisfy a natural curiosity concerning him and his whereabouts.

Margaret got up and played something mournful on a miniature harmonium, a gift from P. T. Barnum. As a girl living in Worcester, she had been taught the reedy instrument, and to my ear, she sounded accomplished.

"Do you play an instrument?" she asked, turning her head from the keyboard.

"I play the lyre," I replied archly.

She finished "The Heart That Is Broken" and took up a sprightly air, "Do, Do, My Huckleberry Do."

"Is it difficult to master?" she asked.

"Necessity is a great teacher." In my voice, I heard self-pity and felt ashamed.

As I lay in bed that night, I pictured Margaret in hers, no larger than a child's. What dreams sweeten her sleep? I wondered. What nightmares disturb it? Does she imagine herself a tiny princess in a fairy tale, waiting for a prince's kiss to undo a curse and restore her to full womanhood? No! I upbraided myself. Margaret is complete in herself and would hate to be thought otherwise. All the same, I was troubled by the notion that a being lay shut up inside her—a fully grown woman impossible to rescue. It was too sad a thought to entertain. I would not let myself ponder the hopeless desires of so famished a heart, nor would I consider the possibility that Margaret might have reason to lament the death of General Tom apart from camaraderie. I recalled the parlor and its contents, which had been sized to accommodate Margaret's humble standpoint, with the exception of a chair and an ornate mirror placed above her head—both objects kept for visiting emissaries from the larger world.

An Object of Curiosity

ON THE FOLLOWING DAY, MR. TIPSON, celebrated narcoleptic, delivered a note from Margaret, asking if she might visit on Friday at one o'clock, "if convenient." "I'd be delighted," I replied. In the brief time it took to compose my answer, Mr. Tipson had fallen asleep, and I had to poke him with Susan's black umbrella to set him in motion again.

The appointed hour arrived, and I was looking anxiously out the window onto the street. The cause of my uneasiness was twofold: I worried that my suffragists would unwittingly pass a remark that would embarrass my small guest, and I feared that Margaret might come calling on board an elephant. I imagined her mistaking Miss Redpath's second-floor apartment for ours and, peering in at her window, startling the elderly spinster into Green-Wood Cemetery. Who wouldn't be terrified at the sight of a little woman seated on an elephant and rapping on the window-pane with tiny knuckles to attract her notice? In my fancy, I heard Jumbo trumpeting in fierce joy for a reason best known to pachyderms in captivity. (What monumental grudges might they harbor in their gigantic breasts! Now that Lincoln is dead, who is there to emancipate them?)

At five minutes past the hour, I watched as a hansom emblazoned with a seal balancing a red ball on its snout drew up to the curb, driven by David Henry Dode, the world's tallest man. He unfolded his long legs from under the dashboard and, having opened the carriage door, lifted my petite guest onto the brick pavement. I was surprised to see a second person exit the carriage, whom Margaret would shortly introduce as Frank Ashton, renowned for his "posturing."

Mr. Dode escorted Margaret upstairs and to our door, while Mr. Ashton, walking behind them, carried a large box done up with string. The brass knocker fell, and I let the strange party inside.

"Good afternoon, Ellen," said Margaret pleasantly.

"Good afternoon. Won't you and your friends come in?"

Having delivered his small charge to the door, the tall man turned on his heels and left.

"Mr. Dode will wait outside," replied Margaret. "Mr. Barnum insisted he accompany me. He's very protective of me, and Mr. Dode is daunting." She turned her head to Mr. Ashton, who was standing in the hallway in an attitude of profound deference. In its exaggeration, it exceeded all bounds of polite usage and, in fact, the ordinary limitations of the human frame. I could not help laughing, a rudeness that brought out in him a smile so broad, I feared his lips, thin to start with, would disappear, leaving behind only a toothy gape such as children love to carve on jack-o'-lanterns. "Mr. Ashton, if you please," said Margaret.

The man, whose parts appeared to have been molded of India rubber and whose face was the color of gamboge, bowed to her and then to me—an obeisance so extravagant that the top of his high hat rested on the floor. It resembled a flowerpot, from which grew a bulbous nose and a pair of ears that could only be described as elephantine. He stood upright and, with tremendous effort, carried the box into the sitting room as though it were packed with cast-iron stove lids. With another scarcely possible feat of agility, he bent over backward and placed the box on a three-legged stool, and then in a fluent movement that seemed to defy the laws of science and anatomy, he shot upright, as if his backbone were a spring, nodded to Margaret, and passed out the door, shutting it behind him with his foot.

Margaret behaved as if this preposterous show were commonplace, which it was in the strange world to which fate, will, or God's carelessness had placed her. She took off white gloves such as children wear to dancing lessons, looked about for a place to sit, and, having chosen a chair that was shallower in its seat than the rest, ascended, as if to a throne, by the footstool Elizabeth had thoughtfully placed there.

"I was not sure how large your appetites would be," said Margaret, glancing at the white box, from which a sweet smell escaped that in a graveyard would have made one gag. In that queasy observation lies a truth that can be profound or trivial according to one's lights. "I have never before bought cake for ladies of substance."

Susan and Elizabeth chose that moment to enter, their arms outstretched in welcome. "We are glad, Miss Hardesty, to make your acquaintance," they said as one. "Ellen speaks highly of you."

I blushed at hearing the word *highly* spoken within hearing of my new friend, though the remark had been an innocent one.

"I assure you that 'ladies of substance' are inclined to eat more cake than is good for them," said Elizabeth. "And suffer the consequences." She patted her stomach contentedly.

"Speak for yourself, Lizzie!" snapped Susan, for whom temperance extended to cakes, if not to her speeches, which were ardent, even inflammatory.

"Shall I open it?" Elizabeth had picked up the outsize box and set it on a taboret.

"By all means!" cried Margaret, rubbing her hands in anticipation. "I've been waiting to try it!"

What a cake! It could have fed Barnum's leapers, tumblers, clowns, and assorted artistes. I guessed that Margaret had estimated our appetites by our gigantic stature, unless she believed that the provender for grossly fashioned beings like us would be equally gross. The experience of seeing myself and my "kind" through her eyes always disturbed me. I did indeed belong to the clumsy race of men with coarse white faces that had shambled among the delicate Japanese in 1853, when Commodore Perry and his men came ashore at Edo. As the comedy of manners played in front of me, I had the curious sensation that I was growing larger, as did Alice after having eaten a slice of cake lettered EAT ME in currants.

Elizabeth and Susan returned to the kitchen to brew a pot of tea. Alone with Margaret, I was timid, as though I were the guest and she the host. I do not know why I should have felt so. Her smile was warm; her goodwill genuine; her manner not in the least haughty or privileged. (Vanity is seldom found in someone who has been looked down on since childhood.) She spoke of her afternoon ride, the loyalty of her two escorts, the consideration of Mr. Barnum, who had arranged for her outing, and of pleasures common to us all. Once again, I admired her wry observations, humor, and good nature, which I supposed had escaped the bitterness and cynicism that blight the hearts of men and women living in an absurd world.

"The ladies seem amiable," she said. We could hear them fussing at each other, like a pair of hens, as two women will who find themselves occupying the same kitchen. "They're considerate." I supposed she was alluding to the footstool.

"They are," I agreed. "I'm lucky to have found such obliging employers."

"What is it that they do?" she asked.

I told her of their endeavors, which impressed her favorably.

"I regret only one thing," said Margaret when I had finished. "That I haven't any work to do of real importance."

I hesitated, thinking how best to reply without seeming to disparage her. "You give people pleasure," I said tentatively.

She glanced at me; she might have even glared. If so, the indignation that sparked her angry look quickly passed into resignation. She sighed and said, "Their pleasure is in feeling themselves—for a moment—lucky."

Yes, I thought. That is the case.

"My role is unfulfilling. I might as well be hanging on a butcher's hook."

I must have looked appalled, because she clarified the gristly image.

"They devour me with their eyes until there is nothing left."

"Who does?"

"The curious who come to view me. They leave with the rapt expression I've seen on the faces of the holy sisters after having eaten the body of Christ."

For the first time in our acquaintance, she had allowed me to glimpse a woman whose contentment might be a pretense. I recalled that, when I had been in her dainty room, I had felt like a spectator of a play performed on a miniature stage—a drama written for a single character whose purpose eluded me.

"I'm sorry," I said, having searched my mind and found nothing else to offer her.

She smiled, and her face softened into a gentle, almost beatific, expression. She waved a hand as a saint would distributing her blessings. "You must not mind me, Ellen. I don't mean half of what I say. You are one of those rare people."

"What sort of people?" I asked, intrigued.

"That inspire confidence in others. I've not known many in your world."

"Mr. Barnum?"

"Mr. Barnum is another one, but then, he is not of your world. We've made room for him in ours."

I could not make out whether "your world" referred to that of the fully grown or to one inhabited by people who see others only in terms of themselves. I had thought of myself as a decent, intelligent woman, mostly without prejudices. Had a war not already been fought to free the slaves, I'd be an abolitionist. Had I a ballot to cast, I'd vote to protect the poor and helpless, whether they were immigrant Irish, Germans, Chinese, Jews, blacks, or nativists festering in the putrid belly of the Five Points. Suddenly, I was conscious of excluding "freaks," in the common parlance of the time, from my sympathies. Frankly, I had never thought of them at all except as circus and sideshow performers who were as irrelevant to matters of prejudice as a trained seal. Then at the spiteful urging of a bad conscience, I turned on Margaret in my thoughts, faulting her for having chosen to live in the private world, the little world, of the circus instead of confronting the cruelty of the big one. My anger was irrational, and I left the ugly words of reproach unsaid.

I glanced out the window and saw the world's tallest man elegantly smoking a cigarette, while Mr. Ashton appeared to be suffering an extremity of boredom. Yawning theatrically and sighing prodigiously, he cracked his knuckles and shuffled his feet, determined to raise the dust, which he regarded with distaste and swatted with his hat, as at a cloud of midges. The horse had its head in a feed bag, its colorful plumes waving this way and that in the breeze, its harness bells ringing each time it lifted its head and snorted. What fun! I said to myself. Maybe a circus life is not such a poor one after all.

Elizabeth and Susan entered with a silver teapot and china cups too large for Margaret's tiny hands. She accepted the situation with the easy manner and good humor of any other fine lady. I cut the cake and dealt out slices on Elizabeth's wedding plates, which we balanced on our knees. We were delighted with ourselves and with one another.

Plates clean save for crumbs and the cups drained to the leaves, I carried the remains of the ritual of hospitality into the kitchen and returned in time to hear Elizabeth inviting Margaret to stay.

"You'll have a room of your own, furnished to your requirements," she inveigled. "I've taken to you, Miss Hardes— May I call you 'Miss Margaret' or, if you would allow me the privilege, 'Margaret'?"

Margaret graciously indicated with a nod of her head that her hostess might adopt the latter familiarity.

"I've taken a liking to you, Margaret, and I know that Susan has also."

"Very much so."

"And, of course, you and Ellen are already friends," said Elizabeth to sweeten her offer.

Margaret looked to me as if for assurance, which I gladly gave.

"What would I do here?" she asked after a pause, in which the two suffragists had leaned forward expectantly.

"You would do what you can," replied Elizabeth, the image of a benevolent grandmother. "We share in the housework, although an Irish woman comes to do the unpleasant chores. You'd do whatever you are able—whatever you found pleasant and profitable."

"Could I assist you in the cause of woman's rights?" asked Margaret, looking at that moment as if she could be of no help at all. The truth is that I couldn't picture her in any occupation other than that of circus eccentric.

"You can do the cause immeasurable good if you would accompany us on our lecture tours!" replied Susan, rubbing her bony hands together so ardently, I expected them to smoke.

"A world of good!" confirmed Elizabeth.

"I don't think I could speak in public. Not in the way you envision."

"You wouldn't need to say anything," said Elizabeth.

"Unless it pleases you to do so," said Susan.

"You would be an example."

"An example of what?" asked Margaret.

"Of abjection!" cried Elizabeth.

"Of humiliation!" croaked Susan.

"But I'm not abject or humiliated!" protested Margaret, clenching her small fists.

"A victim of the exploitation of weakness and a disadvantaged condition, then."

"I don't feel myself to be disadvantaged or especially weak."

"You are a woman," replied Elizabeth evenly. "As such, you are disadvantaged in law and weak in the eyes of men."

"A good man will cosset you; a bad one will beat you," declared Susan. "In either case, you'll be exploited and—whether you are aware of it or not—humiliated."

"Mr. Barnum treats me with consideration."

"We are not interested in whether Mr. Barnum profits by your small stature. We leave that to his conscience. What does interest us is whether or not you are being taken advantage of *because you are a defenseless woman*," said Elizabeth, or Susan. At such times, I could not tell them apart.

"Our conviction is that you most certainly are a victim!" asserted either the gray-bunned lioness or the plump stateswoman with cake crumbs on her lap.

"Ellen, what is your opinion?"

I did not want to give it.

"Ellen?"

I bit my nails.

"Please answer the question!" a voice admonished.

"I don't think it's any of my business!" I retorted. "Or yours!"

Susan and Elizabeth gasped, and their eyes narrowed in disapproval. I wondered if I would be sacked now that the tea party had gone to pot.

"It *is* our business! Her plight is of concern to all women—small, medium, and large." Once again, Elizabeth patted the fabric stretched over her middle section.

I looked to Margaret in my distress.

"What I do with my life is my own affair," she said with a fierce dignity that made her appear the largest person in the room.

An uncomfortable silence ensued. I looked outside and saw Mr. Dode and Mr. Ashton arm wrestling, one of their specialties. The Posturing Man's hyperbolic pantomime expressed strenuous effort, heroic gumption, and—visible in his eyes, which were opened so wide that I feared his eyeballs would pop out of their sockets—profound despair. The horse drowsed between the shafts, its plumes drooping. I wished I were with them instead of in a room electric with barely suppressed antagonism.

"And for your information, ladies, I am not presently faced with a plight," said Margaret, putting an end to the subject.

The suffragists had incensed Margaret, who was now climbing down from her chair and calling for her hat.

"Furthermore, I don't have a problem with men."

In the world of eccentrics, who, in Margaret's view, had been chosen to transform our savage race into a civil one, the sexes may have lived in harmony. In any case, she would not allow herself to be used to further the cause of women outside the tented universe in which she had been placed. I couldn't blame her.

Having put on her hat, Margaret turned her back on us and sailed through the door. Scowling at Elizabeth and Susan, I hurried after her. I caught up to *la petite* just as Mr. Ashton was handing her into the coach with the finesse of a French dandy in the court of the Sun King.

"I'm sorry," I said. "I would not have seen you belittled for the world."

Margaret laughed. "I enjoyed myself immensely! I seldom get among your kind except as an object of curiosity. Mrs. Stanton and Miss Anthony are good women, and I hope they can understand my refusal to be put on display. I would feel a freakishness on a lyceum stage that I don't in a circus parade." She pressed my hand affectionately. "I'd like to show you *my* kind not as you might have seen us at Madison Square Garden or in a fairground tent, but as we are. What do you say, Ellen? Are you game?"

"I'd like that very much."

"Good. I'll stop for you tomorrow."

"Not tomorrow . . . Friday. On Friday, the ladies will be

in Philadelphia, addressing the National Woman Suffrage Association."

"Expect me at a half-past eleven."

Madame Singleton

"ON HER DEATHBED, MY MOTHER begged my forgiveness for having locked me in the root cellar as punishment for my childish misdemeanors. Even now, I can smell the damp earthen floor, the mold and mildew, and the baskets of turnips, carrots, and potatoes. Father said I would grow eyes like the potatoes, which can see in the dark. He was not afraid to defy convention, but he could not stand up to Mother, who, he said, was 'as fierce as an Amazon.' She blamed herself for my 'condition,' she told me as she prepared to molder in an everlasting root cellar. But she was no more to blame for my eccentricity than a malevolent curse such as one encounters in a cruel tale by Heinrich Hoffmann or the Brothers Grimm. My diminutiveness has no external cause, but is, as General Tom maintained, an act of free will. Were it otherwise, I would not be able to call my life my own. I refused Miss Anthony and Mrs. Stanton's offer because I am my own person and not anybody's example."

I was sitting beside Margaret in the carriage that had brought her to Murray Hill three days before. Mr. Ashton sat on the sprung seat next to Mr. Dode. The black horse had been changed for a white one adorned with scarlet plumes fatally plucked from a Florida spoonbill. Margaret held my hand—or rather, I held hers, her white glove enveloped in my fawn. I thought her a precious creature and was instantly ashamed. I reminded myself that she was not a little girl being taken to the stores by a favorite aunt. She was taking me to visit the small world, which I had never before entered.

"Most of our troupe is with Mr. Barnum on a London engagement," she said. "I stayed behind to comfort Tom's wife, Lavinia. Mr. Dode and Mr. Ashton remained to chaperone me, and some six or seven others suffer from seasickness and do not go abroad. They're stopping at Barnum's Hotel, at Twentieth Street and Broadway."

She sensed my nervousness, and, squeezing my thumb with her hand reassuringly, said with a smile, "It will be no worse than your tea party." That is what worries me, I told myself. "I suspect that my friends will take to you, just as I have. You have only to be yourself, Ellen."

And what is that self? I wondered.

I rested my eyes in the shadows of the coach. Margaret relaxed her grip on my thumb but did not take her hand from my palm. My mind was confused by her presence, and I wanted to compose myself. She was both rose and thorn: She delighted and vexed me at the same time.

Margaret's imperious withdrawal from the sitting room had dismayed my suffragists. They criticized her for choosing to remain aloof from the issue of woman's sovereignty; at the same time, they insisted on viewing her as another victim of men, who were incorporated in the shameless showman Phineas T. Barnum. Long after the customary hour of Morpheus's descent, they fretted. At breakfast, they announced that they had failed her. Keeping Margaret's parting words to me a secret, I let them stew. The dish was, I thought then, seasoned to their taste.

By supper, "the unfortunate business" had assumed gigantic importance in their minds. I do believe that if they had not been reconciled with Margaret, Susan and Elizabeth would never have finished the *History*; the ink would have dried to powder in their inkwells. Margaret never did agree to appearing on the lecture circuit, nor did she disavow her affection for Barnum. She gave the two suffragists to understand, however, that she admired their work and would value them as friends. Having met their match, the two firebrands let the matter drop.

Driving down Broadway, Margaret and I passed the Fifth Avenue Hotel, equipped with a steam-powered "vertical railroad" to transport guests to the upper floors, and Madison Square Garden, where the colossal arm and torch of Liberty awaited money to be pledged so that her dismembered parts could be assembled on Bedloe's Island and rise colossally above New York Harbor.

About Bartholdi and Eiffel's gigantic statue, I once heard Elizabeth say, "Thus do men idealize woman, turning her into a symbol, while they imprison her on an island of domesticity."

"Were she real, Lady Liberty would be as disenfranchised as we are," replied Susan with her usual tartness.

The carriage stopped at Twentieth Street, outside Barnum's Hotel. Mr. Ashton helped Margaret down gallantly.
When he offered me his hand, I recoiled and felt a momen-
tary disgust. He responded with a pantomime that began
with surprise and ended in abasement. I hurriedly put out
my hand to him, but he had turned away, crocodile tears
coursing down his ashen face. Margaret touched my elbow
and shook her head, as if to say Pay him no mind.

We left him to his performance and Mr. Dode to see to
the horse's needs. I followed my friend across a wide porch
and into the hotel lobby, where seven guests were sitting
in chairs upholstered in buffalo hide, their heads buried in
newspapers, turned in conversation, or fallen onto slowly
rising and falling breasts in sleep. You could've mistaken
them for an accidental congress of drummers and other
travelers who are ubiquitous in hotel lobbies or the privileged residents at a sanitarium, in various stages of senility
and physical collapse.

Margaret greeted them in general and then introduced
me to each one.

"I'd like you to be acquainted with my friend Ellen
Finch. You may call her—"

She looked at me for approval, and I said, "Please do
call me 'Ellen.'"

They put down their papers and turned their heads
toward me, while those who had been asleep were nudged
into wakefulness. More than polite, the smile they shed
on me conveyed welcome and acceptance—not because
of anything I'd done to deserve it but because their trust

in Margaret was unquestioning. They regarded her with respect and—I could see it in their faces—affection.

"Ellen, please say hello to Miss Etta, the contortionist."

"I am happy to meet you, Miss Etta."

She acknowledged our new acquaintance by tying herself into a knot, shocking in its revelations, which none of the others appeared to notice.

"Mrs. Stoner, snake charmer."

I waited nervously for her to produce her stock-in-trade, but she apologized. The hotel did not allow reptiles. Of all the eccentrics there, she was the dullest. Her charms, I supposed, were dispensed solely for the pleasure of the snake, whose name was Napoléon.

Margaret worked her way around the room, and I became acquainted with Mr. Matchett and Mr. Engelbrecht, scientific fencers; Mr. George Bliss, leaper; Miss Watson, chariot driver at the Hippodrome; and Miss Mattie Elliott, grotesque dancer, who was also renowned for her high kicks.

"Ellen is curious about us," said Margaret.

I felt myself blush and looked at the faces ranged before me for any sign of resentment.

"She is not, however, the least patronizing or malicious. Her curiosity is only that which one human being feels about another. I invited her here—she did not ask to be brought—to see for herself what sort of people we are when we are being just ourselves." She turned to me and asked, "Ellen, do you have any questions for my friends?"

It was a dreadful moment. To say the wrong thing would be devastating, to say nothing rude.

"Miss Watson."

"What would you like to know, my dear?"

"Aren't you scared of driving a chariot? I have an appreciation for the dangers after reading Mr. Wallace's novel *Ben-Hur*."

It was a stupid remark, especially since I had not read the book, but only the reviews. *The Century* criticized it as an "anachronism," and *The Atlantic* as "too lavish."

She smiled tolerantly. "Terrified! If it weren't for the frisson, I would stay at home and knit."

Several of her colleagues laughed—at me, I expect. Their amusement was not spiteful.

"Miss Etta, how is it that you are able to fold up like a—" An apt comparison eluded me.

Miss Etta was kind enough to complete the simile. "Portmanteau."

I nodded in the affirmative. Frankly, I didn't care how the trick was done. Whatever I'd hoped to learn by visiting Barnum's Hotel, this was not it.

"My bones are vulcanized," she said in a confidential tone, as if to conceal her secret from the rest of the eccentrics.

"She is an enterologist," intoned Margaret with a deference that, though sincere, I thought comical.

"I'm not familiar with the word."

"Mine is a very artistic profession!" exclaimed Miss

Etta. "Mr. Barnum says so." I could see that she was pleased with herself. "Allow me to demonstrate."

She glanced at the lobby until her gaze fell on a rose wood cabinet on which a cut-glass vase of nasturtiums sat. I'd guess that the cabinet was about the same height as Tom Thumb at his tallest. Having opened its door, she packed herself inside it. "*Peekaboo*!" she called from between her thighs, and then she stuck out her tongue. The sight produced a disagreeable effect in me. I felt the blood leave my face as the room began to spin.

"Ellen, are you all right?" asked Margaret, helping me to a sofa.

"Forgive me, my corset is too tight," I replied untruthfully. "That and the heat quite overcame me."

She sat beside me and held my thumb until I felt it begin to numb. Her childlike frame was engulfed by the sofa; her short legs, clad in a striped skirt, were barely able to fold over the edge of the seat. Yet she behaved perfectly, as though not the least incommoded by the oversized world. "You went white as a ghost," she said solicitously.

"I'm sorry to be such a bother," I replied, my shamefaced glance taking in Margaret and each of her fellow artistes.

They made noises of concern, which I knew to be genuine.

"Seeing my act for the first time can come as a shock," said Miss Etta after she had unpacked herself from the cabinet.

"Not at all. I was thrilled!" The truth is that the act

had affected me queerly, as if I had happened on something altogether too grotesque for words.

"To put the color back in your cheeks" with a demonstration of scientific fencing, Mr. Matchett and Mr. Engelbrecht each offered me an arm and escorted me onto the porch. I sat in a rocking chair as they produced rapiers— seemingly out of thin air. (It was often so in those days that things came and went without explanation.)

"We have added an *enhancement* to our performance to edify the public, as well as to entertain it," remarked Mr. Matchett smugly.

"A *classical* enhancement!" put in Mr. Engelbrecht, who clearly resented his partner's superior attitude. A livid scar and a missing earlobe hinted that their tempers were not ideally suited to a combative profession.

With astonishing rapidity, Mr. Engelbrecht assumed the character (and strange to say, the costume) of Mercutio; in a trice, Mr. Matchett had transformed himself into Tybalt. (Mr. James once treated me to a performance of the "lamentable tragedy" at the Booth's Theatre in Manhattan, with Edwin Booth in the role of Romeo.)

"We salt our swordplay with Shakespeare for the hightoned crowd," simpered Matchett.

"Edwin Booth praised my fencing!" crowed Engelbrecht.

"Henry Irving said of my performance, 'I could not have been more staggered by Mr. Matchett's Tybalt had I been hit over the head with a sledgehammer such as is used to dispatch oxen.'"

Face-à-face, the pair of scientific fencers began to hurl Shakespearean insults.

> ENGELBRECHT-MERCUTIO: Tybalt, you ratcatcher, will you walk?
>
> MATCHETT-TYBALT: What wouldst thou have with me?
>
> MERCUTIO: Good King of Cats, nothing but one of your nine lives. That I mean to make bold withal, and, as you shall use me hereafter, dry-beat the rest of the eight. Will you pluck your sword out of his pilcher by the ears? Make haste, lest mine be about your ears ere it be out.
>
> TYBALT: I am for you.

They drew their swords and waggled them at each other.

> MERCUTIO: Come, sir, your *passado*.

They fought with ludicrous ferocity until Tybalt gave Mercutio a fatal wound.

> MERCUTIO: A plague o' both your houses! I am sped.
>
> TYBALT: What, art thou hurt?
>
> MERCUTIO: Ay, ay, a scratch, a scratch. Marry, 'tis enough.
>
> TYBALT: Courage, man. The hurt cannot be much.
>
> MERCUTIO: No, 'tis not so deep as a well, nor so wide as a church-door, but 'tis enough, 'twill serve. Ask for me tomorrow, and you shall find me a grave man. I am peppered, I warrant, for this world. A plague o' both your houses! Zounds, a dog, a rat,

a mouse, a cat, to scratch a man to death! A braggart, a rogue, a villain who fights scientifically.

Passersby had gathered on the sidewalk, and as Mercutio crumpled onto the porch and expired with a most
piteous sigh, they clapped and cried "Bravo!"

Not to be outdone by a pair of scientific fencers,
George Bliss leaped from the balustrade over the heads
of the astonished crowd. The poor man landed on a loose
paving stone and broke his ankle. We heard the bone snap
and shuddered. In fakir fashion, Miss Etta rolled herself
into a doughnut for the approval of the gawkers, who graciously overlooked the immodest result of her art. Spurred
by envy, Miss Watson of the Hippodrome had borrowed a
Pierre Michaux "boneshaker" from a cyclist and was rac-
ing hell-bent for election up and down Broadway, like a
cracked-brain Ben-Hur, while the gentlemen ogled Miss
Mattie Elliott's superb legs as she did her famous high
kicks. Only glum Mrs. Stoner had no part in the variety;
Napoléon was in Flatbush, growing fat on mice fed him
by an admirer.

"Hooray for Miss Mattie!" shouted a gentleman wearing a pince-nez, which glittered wickedly in a blast of
sunlight.

"Encore!" shouted a man who could have been either a
drama critic or an aficionado of dogfights.

"More leg!" shouted a paperhanger whose slurred
speech, wobbly gait, and roseate nose betrayed him as a
sot. He sat on his book of samples and sighed for love.

A chorus of sybarites took up the inebriate's theme: "Give us more leg, Miss Mattie!"

She obliged them with a kick of such extraordinary height that her head disappeared into the petals of her skirts. The gentlemen tossed their hats, and Miss Etta, envious of the attention being paid to her colleague, staggered down the porch steps on all fours like a large spider and sang "Father's a Drunkard and Mother Is Dead."

"More leg, Miss Mattie, if you please!"

Margaret touched my wrist. "None of this is what you came to see."

I admitted it was not.

"You mustn't blame my friends; their roles are engrained. Perhaps I was naïve to think that you could get to know them as they really are. If they were to stop playing their parts, they might vanish. Is it the same for you, Ellen, in your world?"

Not wanting to follow the argument to its conclusion, I gave no answer. I had lost my hold on reality and was happier so. At least for a while, I will be free of all *that*, I told myself, unwilling to specify even to myself what "that" might be.

Margaret, however, had not finished with me.

"There's someone else I want you to meet," she said, leading me upstairs by the hand.

We stopped outside room number five on the hotel's top floor. My heart was thudding, my mouth parched, my respiration fast. Something in Margaret's tone had unnerved me, as did the atmosphere of the hotel's upper stories, their dark staircases and corridors, which could have been modeled on Thornfield Hall's. My mind is overly susceptible to the intimations of old houses, easily swayed by other people, and liable to be persuaded of hostile intentions by a neurotic fancy.

Margaret knocked on the door.

"Who is it?" a thrilling voice asked from the other side. I pictured a room done up like one of Barnum's attractions: a papier-mâché grotto inhabited by the resurrected Feejee Mermaid, languid in her bath; a fire-breathing chimaera chained in an asbestos-papered parlor; or, prodigy of prodigies, Jo-Jo the Dog-Faced Boy, "a human–Skye terrier, the crowning mystery of nature's contradictions." Then, having just read *Jane Eyre*, I was certain that the room's unseen tenant was a dangerously distracted creature like Rochester's mad wife locked inside her tower.

"Margaret and a friend," replied the indomitable little person standing next to me.

"A friend to whom?" asked the creature inside the room, which, as I recall, smelled of juniper berries.

"To those who work in circuses."

"You may come in."

I thought my heart would stop as Margaret opened the door and ushered me inside. To my relief, the room was ordinary, as was its tenant. I insist that there was nothing remarkable or grotesque. I felt the blood that had drained from my face returning, my breathing slow, and the vertigo that had nearly toppled me leave me to find my footing on a threadbare carpet that, in better days, had depicted a Mogul paradise in colored yarns.

"Do sit down," said the elderly woman cordially.

I sat in one of the two "grown-up" chairs, and Margaret eased into a small one that the woman had evidently provided for her visits. I thought I should introduce myself and did.

The woman acknowledged me with a smile and nod of her head—a quite ordinary head, neither pretty nor plain. "I am Madame Singleton."

"Madame Singleton is a clairvoyant," said Margaret respectfully. "Her intuitions were recognized by the Fox sisters, Kate and another Margaret, when they were stopping at Barnum's Hotel in the fifties, during the early years of their fame."

Amy and Isaac Post, a Quaker couple living in Rochester, were the first to proclaim the girls' gifts after they had rapped out messages sent by the inconsolable Posts' recently departed daughter. (In another of history's bewildering entanglements, Mrs. Post attended the Woman's Rights Convention at the Wesleyan Chapel in Seneca Falls and signed the Declaration of Sentiments, authored and presented by Elizabeth Cady Stanton.) We now know that Kate and Margaret were frauds, after the third Fox sister, Leah, confessed to having perpetrated the hoax, which had begun as a childish prank.

I could never make out why the girls' "psychic abilities" had excited the interest of many radically minded Quakers of the day, the same faction advocating temperance, abolition, and the cause espoused by those two other controversial "sisters," Elizabeth and Susan. At the peak of their celebrity, the Foxes were championed by luminaries such as William Cullen Bryant, James Fenimore Cooper, Horace Greeley, William Lloyd Garrison, and Sojourner Truth, as well as P. T. Barnum, who appreciated the bamboozler's art. Two of the era's fringe movements—suffrage and spiritualism—became conjoined in the public's mind, to the disadvantage of the first.

"You are thinking that I do not look like a medium and that my room is not furnished as you would expect," said Madame Singleton.

I must have looked surprised, because she said, "Your thoughts are safe, my dear; I would not presume to read the mind of one of Margaret's friends without permission."

"I'm not sure I believe in the supernatural."

"You are an intelligent young woman who knows her own mind."

"I'm not sure that I do that, either," I replied frankly.

"I am not interested in converting you to spiritualism. And you are right to be suspicious; there are a great many charlatans in the field of psychic research."

Pointing to a framed photograph on the side table, Margaret said, "Here is Madame Singleton in costume."

In the picture, she was dressed like an Assyrian sorceress. Her eyes had been made up to exaggerate the intensity of her gaze, and her fingers were adorned with gems, whose miraculous properties were said to strengthen her power of spiritual communion with those who had passed over. Her slender hands rested on a "talking table," with which she would sometimes transmit, as if by infernal telegraph, messages between the quick and the dead. A crystal ball stood beside it, in which Madame Singleton could scry the future. Divination was powerful in her, as was the reach of her uncanny foresight. She was the very image of a medium, spiritualist, soothsayer, or clairvoyant. In that costume and setting, she appeared before the general public admitted to P. T. Barnum's Grand Traveling Museum, Menagerie, Caravan & Hippodrome.

"It's all for show," said Margaret. "Stage props to give the crowd what it expects to see."

"Then it's nothing but a confidence game!" I said indignantly.

Mrs. Singleton spoke in defense of illusion: "The public would be disappointed, even enraged, if Mr. Barnum were to exhibit a man who could fly—not a creature with wings, mind you, but an otherwise-ordinary person able to levitate and soar unaided. He'd need to strap on a pair of cardboard wings covered in chicken feathers, such as children wear in Nativity pageants, to satisfy the 'suckers,' *which they are not*, since they know they are being gulled. People enjoy magic because they know there is a trick to it, and they would burn at the stake the magician who needed none."

There is truth in that, I told myself.

"I require neither costume nor props to interpret etheric transmissions. They bring me secrets that have been locked in the vault of time and also those hidden in the tiny universe inside the human brain."

"Her powers are stupendous!" exclaimed Margaret.

"They're a burden," said Madame Singleton, sighing—without, I hasten to add, ostentation.

"It is your *gift*," concluded Margaret, as though the word comprehended the exceptional ability, grave responsibility, and a fate akin to doom borne by this selfless martyr to the spiritus mundi.

I was far from being convinced. At night, in a lightless room, I might almost believe in unseen, gibbering presences. But they were the stock characters of horror tales. I could more readily entertain the idea of Washington Irving's Headless Horseman or Hawthorne's devils than the talking dead.

"I'll read your palm, if you like," she said. "It's not as revealing as what can be seen in a dish of water or in grains left on the threshing floor or by eavesdropping on voices in another's head—by far the most reliable method. But the lines of the hand are an aperçu of destiny."

I gave her my hand, and, suddenly fearful, took it back before she had glimpsed its palm.

"Don't be afraid, Ellen," encouraged Margaret.

But I was afraid and would not let her read it.

Margaret bravely offered hers. Madame Singleton laid the childlike hand on her own and proceeded to ruminate over the lines of destiny inscribed on her palm.

"What do you see?" asked Margaret, and I could hear in her voice a thrill of anticipation.

"Moments of happiness."

"Is that all?"

"Hours of sorrow."

A human life, in other words.

"Does it matter that the hand is no bigger than a child's?" I asked abruptly.

"If you mean by your question, is a child's hand too innocent to have been marked by life and intimations of the future—you are correct. But Margaret's hand bears time's signature, and her story, albeit writ small, is plain to see on her palm."

"You could have lied to me like the others!" said Margaret peevishly. Madame Singleton was not the only spiritualist in Barnum's circus. Moreover, she was the least popular of them because she would not tell her customers what they wished to hear. I never understood why Barnum kept her, unless he depended on her predictions for reasons of business. Or maybe he loved her. Who can say what truths are radiant in the mind of a mountebank, what passions agitate his heart?

She gazed at me—her eyes gimlets—and said, "If I can ever be of service, please come and see me." She offered me her card, which I took. She may have glimpsed my future after all, because, as it turned out, I would have great need of her.

Krakatoa

SHORTLY AFTER THEIR RETURN from Philadelphia, I told Elizabeth and Susan of my visit to Barnum's Hotel. Their faces darkened like the sky the year following Krakatoa's eruption in the Sunda Strait. Volcanic ash had been blown aloft into the highest reaches of the atmosphere and left for the upper winds to circulate. An immense wave rolled from the Java Sea to the English Channel. If God had instructed a new and pious family in the elements of carpentry, we never heard, nor was a second ark discovered on Mount Ararat.

Even now in 1904, I remember the dreadful sunsets caused by particles of soot drifting high above Earth's surface. The sky might have been set ablaze by aerial troops of arsonists, so spectacular was each day's end. When the Union Pacific tracks reached the hundredth meridian in 1866, the company director, Thomas Durant, ordered the prairie set on fire to entertain the investors who had traveled from Council Bluffs in his Pullman car to celebrate the milestone. Twenty square miles of grassland burned that night. The Pentecostal fires of 1883 were vaster and brighter, though they kindly left the earth unscorched.

On the first night that the fires torched the sky, Holy Rollers thought Heaven had ruptured like a cast-iron stove and was spewing fire through the cracks. Less crackbrained men in New York, Poughkeepsie, and New Haven sent fire brigades toward an ever-receding horizon, hunting futilely for the combustion's source. Franklin and I went up onto the roof and waited for the city to be consumed, while in the street, a congregation of Baptists was on its knees and praying in anticipation of the Four Horsemen and the "great voice from Heaven," which would adjure the seven angels to "pour out the vials of the wrath of God upon the earth." That year, the sun was lavender, the dusk purple, and the moon blue or green. We tasted ash in the air, or perhaps it was only in our fancies, where nothing is ever inconsequential and less than dire. Later, we read that human remains had been found washed up on the east coast of Africa, having crossed the Indian Ocean on rafts of volcanic pumice. (Some stories cannot seem other than lies, and some truths only exaggeration can convey.)

I could be tempted to find in Krakatoa the cause of all that befell me in that eventful year of 1883. I realize the absurdity of so medieval an explanation, but at the time, I judged the truth of things with the rashness and conviction of a sick mind. I am lucky to see things more clearly now.

Elizabeth and Susan frowned on my visit to Madame Singleton's. They had no patience for the occult. Their struggle in the visible world was difficult without "entertaining ghosts" in the bargain.

"Would you prefer it if I had nothing more to do with Margaret and her friends?"

"It's not for us to say with whom you may or may not associate," replied Elizabeth. "That is something men do, especially husbands, although I made it clear to Henry

Stanton when I agreed to marry him that I would not tolerate male despotism."

"It is better to be wed to an idea than a man!" declared Susan.

"I prefer a tyrant of my own sex," said Elizabeth, gesturing toward her soul mate. "Wait and see, Ellen; one day we shall have a woman president."

What a preposterous idea! I thought.

"Women willing," remarked Susan. "For men will never allow it."

"Why not 'God willing'?" I asked, hoping to annoy her. I would grow tired of her misandry.

"He is also a man, and one who sent His ghost to impregnate Mary without so much as a by-your-leave. In this, he was no better than Zeus when he ravished poor Leda."

The heat of indignation rose in me like mercury in a glass column. I'm not particularly religious, but the lessons of the Sunday school do stay with one. "Neither God nor His ghost ravished Mary!"

"I beg your pardon. I get carried away by my own rhetoric. Let us say, then, that God does not think as much of women as He does of men. To be fair, His ministers don't, since—lacking the omniscience of Madame Singleton—I don't presume to read God's mind. But the minds of His *spokesmen*— Do you hear how men have impregnated our language with their sex? Is this not a kind of ravishment?"

"Speak plainly, Susan."

"Is it not a rape? Men cannot help seeing women as a territory to conquer and occupy."

"You're forgetting good men like Cousin Gerrit, Garrison, Lyman, Wendell, James Mott, Frederick Douglass, Henry Blackwell, and my own misguided Henry, who was once a steadfast ally of women and their cause."

"How many of them deserted you when you had the gall to demand a woman's right to divorce the husband who beats her or squanders her housekeeping money on whores and gin?"

"Susan, this is not a lecture platform."

"Forgive me. I become overheated when I think of how I'm no better than a thing in the eyes of most men!"

"A battleax!" said Elizabeth merrily.

"Ellen, you may visit whomever you like," said Susan in a voice that called to mind a starched handkerchief.

"You are a free woman, though the world may say otherwise," agreed Elizabeth with a sniff.

I sensed their disapproval and was curious to know its cause. "Why did you both frown at the mention of Madame Singleton?"

"We have nothing against her," replied Susan. "An unmarried woman must do what she can."

Elizabeth picked up the thread, although by the strength of her conviction, it seemed like the steel cable Roebling used to knit the Brooklyn Bridge. "Our argument is with spiritualism. Men see it as frivolous a pastime as tatting doilies. A séance, in their eyes, is nothing but a hen party or a sewing bee. The Fox sisters would have done better by our sex had they joined us at the convention in Seneca Falls and declared themselves men's equals."

"Votes for women!" yelled Susan.

"Beware, you rapscallions in your boots and whiskers! We will have our day!" cried Elizabeth as she gaveled the table top with a beefy hand.

"Down with tyrants in pants!" shouted Susan, who then giggled like a parson's wife who naughtily shows her ankles. Susan bellowed a verse from a suffragists' anthem:

> Is it because that you can drink
> More whiskey, beer, and wine,
> And not get drunk, and seem to think
> Your majesty divine?

Elizabeth joined her in the chorus:

> Talk not of freedom, equal rights,
> Cold hearted, selfish knaves,
> While in our land, around our hearths,
> Dwell twenty million slaves.

"How is Margaret?" asked Susan, prompted, I supposed, by the song's last line, for she could not view "Barnum's creature" in any light other than enslavement to the great humbug.

"She is as you saw her last."

"Do you mean 'abridged'?" asked Elizabeth, still caught up in the madcap current.

"I mean 'offended.'"

"Does she bear us a grudge?" Both women appeared to have been taken by surprise.

"She did not bother to speak of you," I replied airily.

"Ah!" said Susan.

"Oh?" asked Elizabeth.

The exclamation of the former and the question of the latter amounted to the same thing—chagrin, a response that would have made me smile had I not taken care to put on a severe face.

"We are embarrassed for having insulted her," said Susan regretfully.

"We hope to make it up to her," said Elizabeth contritely.

Unwilling to exhaust the subject, which clearly pained them, I changed it. I wanted to leave something in reserve for their future humbling. As I unfolded the *Tribune,* a complicated mixture of repugnance and morbid excitement stole over me. "Alferd Packer killed and ate his companions." Before the ladies could object, I read the account of the cannibal's testimony:

> Old Man Swan died first and was eaten by the other five persons about ten days out of camp. Four or five days afterwards Humphreys died and was also eaten; he had about one hundred and thirty three dollars. I found the pocket book and took the money. Some time afterwards, while I was carrying wood, the butcher was killed—as the other two told me accidentally— and he was also eaten. Bell shot 'California' with Swan's gun and I killed Bell. Shot him. I covered up the remains and took a large piece along.

Then traveled fourteen days into the agency. Bell wanted to kill me with his rifle—struck a tree and broke his gun.

I was glad not to have been the court stenographer in the case of *Alferd Packer v. the People of the State of Colorado*!

"Packer ate five people. James Gould gobbled up ten thousand miles of railroad track and right of way! The plutocrats have made America their dining table, and each day they sit down and devour us!" cried an impassioned Susan.

"The only difference between Packer and the profiteers is the cleanliness of their linen and the correctness of their grammar!" exclaimed Elizabeth, no less heatedly than her friend.

"Men are cannibals!" snarled Susan, showing her teeth, which appeared at that moment to have been filed. I marveled at the transforming effect of rage on the human countenance.

I chose not to mention Elizabeth Donner, who had cooked Samuel Shoemaker's arm. I was afraid I had lit a fuse that might hoist me with my own petard. The atmosphere in the room was combustible enough to blow Miss Redpath and us to kingdom come. What was Krakatoa's fury next to that of twenty million women "slaves" incorporated in their most ardent deputies? Neither needed me to set them off, however; they had been well primed at the National Woman Suffrage Association convention.

"We rebuked the so-called justices of the Supreme Court for declaring Native Americans to be 'dependent aliens!'" roared Elizabeth, who looked as if she could eat the eminent jurists raw. "It won't be long until the Indians join the bison in extinction, and when both have been dead and forgotten for a century or so, they'll be resurrected on our stamps and coins."

Had she acquired clairvoyance in Philadelphia? I mused.

"Overturning the Civil Rights Act of 1875 is shame enough for one year!" fumed Susan.

The month before, the United States Supreme Court had ruled that the equal protection clause of the Fourteenth Amendment did not guarantee blacks a seat on a 'bus or a train, in an eating house or the necessary one. Only the good Justice Harlan dissented.

"We have Chief Justice Waite and his raven-robed flock of dunces to thank for that particular injustice! There've been too many others for one man to take credit for them all." Elizabeth had worked herself into a rage, which brought color to a usually pallid face.

"Waite would have the negro wait, wait, wait for his rights!" growled Susan.

"Negroes may have been emancipated by proclamation and law, but they've yet to achieve equality with whites!"

"White *men*!" said Susan, glowering handsomely. "In law, women are inferior to black men."

"God took Adam's rib and created woman. Centuries later, man beguiled woman into having one of her ribs removed for the sake of the feminine ideal, which is, in actuality, his own vision of womanly beauty. In exchange

for her rib, he gave her a whalebone corset, the second symbol of her bonded servitude. Now she pants and faints in
wasp-waisted submissiveness, risking death by asphyxiation
for her mate."

Neither Elizabeth nor Susan would submit to the
"murderous contrivances of the corset shop," as Catharine
Beecher described the fashion that kept women delicate,
out of breath, and near to swooning.

I was beginning to fear that my suffragists would rush
out of doors, take the first train to the District of Columbia,
and burn Chief Justice Waite in effigy—or else dispatch
themselves to eternity by a stroke suffered together in perfect accord. Another change of subject was required.

"The other day on Broadway, I saw—"

"What did you see, Ellen?" snapped Susan, whose brain
was nearly pickled in the vinegar of resentment.

I thought an account of the Wild West Show would get
them going down another track.

I had stood in the crowd and watched as a General Custer
impersonator (the real McCoy having reached an inglorious
end at the Little Bighorn), a genuine, if embarrassed, Sitting
Bull, and Buffalo Bill led the Congress of the Rough Riders
of the World down Broadway. Sitting his horse as he now
does his chair in the President's House, the dude rancher
Theodore Roosevelt was conspicuous for his patrician nose
pinched by a glinting pince-nez. A bedraggled band of dis-
couraged Indians and a mangy buffalo completed the spectacle, which fired the fancies of onlookers who saw themselves
as Buck Taylor, the "King of the Cowboys," or Miss Annie

Oakley, the "Peerless Lady Wing-shot," who could shoot dimes from between Frank Butler's fingers.

At the last moment, I stopped myself from describing the cavalcade, foreseeing that it would only increase the ire of the two women for the exploited Indians, as well as the miserable buffalo. I'd heard enough for one day concerning the inequities of the world, which, according to Susan, had begun in Eden, where Adam had been given sway over everything that flew, swam, crawled, and—after the expulsion—bled monthly between their legs.

"What was it you saw?" asked Elizabeth, sensing my hesitation and ready to pounce.

"Alice Vanderbilt's 'Electric Light' gown in Lord and Taylor's window." I was pleased with myself for having defused a bomb as deftly as a Confederate miner in the defense of Richmond. Or so I thought; my fiery suffragists were not so easily quenched.

"Well, I never!" spluttered Susan, looking as if I'd worn muddy shoes into the parlor.

"Electric Light gown, indeed! It's a shocking waste, considering the multitude of poor souls who live in unlighted tenements no better than sties!" raged Elizabeth.

Despite myself, I had provoked them. I blushed shamefacedly and apologized abjectly, asking if they would forgive my frivolity and assuring them both that I was not—at heart—just another "silly female."

Passions spent, they let the matter drop.

"I have a letter to dictate," said Elizabeth. "If it is convenient."

"Yes, of course!" I exclaimed. I would have mucked out the Augean Stables to keep my situation.

"Your willingness does you credit," said Susan, her expression softening.

"As does your ability," said Elizabeth, to show that I was forgiven.

Solemnly, I took my place at the typewriter and poised my fingers above the keys as if waiting for a conductor's baton to release in me the first notes of a heroic overture. The letter, which Elizabeth briskly dictated, was to Julia Ward Howe, president of the Association for the Advancement of Women, a former abolitionist and the versifier who had penned the "Battle Hymn of the Republic," to be sung to the tune of "John Brown's Body." Mrs. Howe was the widow of Samuel Gridley Howe, who had been a member of the Secret Six, which financed the insurrectionist John Brown and who fled to Canada after Brown's attack on the federal arsenal at Harper's Ferry failed.

September 27, 1883

Miss Julia Ward Howe
241 Beacon Street
Boston, Massachusetts

Dear Miss Howe,

I enjoyed the time we three spent together in Philadelphia, and hearing your thoughts concerning the "Ordination of Man as Earth's Plenipotentiary." I agree with Susan's view that the original injustice committed against our sex occurred in Eden with Adam's cravenness. In our opinion, man and woman were created in perfect equality, and only much later was the story of the Fall altered to depict Eve as a treacherous being at the mercy of her appetite. Whether the alteration was deliberate or due to a copyist's error, we cannot know. I would tell the story thus:

"Then the woman fearless of death if she can gain wisdom takes of the fruit. Having had the command from God Himself Adam interposes no word of warning or remonstrance, but takes the fruit from the hand of his wife without a protest.

"When the awful time of reckoning comes, and the Jehovah God appears to demand why His command has been disobeyed, Adam endeavors to shield himself behind the gentle being he has declared to be so dear. 'The woman thou gavest to be with me, she gave me and I did eat,' he whines."

After Adam's despicable conduct, I am amazed that men can claim superiority to our sex or to the meanest dog in the manger.

Sincerely,
E.C.S.

If you are a son, I said silently, apostrophizing the small being growing under my belly's hill, I trust that you will one day be worthy of your Eve. If you're a daughter, I hope you will find an Adam who would shield you from God Himself until you're able to shield yourself with the same laws granted to men. Whether you're a son or a daughter waiting to take up your life, I wish that your time on Earth will be just and that you'll take up your future as heir to a legacy left you by people like Lincoln, Grant, Garrison, Emerson, Frederick Douglass, John Brown, and my two suffragists— an inheritance you are meant to share with others. I wonder if those names will be remembered or expunged from the nation's faulty memory.

You should know this much at least about Elizabeth and Susan: They were famous (or notorious) for their militant dedication to the rights of the disenfranchised. In 1848, as a young married woman, Elizabeth found her voice and purpose at the Seneca Falls convention, which sparked a slowly burning fuse that has yet, in 1904, to touch off the powder keg of revolution but must do so in the fullness of time— not God's, but that of women, who are more patient than He and infinitely more long-suffering. Three years later, Elizabeth and Susan met by chance on a street in Seneca Falls, where each had gone to hear a lecture given by William Lloyd Garrison, who before the war had been slavery's gadfly and abolition's fierce and fearless spokesman. As he had done in aid of abolition and suffrage in the pages of his newspaper, *The Liberator,* so the two women would do in theirs, *The Revolution,* which they published together in an office of the Women's Bureau, near Gramercy Park.

I would not have believed that words could accomplish anything much to ameliorate the conditions of an unjust world—not the hundreds of thousands strung together in knotty sentences by Henry James or the incendiary ones of two elderly women in Murray Hill that I typewrote on my Sholes & Glidden. "You must believe that words can change the world," said Elizabeth, "if not for the world's sake, then for your own. The fruit of which Eve ate was a book."

A Minotaur in Bellevue

TOWARD THE END OF OCTOBER, we were visited by Jacob Riis, a police reporter for the *New-York Tribune*. In a rented room on Mulberry Bend, called "Death's Thoroughfare," he wrote about the slums, especially those of the Lower East Side, and photographed the poor who scrabbled in the noisome tenements. His grim pictures—not easy to look at—were pricking the conscience of those who had one and inciting reformists to demand the enactment of laws against exploitation by landlords and sweatshops.

When we four had seated ourselves and made polite inquiries into one another's health—even revolutionaries will observe the rudimentary social conventions—Riis explained the reason for his visit.

"I do not involve myself with the subjects of my photographs," he said without apology, his English muddied by the Danish he had grown up speaking before emigrating to America. "It is for people who see my photographs to involve themselves. I take a picture, like a burglar breaking into a house; I have time to steal only one, and then I must quickly leave. If I asked for permission, the tenants would be suspicious and not let me inside. If they did, they might turn their faces away in shame or put on false ones, which would not tell the truth about themselves. Do you understand?"

"Yes," said Elizabeth, and Susan concurred. His question had not been addressed to me, so I thought it best to say nothing.

"Good!" said Riis. "I knew you would."

He opened a worn leather case and took out a print he'd recently made from a dry-plate negative of a girl lying in a stairwell. The way she had folded her arms and legs to make herself compact reminded me of Miss Etta, only the girl was dirty and miserable.

"She's no more than fifteen or sixteen," said Riis. "She is skin on bone, sick; her eyes are sunken. I took the picture and hurried away, as if I'd stumbled on a corpse. Something must be done! I told myself. But what? Would the Female Almshouse on Blackwell's Island be better than her filthy place under the stairs?" He opened and closed his hands helplessly. "I wonder. Good ladies, what's to be done?"

The photograph had spoken in tongues of fire, inflaming the suffragists.

"In the morning, we will see what can be done!" vowed Elizabeth and Susan, as if they were Grant and Sherman preparing to take Vicksburg. "Mr. Riis, will you show us the way?"

They arranged to meet at ten o'clock at the corner of

Mulberry and Baxter streets, near Ragpickers' Row. In back alleys, stable lanes, and byways—familiar to rent collectors, if not to health inspectors—men, women, and children hunted for anything that could be eaten, burned, sold, or pawned. Inside ramshackle, foul, lice-infested cavities, the poor (in possessions as well as in spirit) sat waiting, sullen and oppressed, surrounded by the "amenities" the city's ash heaps and refuse barrels afforded them. For what were they waiting? Eviction, the asylum, death, potter's field. Perhaps a few Christian hearts still waited for Jesus to roll away the stones from their tombs.

I recall reading in the *Herald* from a speech given by Clarence Harrington, whose opinion of the city's multitude of indigents was uncharitable, though not exclusively his own.

> The poor are our common enemy. They must be dealt with harshly before their desperation turns into enmity; in other words, we must defeat them and drive them out before their self-hatred can be turned against us. Henry George, the communist, speaks of "wage-slavery" and the "tyranny of non-producers over producers." He accuses us of a "crime against the poor," and he would have you empty your pockets in redress. He and the Mugwumps would have you tithe, like the papists, a tenth of what you earn by your labor and industriousness. And should a tenth not be enough, because the poor are many and you are few by

comparison, then give them twenty, thirty, fifty per cent—give all that you have until you and your family are the poor!

The tenement house where Riis had photographed the girl stood—or rather, slumped—at number 79 Baxter. The girl was lying under the stairs on torn newspaper. I've seen dogs do as much in preparation for their newborn. The sight and smell were too much even for the suffragists, who blinked, pinched their nostrils, and stepped backward into the comparative spaciousness of the cellar, whose earthen floor was crowded with crates, battered and mildewed furniture, and old tools too rusted from neglect to be of use. The New Jerusalem would never be built here.

Inured to the stink by his frequent visits to the city's rankest slums, Riis bent over the girl and felt her forehead. "She is burning with fever." She was muttering—call it "gibbering," since the effect it had on me was terrifying— the same words over and over: "I lost my baby. I lost my baby. I lost my baby."

We heard footsteps on the stairs. Raising our eyes from the wounded animal—forgive the word, but in her help-lessness, she seemed like one—we watched an old woman descend, carrying a plate of soup and a cup of water.

"Two days she's been like this," said the woman, whose dress looked as if it had been fished from a barrel with a stick. "She won't eat or drink, poor thing."

With few to pity them and still fewer to help, the poor

pitied one another. I hope there's a Heaven and a big gate to slam in Clarence Harrington's face.

"She says she lost her baby."

"I don't know about that," said the woman, whose face was as crazed as the china cup she had set down next to the girl, together with the bowl of soup, which looked revolting. "She was here when I came down to look for something to burn in the stove."

"You never saw her before?"

The woman shook her head. "There be plenty that look like her, though."

"But not so many who would look after her." Riis's remark was meant in praise of the old woman, whose eyes registered nothing except weariness—and maybe a little wariness, since she could not make out what these fine people were doing in the cellar.

"The well-to-do want the poor to be well behaved and deserving of their charity," said Elizabeth, who could mint epigrams in the most direful situations. "This girl would have been neither."

"Maybe not," said Riis.

"Which is her right!" Defiance was never far from Susan's reach. "We're not here by the sufferance of the rich!"

I thought the girl was likely to die before the argument was finished, and said so.

"We must get her to the hospital!" declared Elizabeth capably.

"I'll get my old man," said the woman.

Her husband looked frail. But the girl weighed almost

nothing, and he and Riis carried her outside and put her into a coach for hire. Susan opened her purse and handed the old man a two-dollar bill. He hesitated. I guessed that he felt a remnant of shame, but his wife's had died an unnatural death, and she snatched the bill and gripped it in her fist.

When we were seated inside the coach, Elizabeth called to the driver up on his box, "To Bellevue, and don't spare the horses!"

He touched his whip to the horse's rump, and the coach jumped forward; its wheels sent up a cloud of grit. The girl's head lolled on her breast as we bounced over cobbles. She was the incorporation of the misery of a million people jammed into 37,000 tenement houses—a scale of pauperism too vast to help or even comprehend. Forty thousand bodies filled the city's asylums and workhouses; half a million beggars and ten thousand tramps passed among us, eliciting disgust, if they were noticed at all. More bodies—call them that, since they appeared to be more dead than alive—crowded the Lower East Side than Bombay. But our attention was centered on this girl, gratefully. To have only a single life on one's conscience is a convenience in the same way that one pesky fly is easier to swat than a swarm, one itch less irksome than a rash.

Located in Kips Bay, on First Avenue, near the East River, Bellevue Hospital had been an almshouse and, along with the penitentiary and pesthouse on Blackwell's Island, had served Gotham's poor by making the sick well or, from its morgue, by sending them to the potter's field on Hart

Island, in Pelham Bay. Whether they went thence to glory or perdition was a matter for theologians. The girl, whose name we could not discover, was attended by Dr. Jasper Garmany, a surgeon whose competence extended even to the brain, which he would trephine with a drill resembling a carpenter's. He was a decent sort, and I suppose skillful at his trade, if daunted by the number of patients and the seeming futility of his work; no sooner had he treated one of them than three others took his or her place. The poor are often sick and not always articulate; like drunkards, the insane, the febrile, or those stricken by religious mania, they often speak in an alien tongue. The girl continued to bemoan the loss of her baby, whose whereabouts never would be known. (Sentimentalists may like to imagine that the infant was rescued from the alley where it had been rudely loosed into the world and, in time, would become the scion of a Fifth Avenue millionaire.)

We stayed with her in a whitewashed room while she alternately thrashed and went limp in the bed, which seemed, in contrast to her small, gaunt body, enormous. There was nothing we could do, and as it turned out, nothing Dr. Garmany could do, either. She died before he could allay her fever, reverse the course of sepsis, undo the effects of hunger and poverty, relieve the pressure of blood blooming inside her skull, or stitch up her broken heart. Despair, too, could have been sufficient cause of death, a canker not even the finest surgeon in the land can lance.

"I'm sorry," he said as a nurse drew the bedsheet over the girl's head. I was glad he hadn't shrugged, a gesture often revealing an unsympathetic character, or a demoralized one.

Elizabeth was upset by the death of the girl, who shortly would be buried as Jane Doe, wife of John Doe—names bestowed upon the nameless since the time of King John of England. I supposed that my suffragists were disappointed not to have had the chance to parade the girl—in her misery and degradation—before lecture audiences. In those days, I was often cynical.

"Will you be claiming the body?" asked the surgeon.

Putting their heads together, Elizabeth and Susan conferred in hushed voices. When Riis discreetly left the room, I followed, hoping that they would not make a tour of the lyceums with the dead girl. I shuddered at the thought of her sitting in a stifling Chautauqua tent in the dog days of summer, her spoiled condition a reproach to faithless men and hardened hearts.

I walked down a corridor until I came to a room in which the more docile of Bellevue's lunatics were permitted to sit and take the sun streaming democratically through barred windows. I smiled at a young man, who responded with a look so serene, it could only be called "beatific."

"Good morning, madam," he said, and added anxiously, "It is, is it not?"

"It *is* a good morning, sir," I replied cheerfully. "I hope it finds you well."

"It does not find me at all," he replied, touching a finger to his nose. "I am too cunning for it."

"I see," I said, preparing to be amused.

"What do you see?" he asked, nervously looking around him.

"I see *you*," I said.

My answer appeared to reassure him. "Ah! I'm glad. They do not allow glasses, you know."

"Glasses?"

"Looking glasses. Without one, I can't be sure that the person who is here is I and not an impostor. 'Seeing is believing,' as Thomas Aquinas said—and quite right, too. Unless it was Mr. Krueger who said it. Mr. Krueger gives me my baths. They're therapeutic, you know; they open the pores. I would suffocate otherwise."

I could not help laughing; he was so droll.

"I would like to see you this evening, if it can be arranged," he said, like a philanderer in one of Douglas Jerrold's melodramas.

"I'm sorry. I have a previous engagement." He seemed such a boy; I didn't want to hurt his feelings.

"Would it be difficult to break it?" He gave me a knowing glance.

"I'm afraid that would be quite impossible!" I felt like an actress uncertain of her lines.

"So much is impossible for humankind, when every day a spider climbs the Himalayas."

I had been about to leave, but the cleverness of his remark stayed me. He was a charming and plausible young man.

"I want to draw you in the nude," he said, and this time there was a sinister quality in his tone. He continued airily.

"I am an artist, you know, or I would be if they'd give me back my pencil." Again, he touched a finger to his nose and whispered, "The blind man has it and will not give it back."

I felt—well, you can imagine!

"Your breasts are said to be very fine, and I have heard that the dank place between your legs is magnificent! I once painted a woman who had a tiny crèche there. An angel showed me it. I was astonished. Who wouldn't be? Because I'm devout, I bowed down and worshipped it. I sent the painting to the Vatican, in care of Pope Leo the Thirteenth, to be hung in the College of Cardinals. I'm still waiting for His Holiness to acknowledge the gift."

He covered his face with the palm of his hand like a saint in contemplation. "*Peekaboo*, I see you!" he said gleefully, his eyes peeping through his fingers. "God the Father has lain with you, you naughty girl!"

I hurried from the room. I heard his footsteps behind me, but I dared not turn around. The perspiration stood out on my forehead, my heart beat fast, and I felt my chest and throat tighten. I considered calling for help, but the hallways were empty, the doors to the patients' rooms shut. In my accumulating fear, I ran from one empty ward to another. In the amphitheaters, surgeons dressed in bloody aprons were sawing arms and legs and tossing them into buckets. I rushed up a stairway, only to find myself in the basement morgue, where row after row of shrouded corpses lay in eerie silence until, one by one, they shouted "*Peekaboo!*" from underneath their sheets. I screamed, but no one came to my aid.

I wandered like a child in a garden maze, too small to peer over the hedge tops. Endless corridors were spawned by rooms that multiplied on either side. Behind closed doors, moans, gibbers, and guffaws made my blood run cold. I ran down a flight of stairs that led, perversely, to the roof, where chimney pots, each a miniature Krakatoa, were spewing ash. The East River had turned to blood. I would not have been surprised to see Aaron stirring the water with his stick while Moses snickered. I felt like the poor Minotaur lost in the Labyrinth, waiting for Theseus to come and slay it. I roamed the balconies on which inmates would gather to watch Barnum and his circus perform, as they sometimes did to prove the impresario's munificence. The balconies could have been on the moon, so very desolate they seemed. Exhausted, I went inside the sprawl of brick and iron and lay down on an empty bed. I shut my eyes and, after a time, opened them.

"Why, Mr. James!"

Henry James was standing by my bed, one hand on its rail, the other clasping a bunch of primroses wrapped in sheets of *The New York Evening Telegram*. His overcoat exaggerated the stoutness to which he is prone. Having remembered his hat, he took it off and looked about for a place to hang it. Finding not so much as a peg, he put it down—with an odd tenderness—on the room's only chair.

"Mr. James, you startled me!" Although I had been employed as his stenographer and typist, I would no more have called him Henry than I would have presumed to criticize his prose, which I thought tedious, or to kiss the novelist's face, which, with its wide mouth, thin lips, and goggling eyes, reminded me of a frog's.

"My apologies, Mrs. Finch. I've been meaning to visit you ever since your confinement, but the work, you understand, was in a critical phase. I hope you are recovering."

"I'm not ill."

"I was given to understand your wits were turned." Had a look of disappointment briefly clouded his face and glazed his eyes? "I made inquiries at Mrs. Lang's and was informed that you are being treated for hysteria."

"I assure you I am not!" I replied indignantly.

"At present, you *are* residing in the Bellevue lunatic ward."

"I'm merely resting. Today has been quite exhausting."

"Be that as it may, I have missed you, Mrs. Finch—your skill and complaisance."

My face registered surprise, a reaction that prompted him to explain himself.

"Mrs. Lang sent me a 'Miss Maisie,' and she has proved a dullard. She does not grasp what I am saying—or rather, how it is that I am saying it. It's not necessary that she understands me, only that she takes down my dictation accurately. It's a nuisance, and she fusses overmuch about her working conditions. I had to have the Carlton desk relocated because of the glare of the late-afternoon sun on her machine, and I've had the devil of a time about the chair. The chair, she claims, is unsuitable for a person operating a typewriter. You, Mrs. Finch, made no such demands. Moreover, you could always be depended on to keep your head above the 'stream of consciousness,' as my brother calls my narrative method, while this Maisie person drowns in it. She is unsatisfactory, and, I suspect, a socialist. I am hoping you will return to Washington Square forthwith, so I can sack her, sans reference."

He had reached the end of his preamble, for so I felt it to be, having sensed his reluctance to pick up his hat and leave me in peace. With the primroses still in the clutch of his meaty hand, he made a noise in his throat, reminiscent of the rumbling of the Numidian lion I had seen at the menagerie in the Central Park or, to be less fanciful, in the pipe conveying steam to the radiators in Rothschild's millinery store.

"Is there something else, Mr. James?" I asked when I could no longer bear the sight of his discomfiture. He signed piteously. "Why don't you sit?"

As before, he surveyed the room, dismayed by its austere furnishings, which consisted of the bed, a table on which sat a water pitcher and a glass, a chair used by consulting physicians and presently occupied by his top hat, and a walnut cabinet, whose contents were known by the medical staff, though not by me. He was still clutching the bouquet.

"Why not put them there?" I suggested, indicating the glass pitcher on the table.

"But, madam, your thirst. It may become intolerable."

"If it does, I shall drink champagne!" I said gaily.

He regarded his hat, a lovely fawn derby.

"Perhaps it would be safely out of the way underneath the bed," I suggested.

He took the hat in his hands, sat on the chair, and bent forward to stow the hat beneath the bed. Having glimpsed the bedpan there, he recoiled and decided to sit with his hat on his lap.

I had found the little farce wonderfully entertaining and smiled at him, grateful to have my mind distracted from the confusion of the morning and the mounting sense of panic that had ensued. "Now tell me, Mr. James. Whatever is the matter?"

"I had hoped to find out whether Galen or Kos was right concerning—" He buttoned up abruptly.

"Concerning what?" I asked with a gracious wave of my hand, as a queen would use to bid her subject to continue without fear of the executioner's ax.

"Your womb . . ." He had gone quite red in the face.

"My womb?"

"I beg your pardon!" he stammered, his old impediment reasserting itself.

"You were inquiring after my womb," I repeated pleasantly. We might have been talking about my tonsils.

"Forgive an author his curiosity, but I would have liked to know whether it wanders, as Hippocrates of Kos maintained, or is the stationary organ Galen declared it to be."

"I've no idea, Mr. James." I was determined to be agreeable.

"Aretaeus conceived of the womb as an organ of the body closely resembling an animal, for it is moved of itself hither and thither in the flanks and, in a word, is altogether erratic. Many physicians still believe this to be the case."

I stared at him as one would at a talking ape. By this time, I may have even gaped, an undignified rearrangement of the human features alien to polite society.

"In that you are sane—I trust that you are?" he asked, his tone conveying the wish that I were not.

I bristled. "Perfectly!"

He went on in that pedantic way of his, which at the best of times irritated me. At that moment, the time was of the worst. "Hysteria, whose Latin meaning is 'belly,' is believed to be caused by a wandering womb."

"I'm afraid I can't help you, since I am not hysterical."

"Ah!" He was crestfallen. "Hysteria would make a wonderful subject for a horror tale, don't you think? I would have called it *The Turn of the Screw* had you been able to furnish a firsthand account of the various sensations experienced during your madness."

"I'm sorry to disappoint you."

"No matter. But if you should ever feel that wandering sensation in your belly—I beg your pardon—please take note of it."

He gathered up his hat and coat and left. I shut my eyes, the better to be alone with my thoughts. After a while, which could have been ten minutes or two hours, I opened them. For a moment, I feared that I had imagined Mr. James's visit; novelists in the flesh were hard enough to manage. Then I detected the ghost of cigar smoke that his clothes habitually gave up, and on the table beside me were the yellow primroses. He was not a figment, I thought, much relieved.

I left the room, only to find darkness, particulate and writhing, in the corridor. I felt my way like a blind woman through twisting passages that, in their form, resembled tripe, until I found an unlocked door. I staggered onto First Avenue and blinked in the blessed light of day. The pavement heaved and then fell flat like a blanket shaken to rid it of leftover dreams.

I was distraught, as anyone would be after having escaped a nightmare of uncommon terror. So vivid had it been, I could not believe, at first, that I was not still caught in its toils, no matter how furiously I shook my head to clear it of the remnant fear. Not even in Edgar Poe's horrors had I read anything to equal what I'd experienced at Bellevue. I walked the hospital's frontage and the riverside esplanade, but Riis and the two suffragists were nowhere to be seen. Passersby kept their distance. When I saw myself reflected in a store window, I understood their caution. My hat was gone, my hair had come undone, and my shirtwaist was ripped, my skirt bedraggled. I could easily have been mistaken for a heroine in a sensational novel or an escaped lunatic clutching a yellow primrose in her hand.

I walked down Avenue A to Tompkins Square, where the draft riots of 1863 had started. Weary to the bone, I chose a bench shaded by poplar trees and made myself presentable. Thirsty, I drank from the fountain beside a horse trough. Beside me, a horse noisily sucked up water. I turned in time to see a splendid woman giving her arm to a gentleman, the snowy egret feather of her hat dazzling in the noonday sun. Somewhat revived, I took a 'bus to the Brooklyn Bridge, which had opened five months earlier. I felt a sudden need to visit the house of my childhood across the river on Vinegar Hill.

The Memorial Day panic on the roadway of the bridge a week after its inauguration was fresh in the minds of citizens on both sides of the East River. That October afternoon, I crossed it for the first time. I was too preoccupied by the strange occurrences at Bellevue to worry about the integrity of Roebling's colossus, which, at the outset of his thirteen-year Herculean labor, had been called his "folly."

The smell of New York Bay, arriving on a northerly breeze, recalled the People's Day, when Franklin and I had stood on a rooftop in Printing House Square. We were in mourning for the death of his brother, Martin, who had "met an untimely end," as scribblers for the two-penny papers like to say. We'd gone up on the roof in the hope of giving grief the slip—at least for the afternoon. We watched President Arthur, Governor Cleveland, and their frock-coated entourage step from the Fifth Avenue Hotel, across the street from Madison Square, into a blaze of bunting, banners, shiny commemorative medals, and madly waving flags. On Broadway, down which the illustrious would ride to the bridge's Chatham Street entrance, Old Glory hung at every window. The citizens of Manhattan and Brooklyn were choked to maudlin tears with a patriotic sentiment not felt to this degree since the opening of the Erie Canal. Not even Lee's surrender to Grant at Appomattox Court House had ignited civic enthusiasm to equal the bridge's grand inaugural day.

Nearby our aerie, a mob of "sporting men" soused to the gills were pouring champagne down their throats from hundreds of bottles, breaking chairs for firewood, and roasting an ox on the roof of the *Police Gazette* Building. From midtown to the Battery, Manhattan was overrun by fifty thousand gawkers who had arrived by steamers and milk trains. Rural swains in old-fashioned cutaways and green ties, assorted rubes, hayseeds, and country bumpkins were buying five-cent souvenirs and scratching their chins in wonder. The streets surrounding Chatham Square— Bowery, East Broadway, St. James Place, Oliver, Mott, and Worth—were packed past all hope of unpacking till the next day. Franklin and I were stunned by the shrill uproar of steam whistles, calliopes, and regimental bands and by the clamor of a multitude thick as the masts of ships crowding the river from Red Hook to the Navy Yard. At midnight, Thomas Edison threw a switch at the Pearl Street generating station, and the great bridge blazed forth—a new constellation heralding the "American Century" to come and our inexorable destiny. Fourteen tons of rockets hissed and wheezed in a bombardment sufficient to crack the walls of a citadel. We stuffed our fingers in our ears and shouted "Hooray" like children. Martin was absent from our thoughts—no memory could survive the din—and afterward, we were ashamed.

Vinegar Hill

I CROSSED THE BRIDGE TO BROOKLYN, my mind oppressed by thoughts of Martin, the dead girl, the sight and smell of the tenement house, my wandering womb, and the morning's hysteria when I could not find my way out of the hospital, as if its staircases and corridors had been copied from the twists and turns of a human brain disordered by lesions beyond Dr. Garmany's surgical skill. I recalled with fondness Martin's friend Shelby Ross and our summer picnic in the Central Park, where he and I had played innocently at being a shepherd and a shepherdess, while Franklin had walked to the refreshment stand in the Ramble to eat ice cream. I'd been happy then. Martin had not yet died, nor Shelby gone to prison for avenging his murder. Franklin was still in New York City, and I was not carrying a child conceived by "fornicating" with my own husband. You see how things stood.

Tomorrow I will take the train to Sing Sing and visit Shelby, I promised myself.

I went north along the heights to Vinegar Hill, a short distance from the Brooklyn Navy Yard. I had last walked that way on the day that Franklin and I were married. There had been a small wedding party at Mother and Father's house. For all his great size, Franklin was shy. I, too, was shy, afraid of his hands and the muscles visible under his shirt sleeves. I knew him to be a gentle man; his gentleness was one of the reasons I'd fallen in love with him. But I also knew, as every woman does, that a man can sometimes forget himself. I was afraid—he was such a big man! In time, I grew to love the strength of his hands and arms and the power of his body, which, more often than not, he held in check to please me. Sometimes I wonder if it did, in fact, please me to have been handled like a china cup. I did love him—I do so still, despite love's complexity.

On Vinegar Hill, I gazed across the river at Manhattan, where the Trinity Church spire would later turn pink as the afternoon grew into evening, and at Wallabout Bay, where ships of the North Atlantic Squadron were docked. Father had been a carpenter at the yard till he came down with yellow jack and died. Afterward, Mother went to live with a widowed sister in Michigan. When I was a girl, I would walk down Columbia Heights to stare at the second-floor window behind which Washington Roebling, the famous invalid, sat by the hour and watched his prodigy slowly taking shape until, at last, the granite towers were strung with steel cables and the bridge resembled the Irish giant's magic harp, on which the winds used to play their ancient airs.

I turned off Fulton and walked in the direction of the city park. Charred timber and fallen stones marked the place where my house had once stood at the corner of Pearl Street and Nassau. After Mother left, a tramp acquired the property, claiming that his manifest destiny demanded it. Later, he fell into a drunkard's sleep, leaving his tobacco pipe unquenched. I walked to the post office on Washington. Megan, a childhood friend, lived nearby, together with a loutish husband and a sickly infant. When she answered my knock on the door, I was surprised at how she had aged;

she was only three years older than I, but her expression was hangdog and careworn. Her chestnut hair was dull; dull, too, were her eyes. Had I not known they were blue, I would have said they were gray.

"Hello, Meg!" I said with a cheerfulness I didn't feel. I knew at once my visit was a mistake. She needed jollying, and in my present mood, I was not the one to do it. She let me inside, and I sat on a threadbare couch in a gloomy room and felt dampness working its way into my bones, though the October day was warm. I studied a face that had once known the bright and buoyant loveliness of a girl in bloom, but at the time of my visit, the bones of her cheeks and jaws were sharp beneath the yellowish skin. I wondered if she, too, was sick. I'd heard that her husband, a layabout and a drunk, sometimes showed her the back of his hand, as the Irish say, without the sting of rebuke abuse deserves. I discreetly searched her face for bruises and was glad to find none.

"It's been some time," she said, as if she had been counting the days since we were girls and played on the Heights and the gravel shore of the river below. "You look well, Ellen." Had she spoken grudgingly?

Not meaning to, I blurted, "I'm expecting!" We had never kept secrets from each other, and I suppose the intimacy that can, in women especially, override embarrassment, even shame, reasserted itself, although five years had passed since we had been in each other's company.

She smiled wanly and tried to find the proper tone for congratulations, but it rang false. It occurred to me that she was lucky to have only one child, and I could have prayed, then and there, that she would have no others, because, by the look of her, she could not bear it.

"And Tom?" I asked for form's sake.

"At work," she replied. I knew that she had lied. I hoped he was not in the other room, sleeping off a spree. I began to grow anxious that he would awaken and find me there, "putting ideas" into his wife's head. I grew more anxious still that he would come strolling through the front door on his long legs, in his big boots, and shout down the house for his supper. I wanted to make some excuse and go, but I stayed awhile longer for Megan's sake. She may have wished me gone as much as I did. We sat, each with her heart in her mouth, trying not to chew the tender thing to pieces. Regardless of how bruised and hardened it can become, at the heart of the heart, there will always be a morsel of tenderness—a foolish thought, perhaps.

"How is Franklin?" she asked when the silence had grown too loud.

"He's in California, looking for work."

She nodded indifferently, as if I'd said he'd gone down the street to buy a cigar. Five years have done for her, I thought. Five years or a little less and the light had died in her eyes and in her heart, and I did not have the heart to see if I could find a vestige of innocence there.

"How is Little Tom?" I asked, to have something to say.

"He's been poorly. He's asleep. The doctor came yesterday."

"What did he say?"

"Some kind of fever."

"Well, I hope Little Tom will feel better soon."

Megan made a face and shrugged her shoulders, and in that face, I saw her helplessness, and in that shrug, I understood that her helplessness extended throughout the universe, which she did not understand.

My only thought was how to take my leave without hurting her feelings, assuming she had any left to hurt. That was unkind. But nerves can become raw, till they eventually grow calloused. How could we go on otherwise? She must have seen the thought in my eyes or in the nervousness of my hands, because she stood and said, "I best get Tom's supper on the table."

Relieved, I could reply cheerfully, "It was good to see you again, Meg!"

Only then did I realize that I was holding a yellow flower in my hand. I'd carried it all the way from Bellevue. I handed it to Meg. She regarded it rather stupidly, I thought.

"You must look in again," she said. "It was nice to catch up."

I nodded cordially, knowing that I would not look in again and that catching up had been a torture neither of us would wish to repeat. I left the house, trying not to hurry. When I turned the corner onto Myrtle Street, I began to breathe freely. I put Megan out of my mind, since there was nothing I could do for her.

By this time, I was hungry. I walked to a German eating house at Fulton and Sands. Franklin and I had gone there during our courtship to eat chops and dark bread and drink the bitter German beer. The table was scarred by heavy knives, cigars, and long-stemmed pipes called "*Lese-pfeife*" wielded by generations of emigrants who had found, inside the tobacco-darkened walls, the tastes, smells, and guttural sounds of Prussia and Saxony. I recalled the plea-sure we had taken in that place where the language sounded like gravel. Afterward, we'd walk up Vinegar Hill to watch the sun set on the far shore of the Hudson and, in a reces-sional as inexorable as it was majestic, redden the waters of the Hackensack, Passaic, Delaware, Lehigh, Susquehanna, Allegheny, Ohio, Illinois, Mississippi, Missouri, Arkansas, and Colorado until, having sunk below the trembling rim of the Pacific Ocean, it swam up into someone else's day.

I ordered blood sausage and potatoes, which I ate with relish between gulps of lager beer.

"Mrs. Finch?" I had not seen the man approach my table, but I now recognized him as Herman Melville. He had been Martin's and Shelby's superior at the Customs office on Gansevoort Pier. "It is Mrs. Finch, is it not?"

"Yes."

"We met at your brother-in-law's viewing."

"I remember you, Mr. Melville."

"May I join you?"

I had not wished for company, but his handsome face and kindly manner overruled my reluctance. "Please do."

He sat and looked me squarely in the face. His gaze was neither shameless nor intended to satisfy a man's curiosity. He looked at me with a sympathy so quick and genuine, it could only be habitual.

"Martin was a fine young man," he said without pre-liminary. "Now and again, I would stand outside St. Paul's Chapel just to hear him sing. He had the voice of an angel. No, he had the voice of someone who could discover the godliness in us, of which only a few are aware."

It was my turn to look deeply into Melville's eyes, and I did so gratefully.

"He was a sweet person," I said. "Franklin and I are lost without him."

"I'm in touch with Shelby Ross. I understand you and he were friends."

"And Franklin!" I said with unnecessary emphasis. "Mr. Ross visited us at our house on Maiden Lane. I said nothing about Shelby and my fête champêtre in the Central Park.

"He has behaved admirably. I have nothing but good things to say about him."

I don't know why, but I blushed—perhaps because of the intensity of Melville's gaze. He *is* handsome, I thought, with his broad brow and grizzled beard, and those eyes of his see right down into one. I had always been curious about the man who had written *Typee* and *Omoo,* books that decent Christians shun for their immorality. How fine it would be, I thought, to typewrite the stories of such a man! What a relief from the gentility of Mr. James's world.

"How is Mr. Ross?" I asked, employing the tone of voice one would use to inquire after a grocer's lumbago. "I've heard nothing since he went to prison."

Melville seemed surprised. "I imagined you would have written to him, and he to you."

Embarrassed, I shook my head.

"He's well and in good spirits. I visit him now and then in Sing Sing. He has a job in the warden's office, keeping the accounts. Shelby is a likable fellow. I am convinced he will make something of himself yet."

"Franklin and I are grateful to him."

"It would do him no end of good if you were to visit him."

"Why, this morning, I resolved to do just that! I was unkind to him when you and he visited us in Maiden Lane to offer your condolences."

"Excellent! If I were not otherwise engaged, I'd accompany you." He sensed that he had presumed. "If your husband would allow me the pleasure." I suppose he could not help himself: He smiled, but not as some men do—those, I mean, who leer.

He took a cigar case from his pocket. "Shelby is fond of cigars. Whenever I visit, I take him a box." Causing the waiter to frown, Melville tore a linen napkin into strips and carefully wrapped each cigar. He used his teeth, and I shivered at the sight of them. "There! Just like a pair of Egyptian mummies. Unscrupulous businessmen used to grind the ancient bones into powder and hawk it as medicine, then sell the cloth windings to the paper mills. Thus were the pharaohs and the pharaonic cats resurrected not as lords and minions of the sacred reed fields, but as two-penny rags advertising Fairbank's Fairy Soap and electric corsets."

Melville was an amusing man when he was not a gloomy one.

"If we can believe Mark Twain's account in *Innocents Abroad*, contemporary Egyptians buy three-thousand-year-old mummies by the carload to stoke the boilers of their locomotives. But perhaps you don't care for history." His glance was so sharp, one could feel like a prize moth transfixed by a pin.

"I care for it as much as the next *wo*—" I had meant to say "woman," but I realized that Melville, like nearly all his sex, would take my words to mean that, like most women, I cared nothing at all for intellectual topics. I finished my sentence: "—*begone* prisoner of it."

Melville smiled wryly. He did really seem to read my thoughts, which were chasing one another like children in a schoolyard or geese on a lawn. He handed me the mummified cigars. "Please give Shelby these, along with my good wishes."

I put the cigars in my purse.

"Are you traveling back to Manhattan?" he asked. I nodded in the affirmative. "Will you allow me to ride with you?"

"Of course, Mr. Melville." What else could I have said?

"Call me Herman."

"If you don't mind, I prefer to call you Mr. Melville."

"As you like," he replied with a smile that could only be described as inscrutable.

We walked down Sands Street to the bridge's Brooklyn entrance, built on the site of St. Ann's Church, in which my parents had been married and in whose yard their parents had been interred without much pomp or fuss. The dead had been uprooted and sent by wagon to Green-Wood and Evergreen cemeteries to continue their sentences, which were as long as eternity and impossible to commute. I recalled Elizabeth's having said that her family's church in Johnstown, where she was raised, became a mitten factory. "Better that hands should be kept warm in winter than minds frightened into sanctity."

I was glad that Melville suggested we cross the river on one of the new bridge trains; I was nearly dropping from exhaustion. From Sands Street to the Chatham Street entrance on the opposite side of the river was more than a mile. We sat by the southward-facing windows, open to a tonic ocean breeze, and admired, as people do, the sights that passed before our eyes as if the scenery had been painted on a scroll that was being unrolled for our pleasure by unseen hands. I had the window seat. Melville sat beside me, stretching his long legs into the aisle. He talked easily of this and that, and I replied with equal cordiality. He seemed an affable man, although I recalled that Martin and Shelby had experienced a darker side of him. I thought that any man who could have written *Moby-Dick* would need to take a comprehensive view of human nature.

"Living on Maiden Lane, I suppose you and Franklin could not help being swept up in the fuss and folderol of the People's Day."

"Yes." I told him how we had stood on a roof in Park Lane and smelled a roasting ox.

"Sporting types are actors without talent. Denied a legitimate stage, they shout, shove, bellow, and brawl in a barroom or on a rooftop and think they are great fellows, when they are merely fools. What a shame that John Wilkes Booth could not have been content on a less momentous stage than history's! Bored with the smell of greasepaint, he wanted the stench of blood in his nose. Well, history is a raree-show where men are remembered for the enormity of their crimes. I'm exaggerating, of course, but truth in our time is best told as Mark Twain tells it."

He made several other remarks that struck me with their bitterness. He also recalled how the river on the day of the bridge's grand opening had been bright blue. "I can't remember its having been so before."

We got off the car and stood awkwardly on the pavement. I sensed that he was reluctant to part company. I wished only to go home and sleep; however, I didn't want Melville to know that I was living with two suffragists. I've no idea why I should have cared.

"Can I escort you home?" I guessed he thought I was living still on Maiden Lane, which was not far from where we stood and dithered. "There're many rats and roughnecks about."

"Thank you, Mr. Melville, but I'm stopping at a friend's."

"Then I wish you a good night, Mrs. Finch." He tipped his hat and took a few steps down Chatham before turning round. "If you do see Shelby, please tell him that I'm doing what I can for him. And don't forget the cigars." He tipped his hat again, and I soon lost sight of him in the crowd.

Angel of the Waters

NEXT MORNING, I TOOK the Hudson River Railroad train to Sing Sing. In my purse were Melville's gift of cigars, a book of Longfellow's poems, a cabinet card showing Martin at Coney Island, and a molasses cake Elizabeth had baked "to cheer up the gentleman," as if I were visiting a shut-in and not a prisoner convicted of manslaughter. Despite the dreary brick pile of the penitentiary, the town is admired for the beauty of the Upper Hudson, with its views of the high bluffs, Hook Mountain, and Croton Bay. Beyond the bay, the river widens at Haverstraw to more than three miles from shore to shore. Ships, barges, and packet boats travel thirty miles upriver from New York City, stopping at the port towns along the way, and thence north to Albany, Lake Erie, and the Ohio Valley wheat fields.

When I disembarked at Sing Sing, a light rain had begun to fall. By the time I arrived at the prison and took an uncomfortable seat in a dismal waiting room, I regretted the three-hour trip from the city. Elizabeth and Susan had urged me to rest after the previous day's exertions. Concerning my panicked wanderings inside Bellevue Hospital and having met Henry James, I said not a word. Seeing that I could not be dissuaded, the two women went with me to the depot and waved their handkerchiefs as the train shuddered into motion. I settled into a plush seat and fell asleep, heedless of the monumental Palisades and the western bluffs. I didn't wake until the train stopped at Tarrytown to take on passengers—a drummer in hardware wearing a checkered coat and a derby hat and a woman who struggled with a Gladstone bag and would not surrender it to an amused porter who followed behind her with a creaking baggage truck.

As I waited for Shelby to be brought down from the cells, a guard handed me a dingy towel to dry my face and hair. When I thanked him, he replied gruffly, like a man embarrassed by his own kindness.

An interval of dreadful expectancy ensued, which in retrospect always brings to mind the first verse of the eighth chapter in the Book of Revelation: "And when he had opened the seventh seal, there was silence in heaven about the space of half an hour." At last, the guard, who did not utter a word as he led me along a dim bricked passage smelling of carbolic, motioned me toward a small room, like an usher showing a lady into a box at the opera. Shelby was sitting on the other side of a wire screen. "You have ten minutes," said the guard.

"Only ten? I came such a long way," I said meekly, because bears—and the guard was a bear of a man—prefer honey to vinegar. The bear must have had a toothache, since he repeated, "Ten minutes."

"I have a cake." He took it "to be examined." I'll never know if Shelby tasted it. "And two cigars from Mr. Ross's friend." I turned to Shelby. "Mr. Melville sent them."

"I'll see that the prisoner gets one."

I held the photograph up for the guard's inspection. "A

picture of my late brother-in-law." I showed it to Shelby. "I thought you'd like it."

"Thank you kindly," he said. His face was ashen, like his prison clothes, but maybe the murky light made it appear so. The rain falling hard on the roof sounded like nails spilling from a barrel.

"The prisoner can keep the picture," said the guard, taking it from my hand with a studied brutishness, which I sensed was only partly intended. He may be spied on through a chink in the wall by the Grand Inquisitor of Sing Sing, I told myself. "I'll leave it in his cell."

"Thank you, sir," I said timorously, a counterfeit of a helpless woman, which would have infuriated my suffragists. I pictured Susan beating the blockhead with her umbrella.

The guard took a seat behind Shelby and, taking out his pocket watch, noted the time.

"You look well," said Shelby, smiling in that endearing way he had.

He did not look well, so I didn't return the compliment. "Are you all right?"

"I am. It's good of you to come. How is Franklin?"

"He has gone to San Francisco to see about a job," I said, and immediately wished I had not. Martin and Shelby had been planning to move to San Francisco; they'd had jobs waiting for them there. "I'm sorry, Shelby."

"Water over the dam," he said with forced cheerfulness. "Or under the bridge, if you prefer. I'm looking ahead now."

"It was a mistake to have brought Martin's picture," I blurted.

"Not in the least! He was a good friend—a better one than I realized at the time. I can't forget him, nor do I want to. I am glad you brought it. And please tell Herman that I continue to be grateful. He, too, has turned out to be a friend. I would never have believed it possible!" He laughed good-naturedly. "He can be a cussed so-and-so!"

I told him about my encounter with Melville and mentioned that he was doing what he could to help Shelby. As we talked, I would glance at his face to satisfy my curiosity concerning his welfare. His eyes appeared lusterless and sunken, the sockets deep and black. He had lost flesh; his chin and cheekbones were prominent. He had the pallid complexion of someone who has not been outside for a long time. Overall, he seemed listless, although I could see that my visit pleased him. I was glad I had come and gladder still that I did not feel the excitement I'd once known in his presence. You are cured of *that*, I told myself, and hastened to add that there had been nothing between us except an innocent flirtation. My composure strengthened my belief in my virtuousness. I could afford to be solicitous, even to show him the affection that a sister can a brother whom she has missed.

"What will you do when you leave here?" I asked, determined to be as forward-looking as he.

"I haven't thought much about it. I suppose I'll take up some business or other. I have a cousin in Texas. Perhaps I'll be a cowboy like Theodore Roosevelt."

We laughed, and I realized that anything important we might say to each other had been said before he went to prison. I don't recall our parting words or having walked the wet streets to the depot. As the southbound train left Sing Sing, I drowsed. I was very tired and wondered whether the trip—the effort I'd made and the nervous anticipation I'd felt beforehand—had been worthwhile.

I awoke to the crying of lambs in Sheep Meadow. Shelby and I carried crooks to hook about the necks of those that had fallen into a ravine. We said words to each other, which I did not understand. I knew they were without comfort. The Angel of the Waters had left her place atop Bethesda Fountain. She gave me a yellow primrose and announced that I was with child and must go to Bethlehem. Beside her stood the cherubs Peace, Temperance, Health, and Purity, which had accompanied her from Emma Stebbins's fountain in the Central Park.

I was sitting in a drafty waiting room. I held an infant on my lap. Far away a man who might have been King Herod told three commercial travelers wearing checkered suits and derby hats, "Go and search diligently for the young child; and when ye have found him, bring me word again, that I may come and worship him also." And there was much sniggering in Jerusalem among the Pharisees.

Once again, I fell asleep, and when I awoke, the train was hurtling south. I passed New York City. Elizabeth and Susan waved their handkerchiefs. Little Margaret sat on an elephant's trunk. The next minute, I was riding through tobacco fields. Black men, women, and children were laboring in the sun. Though I was sitting inside the train, I could feel the heat on my face. The conductor approached me and said that I was needed in the locomotive. I carried my baby to the front of the train. He was wrapped in cloth strips, and his face was covered—I supposed to keep the flying grit from his eyes.

"Don't let the fire go out!" admonished the conductor, who delivered me into the hands of Mr. Roebling, the chief engineer.

"It will be too bad for you if you let the fire out," said Roebling, his hands inside dainty white gloves that, in spite of the oil and coal dust, were immaculate.

I put my baby down and, looking behind me into the coal tender, saw that it was piled high with mummified cats, stiff in ragged shrouds. I began throwing them into the firebox, one after another—there seemed no end to them. Dust rose from the windings and brought tears to my eyes. The linen cloths rustled in my hands. At last, the tender was empty.

"Don't forget that one," said Roebling, pointing to a child wrapped in swaddling clothes.

"No, sir," I said sweetly. "That is *my baby*."

"It's dead as a stick," he replied. "Give it to the purifying flames."

"It will make no difference to the fire," I said cannily. "The sons of Adam are small."

"The oven has a mind of its own," said Roebling, his face revealing perplexity before the god of steam called Moloch. "Once kindled, it will not be denied."

I laid the swaddled babe in golden straw, which crackled pleasingly as it burned.

"Now dry your eyes," said the guard, handing me a towel.

"Who's watching the prisoners?" I asked him, laying a hand flirtatiously on his arm.

"They have all been put to death."

My shoulder began to shake. "Are you all right, my dear?" asked Roebling.

"I've lost my baby," I replied, sobbing.

"Wake up! You're dreaming."

"I tell you, I have lost my baby!"

Light peeped in at my shuttered eyes. I opened them and saw a woman gently shaking me by the shoulder.

"Your head is hot," she said. "You have a fever." She mopped my damp brow with a handkerchief. "You must've caught a chill walking in the rain. Can you hear me?"

"I lost my baby," I repeated stupidly.

"I get off at the next stop. You'd better come with me. My house is nearby the depot. You can rest till the fever passes. I'll call a doctor if need be. You better get off the train with me."

I mumbled something and shut my eyes again. I felt her arm around me and some other's arm, too. I was being helped from the train. A porter offered to wheel me in his baggage truck. I lay on rough planks. They smelled of tar. A blanket smelling of horses covered me.

"Am I going to the stable?" I asked.

"Hush!" said the woman's voice.

I rumbled over cobblestones, over paving, over gravel. The gravel greeted me cheerfully like an old man who had fought in the war and no longer cared a whit what people thought of him. I heard singing, but maybe not. The gravel spoke in a crackling voice. Try as I might, I could not make out the words. They were drowned in the roar of the firebox.

A door opened. I was borne aloft like the queen of Egypt visiting the house of her grand vizier. A door closed, and the fire, whose voice was alien to my ears, fell silent.

I heard grunting; the inflection suggested that a question had been asked.

"She's delirious, the poor dear."

I smelled smoke.

"They're burning mummies!" I cried.

"There, there! Put her in Louisa's old room," said the woman. "And put our your cigar."

I was lifted in a man's strong arms and carried lightly up the stairs.

The Shower Bath

LILIAN HEIGOLD, WHO HAD TAKEN ME off the train at Dobbs Ferry, sat by me until morning, when, satisfied that my fever had broken, she went to her own bed and slept. As I lay in mine, I was aware of her husband's presence, a mute one as it turned out: Fred had lost the power of speech at Gettysburg, after a rebel's minié ball nicked his vocal cords. There was kindness in his eyes and in his hands as he brushed the damp hair from my brow in a wordless gesture of compassion, which speaks for the heart. I thought Mrs. Heigold was fortunate in a husband who could never scold or belittle her.

By the afternoon, I was well enough to sit up and break my fast with ginger biscuits and elderberry tea, a remedy for fever. The room used to belong to the Heigolds' daughter, Louisa, who'd married and moved to Ohio, where her new husband, a Unitarian minister, had a church in Oberlin. The room was pretty and bright; the walls were papered in pale pink roses; the brown wainscoting and windowsills had been painted white, as though to hide an ugly truth—namely, that Egyptian brown paint was made from ground-up mummies.

Through a window, I saw the Hudson shine behind a screen of willows. A coal barge disappeared below a reach; black smoke from its funnel marked its progress south toward the city. Passersby walked along the street in haste or idleness. A young woman had paused in her outing with a collie to speak across a hairpin fence to a young man holding pruning shears. A boy in knickerbockers rolled a hoop. The dog barked at him. The man said something, and the woman laughed. A postman hurried self-importantly down the sidewalk, as if he had the Treaty of Guadalupe Hidalgo in his bag. A delivery wagon bounced on rubber tires down the bricked-over street. The driver's head was sunk between his shoulder blades; the horse's head hung low—the man and his beast a picture of dejection. A whistle shrilled; a crow shied, cawing, from a mansard roof; a train pulled into the station and briefly vanished in a cloud of smoke.

"May I ask what you were doing in Sing Sing?" inquired Mrs. Heigold.

She meant the prison, not the town. "I was visiting an acquaintance."

"I saw you leave. I almost came up to you because of the rain, but I thought you might not wish to share an umbrella with a stranger." She meant that I might have been embarrassed to be seen leaving the prison.

I managed to smile. I may have taken her hand. I understood that a show of gratitude was required of me; however, I knew nothing about the woman except that she had done me a kindness. For all I knew, she might have been one of the officious tribe who like to stick their noses into other people's business—the more tragic or scandalous, the happier they are.

"Ellen, please forgive me," she said, having sensed my uneasiness. Say what you will, the compassionate gift is greater than any possessed by a clairvoyant, medium, or spirit rapper, and just as rare.

"Why were *you* there?" I asked, turning the tables.

"The warden and the board of governors allow me to visit the prisoners once each week. Sing Sing is a dreadful place! The name derives from the Algonquin phrase *sinck sinck*, which means 'stone on stone.' Their shamans must have foreseen the prison that would be raised on the site of their village two hundred years after the tribe sold it to a

Dutchman. Naturally, they were cheated, and the Dutchman prospered."

"Are you a Quaker, Mrs. Heigold?"

"I'm not religious, although I pretend to be. Otherwise, the authorities would not let me inside. Ostensibly, I'm there to lead the men in Bible study, but my purpose is to monitor their well-being as far as I am able. I need to be discreet. Questioning them about conditions at the prison is forbidden. I've learned to be alert to signs of mistreatment."

"How long have you been doing your good work?" Thinking of dear Shelby, I saw it in that light.

"Ever since attending the National Conference of Charities and Corrections in Louisville. During the war, I was a nurse at the Union Hospital in Washington. I met Walt Whitman there. I also met Louisa May Alcott. We became friends and allies in the woman's suffrage movement. In Concord, she was the first of her sex to register to vote. Among modern women, Louisa is by no means 'little.' We named our daughter after her."

My ears had pricked up at the words *woman's suffrage*.

"I send my appraisals to Mr. Brockway, warden of the Elmira Reformatory and one of the few prison administrators who oppose the brutalities that are commonplace at Sing Sing. The so-called shower bath is especially cruel. It's given most often to negro inmates, who are said to be in need of it."

I didn't see the harm in it and said as much.

"It is a punishment, an extreme one, judging by the number of men who die from it."

With a stick of chalk, Lilian sketched the apparatus, which would have gladdened the heart of Torquemada, on a slate. (The house was furnished with chalkboards for Fred to use.) "Picture a fairground booth like one where a fortune-teller sits turning over cards. Bound hand and foot and pilloried by a wooden collar, the prisoner sits inside it on a stool. From a large funnel, a torrent of water pours onto his head with such force, he can hardly breathe.

"Now imagine the poor man showered with ice-cold water for a half an hour or more. It's not unheard of for prisoners to drown or die afterward in their unheated cells of pneumonia or the inhuman strain on their bodies. Christ didn't die of His wounds, but from His struggle to draw breath." Careless of the dust, Lilian erased the slate with her sleeve. "The shower bath is a refinement of the ducking stool once reserved for women, but I take no joy in the fact that men are made to suffer it."

"Do you know Elizabeth Stanton and Susan Anthony?" I asked.

"I know them well. Are you a suffragist, Ellen?"

I waited for an answer to emerge from the mind's darkroom, like a photographer for an image to bloom in the developer bath. "Yes," I replied, although the image was blurred.

"I'm so glad to hear it!" With a joy of recognition, she embraced me like a Jew finding another of the tribe in a dungeon beneath the Vatican. When I told her of my arrangement with Elizabeth and Susan, I sensed that her enthusiasm became cooled, if not chilled, by something she preferred to leave unsaid.

"I ought to be getting back to New York."

"I'm going to the Tarrytown Lyceum this evening to hear Emma Hall speak on the reformation of criminal girls. Why not come with me? Tomorrow, after a good night's sleep, you can take the boat back to the city."

Although I was not tempted by the opportunity to sit through a lecture on "an important issue of the day," I was by the thought of awakening in Louisa's cheerful room to the piquant odors of river water and gardens gone to seed and to a breakfast such as I had envied when I came downstairs and saw Mr. Heigold finishing his. So I agreed.

"You must let Mrs. Stanton and Miss Anthony know you're here. They're sure to be worried."

We walked to the Western Union office, on Palisade Street, and I composed a telegram with the laudatory terseness preferred by God for His pronouncements and by merchants for theirs, if not by writers who are paid all too meagerly by the word.

CAUGHT CHILL STAYING WITH LILIAN HEIGOLD
DOBBS FERRY RETURN TOMORROW (STOP) = ELLEN

Not since news of Custer's defeat at the Little Bighorn had hissed over the wires from the Crow Agency in Montana to the far corners of the American Empire had a finger tapped at so frantic a rate as the one, stained yellow by tobacco, belonging to the crusty telegraph operator at Dobbs Ferry. I pictured him at a spirit table, rapping out messages to the bereaved from their dearly departed, who had left Earth without so much as an overnight bag. For thus it is written: "As he came forth of his mother's womb, naked shall he return to go as he came, and shall take nothing of his labor, which he may carry away in his hand." And don't think, ladies, that the masculine pronoun *he* used by the holy scribblers exempts you from the laws governing property in the afterlife. Thou shalt not take so much as a thimble with you! As a woman is on Earth, so shall she be in Heaven— owning not even the shift in which she was buried. (In *The Woman's Bible*, Elizabeth granted our sex pronomial equal- ity; suffrage, however, still waits for the coming of a more enlightened age.)

I exaggerate and exaggerate until I begin to see a truth emerge.

In the afternoon, Lilian and I rambled to North Brook in the shadow of the Croton Aqueduct whose route she sketched in the dirt with the stick she carried. The great iron pipe begins at the Croton River Dam near Sing Sing, skirts the Tappan Zee, crosses the Yonkers River into York- ville, veers toward Manhattan, and empties into the Murray Hill Reservoir, at Forty-second Street and Fifth Avenue, decorated in the style of the pharaohs. The forty-one-mile gravity-fed works had been the marvel of our modern age till the Roeblings—father, son, and the son's wife, Emily— erected their own colossus.

"New Yorkers owe their drinking water to the Wom- an's Christian Temperance Union and the great fire of 1835, which turned seventeen city blocks into charred ruins," said

Lilian, poking a jack-in-the-pulpit with her stick in a manner that made me shiver. "Property owners demanded an adequate water supply to safeguard their real estate, and temperance crusaders clean water for New Yorkers relying on ardent spirits to quench their thirsts. What cholera and yellow fever stewing in dirty water couldn't accomplish, fire and liquor did: The city's noxious springs, wells, and cisterns were condemned and bricked up."

The previous day's storm was visiting its miseries on some other place. The grass and the remaining red chestnut leaves had dried in the high noon sun. The leaves at our feet spoke of copper and bronze amulets like those Martin and I had once seen among the Egyptian antiquities displayed at the Mercantile Library. I was tired of causes, regardless of how noble. You mustn't think me insensitive. I'm sorry for the sick and needy and for those wounded in body, mind, and spirit. My compassion takes in the elephant and also the gnat, to speak fancifully, as my brother-in-law used to do. But my heart was bruised by his death, by Shelby's imprisonment, by the loneliness I had felt ever since Franklin left, and by the cup that Elizabeth embittered each time she complained that she was "as deserving of the vote as any ignorant negro man or nativist lout." I missed the suave words of Mr. James, which, in the tobacco haze between us, would gather into an edifice as grand as the brick and iron arches of the Croton Aqueduct. How that dumpling of a man can sing!

I regretted having agreed to go to Tarrytown. I couldn't fan the least ember into a flame of enthusiasm for prison reform. The more Lilian went on about it, the more irritated I became. I did admire her courage; she needed it to walk among cutthroats and murderers. At Sing Sing, I'd been terrified as I followed the guard down a brick corridor pierced by iron doors. I nearly jumped out of my skin when his heavy keys clanged against one another in that narrow place, a cave of echoes that could have unmanned Hercules—or unsexed an Amazon.

"What do you think?" asked Lilian.

She'd stopped beside one of the masonry ventilation towers that draw fresh air into the pipe to sweeten the water and keep it flowing toward the distant city, where it slakes the thirsts of good men and bad alike. In water, we flourish or drown. It's careless of our kind and obedient to no law save gravity, which neither governments nor engineering geniuses can annul.

"Ellen, you're miles away," said Lilian, thankfully without reproach.

"Forgive me," I replied, jerking my head as I would to break a spider's web touching my face. If only the snares of the wicked were gossamer! "I was thinking of something else."

"Your friend Mr. Ross?"

"Yes." She was welcome to believe that Shelby and I shared an attachment. In a way, we did, though not the sort relished by vulgar minds. Call it a "virtuous" one, as Mr. James does in his novels. Most of us measure our happiness by the number of friends we make and keep; the vicious, however, do so by the number of people they shun.

"Would you like to rest your feet?" Lilian pointed her stick at a fallen tree. "I should like to rest mine."

"Do they trouble you?" I asked, glancing at her walking stick.

"I turned my ankle, helping you from the train."

"Oh, I am sorry!" I said, regretting my previous annoyance with her.

"It will soon mend."

We sat in silence. Studying her face and figure, I decided she was pretty. The years of controversy had neither coarsened nor unduly aged her.

"I'm a lucky woman to have married the man I did. Fred has always treated me as an equal partner in a marriage that brings us both joy despite the sorrows that beset every living soul. He lets me do what I must. I hope *you* will marry as well as I did." She glanced at me slyly. "When will the baby arrive?"

"At the end of December." I stroked the gravid hill. I'd decided to be faithful to the lie that I was unmarried. I didn't want Elizabeth and Susan to think less of me for being other than the unwed mother they supposed. The distance from their cheerful apartment to the fetid cellar at 79 Baxter Street was less than it appears on a street map of Manhattan. A woman could fall out of a feather bed and land in a nest of torn newspapers in the time it takes to unlace her shoes.

"You should not have been traipsing through the streets of Sing Sing in the rain!"

"It was foolish of me," I admitted contritely.

"It certainly was, young woman!" Her disapproval silenced me. She dug a furrow in the dirt with her stick, cutting an inchworm in two. A jay squawked; a squirrel rustled in the rusty leaves; the wind shook the tassels of timothy grass at our feet, as though nature were censuring me for a carelessness shown toward her priceless gift.

"Lilian?"

"Well?"

"Have you ever lost a baby?"

"A boy to diphtheria. Why do you ask?"

"What did you do?"

"Cried, cursed God, and then I clung to Him, whom I was sure did not exist."

"My husband's in San Francisco!" I blurted, afraid that God, even a nonexistent one, might rebuff a wife who disavows her spouse. God's a man, after all, if an exceptionally tall one. (I pictured Henry Dode.)

"And your Mr. Ross?" Her tone was neutral, and I could not guess its meaning.

"A friend of the family."

"It's no business of mine in any case," she said, getting to her feet.

"No, it isn't," I replied with an insolence I immediately regretted. She glanced sharply at me. "I beg your pardon, Lilian."

"It is usual for the nerves of an expectant mother to be finely strung." Flailing her stick, she rid a burdock of its leaves, a plant country people call "beggar's-lice," and I understood that the subject of my pregnancy, whether sanctified by marriage or not, was closed. "Shall we walk on?"

Grief is a complicated emotion, whose course and outcome can baffle us.

At Palisade Street, we left the road that continued along the aqueduct. I went inside the Western Union office, where a telegram awaited me.

EXPECTING YOU TOMORROW REGARDS TO MRS H (STOP) = E.C.S.

"You won't tell them I'm married," I said hopefully.

"I do not tattle!" she replied indignantly.

I felt she deserved an explanation for my unusual request. "They would not have hired me otherwise."

"They move in mysterious ways."

At the ferry slip, deckhands unloaded trunks from a steam packet just arrived from Castle Garden, located off the Battery, where immigrants stepped into America before Ellis Island was opened in 1892. Three families, whose lilt betrayed their potato-famished origins, were getting off the boat. A pair of good-for-nothings jeered at the newcomers while hooligans recited a singsong piece of doggerel about cat-licks and mackerel snappers.

"Not all my neighbors agree that a stock is made richer by variety," said Lilian. "They look down their noses at an Irish stew." She harried the brats with her stick and stared down the two loafers until they turned and left, but not before shouting "Green niggers!" at the bewildered families on the dock.

I listened to the river lapping over gravel, its soughing among the reeds. I wrinkled my nose at the odor of a rat rotting on the boggy shore. I remembered the stench at the bottom of the cellar stairs where the wretched young woman had gone to die.

"Mrs. Stanton is devoted to the cause, but her privileged childhood blinkers her. We fell out after the war, when she declared that the right to vote should be given to 'educated women first, ignorant men afterward.'"

I stood near enough to see the face the rat had made at Death. Was that what passes in a rat for fear? I wondered. The fierce eyes, the bared teeth I'd seen in one as my father poked it with a broom to drive it from the shed weren't there. Perhaps despair is felt by creeping things, as well as by those who kneel at altar rails or shout "Green niggers" at their fellows.

"Don't imagine for a minute that workingwomen can afford to leave the mill, factory, or sweatshop to sit in a schoolroom and be educated!"

I should have gone to California with Franklin. I was sick of the clamor of principles. I longed for the days when the house in Maiden Lane was noisy with two good-natured men and Franklin and I could fall to sleep with a clear conscience.

"What is it, Ellen? You look white as a sheet."

"I feel sick," I replied, and said no more about it.

"You need a tonic and a digestive biscuit." She led me home, an arm around my waist.

I rested on the sofa while she made beef tea. I heard the

mantel clock tick out its slow measure of domestic tranquillity and sighed.

"I don't think you should attend tonight's lecture," said Lilian, eyeing me with motherly concern.

"But I was looking forward to it!" I said, feeling relieved. I was quite the dissembler in those days.

"You need to think of the baby; your moral education can wait till after it's born."

"I suppose you're right." Fanny Kemble could not have been more convincing as a delicate creature on the verge of a swoon. She was a great friend of Mr. James.

"Fred went to the county seat to fix the courthouse clock. I hate to leave you alone."

"Don't worry about me. I'll be safely abed by the time you get back."

She felt my forehead. "I guess it will be all right. The ferry leaves Tarrytown at nine-thirty. I'll be home before eleven."

After getting me into bed and filling the pitcher with water, she went into her room to change her dress. I waited until two hoarse blasts of steam announced the Tarrytown packet's departure and then set about to explore the house. I was not myself. What other explanation could there be for betraying my benefactors' trust? It would also explain the odd sensation of watching myself perform like an actor in a play that might be either comical or tragic.

As I hunted in the closets and drawers, I yielded to an emotion apart from shame—an excitement such as I'd felt when Franklin and I had kissed on the Heights above the

East River. So vivid was the recollection, I sat on the stairs to catch my breath before going up to the attic, where I found a mildewed box of photographs. Sitting on a trunk by the glowering window, I studied them, as if to find a meaning larger than what was visible in the chiaroscuro dramas told in tableaux and pasted on gray rectangles of cardboard.

In a tintype, a pretty girl was wearing a frock dress and a big bow in her hair; by her eyes and mouth, she could only have been Lilian, and by her smile, she was happy, at least on the day she'd sat for the daguerreotypist. I saw the telltale eyes and mouth again in a photograph taken on her wedding day; she sat uncomfortably in a straight-backed chair while Fred, wearing a black sack coat, stood beside her, his hat held in the crook of his arm like a small black dog. Husband and wife were stiffly posed, their heads restrained by unseen iron clamps; their faces were tense with the effort of stillness as the light slowly drew their likenesses on a pane of silver-coated glass.

In another picture, Fred wore the uniform of a private in the Tenth New York Infantry Regiment, taken before he went to war and could still speak words of love and regret, resolution and acquiescence prompted by the mixture of desire, fear, and audacity that made Fred uniquely himself. Not so much as a thin shadow of doubt appeared in his clear and callow eyes.

Next, a young Lilian stood defiantly on a lecture plat-form between Elizabeth and Susan before they fell out over politics. The three firebrands were genteelly framed by a lectern and a fernery.

Taken by Alexander Gardener on July 7, 1865, the last photograph showed Lincoln's four assassins, hands and feet bound in cloth strips, poised on the brink of extinction, on a scaffold in the Washington Arsenal courtyard. Someone had drawn a circle around the head of Mary Surratt, at whose Washington City boardinghouse John Wilkes Booth and the other conspirators planned to murder the president. Her dark hair and eyes were not yet covered by the white hood. Union soldiers lined the arsenal wall to bear witness to the final reckoning. Four men held umbrellas in the lightly falling rain. On the back of the photograph's gray cardboard mounting, someone had written:

> There are thoughts too hopelessly discordant to
> be harmonized, individuals too firmly disaffected
> to be restored to the world, & riddles too galactic
> in their spite to be solved by a human being.

At the bottom of the box lay one of a thousand tickets admitting the morbidly curious to the hanging as if it were a Barnum spectacle. I couldn't imagine why Lilian would have it or the photograph, although she was in Washington at the time, working for the Sanitary Commission, while Fred was away in the army.

That night, I hardly slept, afraid to be alone in the house with Lilian when she returned from Tarrytown. Fred was staying in White Plains till morning. My fear was ridiculous. I could not account for it, but there it was. I locked the door to my room and listened to a distant bell toll the hours.

I woke, ill at ease. The house was silent, though the

time, by the banjo clock, was nearly ten. Having dressed, I looked into the downstairs rooms and found them empty. I went upstairs and knocked on the Heigolds' bedroom door. The bed had not been slept in. Where can she be? I wondered. I walked to the boat landing and asked the man who sold tickets if the 9:30 boat from Tarrytown had arrived the previous night. He said it had.

"With all passengers aboard?"

"No way of telling," he replied. "The Tarrytown packet is not the *Grand Republic*." He did everything but spit tobacco juice to show his contempt for the packet boat or me or both.

I went to the Western Union office and asked if there was a telegram for me.

"Not since yesterday's," said the telegrapher.

"Did you get any last night or this morning from Tarrytown?"

He consulted the book in which the night operator made his entries. "Nope."

"Any from White Plains?"

He ran his finger down the lines of ledger paper. "No, ma'am. Not from there, either."

I walked back to the house. As I waited for Lilian or Fred to come home, I asked myself, What is a photograph of Mary Surratt on the gallows and a ticket to her hanging doing buried in the attic? I felt sure that the answer lay where reason and unreason hold hands, logic and illogic kiss—a place in the mind where impossibilities are entertained and sometimes reconciled. There Lilian and Mary

Surratt were friends who had met by chance at a tearoom, bookseller's, lecture hall, or a musical evening when they were both living in Washington. For a time, Lilian had stayed at Surratt's boardinghouse, where she overheard John Wilkes Booth and Surratt's son, John, Lewis Powell, David Herold, and George Atzerodt plotting to kill the president. There, too, Mary Surratt persuaded Lilian to meet Jefferson Davis in secret at a farmhouse near Falls Church.

I closed my eyes and was no longer at Dobbs Ferry, but at Barnum's Hotel, sitting on a maroon sofa, with Madame Singleton's crystal ball on my lap. In its depths, I saw Jeff Davis disguised as a woman, as Abe Lincoln had been in '61 to foil an attempt on his life when he arrived in Washington to begin his presidency.

"I know of your loyalty to Mrs. Stanton," said Davis, taking off his spoon bonnet. "I also know that she's a reluctant abolitionist."

"Mrs. Stanton abominates slavery!" replied Lilian fiercely.

"Didn't she say 'It is better to be the slave of an educated white man, than of a degraded, ignorant black one'?"

"If negroes are degraded and ignorant, the land of cotton made them so. What is it you want, Mr. Davis?"

"I want you to convince your friend that it's better for her and for all her sex to oppose abolition. If the South prevails, I pledge the immediate enfranchisement of white women by my executive order."

"We want more than the vote."

His tongue flickered like the Serpent's. "In the new

South, white women will be afforded the same rights as white men in every department."

The glass grew cloudy, and I could see no more.

We know what happened. Lincoln was assassinated. Surratt and her coconspirators were tried and put to death. Jefferson Davis became president of the Carolina Life Insurance Company. But still a question remains: Did Lilian go to the Washington Arsenal that day to stand in silent grief as revenge was taken or in speechless joy as justice was done? Or was she standing in the rain in gratitude to the Almighty for having given her the strength to resist Jeff Davis's shiny sour apple? My brain, with its wall of bone between what is reasonable and what is absurd, no longer seemed my own. I thought of Mary Shelley's gothic horror and shuddered.

At one o'clock that afternoon, I unlocked the front door and opened it to Fred. He looked tired and distressed. His clothes were in need of the iron, his boots of the brush, his face a razor; in his haste, he'd buttoned his coat amiss. He put down his tool bag and handed me a telegram from the Tarrytown magistrate. In several curt sentences, he stated that Lilian had been arrested for disturbing the peace and causing grievous bodily harm to an officer of the law. I couldn't imagine that kind soul disturbing anybody's peace even if she had savaged a burdock and cut an earthworm in two. Fred took the slate he wore around his neck on a string and wrote in chalk, "Going to Tarrytown. Will you come?"

I agreed. He hurried up the stairs to make himself presentable. The stair treads creaked as he came heavily down them, carrying a valise packed with clothes and necessities for Lilian. We left the house and hurried to the ferry slip. I had questions, but there was no time for him to stop and answer them on his slate. The boat to Tarrytown would shortly depart; its steam whistle was urgently sounding the final boarding call. Suddenly, I was overcome by misgivings and a profound weariness.

"Go without me, Fred," I said, laying my gloved hand on his sleeve.

Puzzled by my change of heart, he stood aside to let the other passengers board.

"I must return to New York. Mrs. Stanton and Miss Anthony are waiting for me."

He nodded that he understood and walked up the gangway and onto the deck.

"I'm grateful to you both!" I called after him. "I hope everything will be all right."

Fred smiled and waved good-bye before taking a seat under a canvas awning.

As I waited for a boat, I read the book of Longfellow's poems I'd forgotten to give Shelby.

Mrs. Heigold's Stick

I WOULD HAVE LOOKED A SIGHT as I took off my hat and fell into a chair. Elizabeth and Susan put down their newspapers and regarded me with a certain wariness. I folded my hands over the "rotundity" and sighed with fatigue and contentment at having come at last to rest in a pleasant sitting room smelling of violets, the delicate must of old books, and a savory cobbler. The two women could not make up their minds whether to scold or offer me tea. In a silence invariably said to be "uncomfortable," the sounds of the house were overcome by the declamations of the street—the shouts of coachmen, the whicker of their nervous beasts, the high-pitched voices of soap-locked boys hawking the evening editions, a rumbling Third Avenue elevated train, the shrill whistles of policemen, and the mournful long-held note of a steam tug's horn.

"You look peaked," said Elizabeth, frowning.

"Your telegram worried us," said Susan reproachfully.

"We wondered whether we ought to go to Dobbs Ferry."

"To fetch you home."

"Or a doctor."

"We were in a quandary."

"Would you like a cup of tea?"

"Or coffee to stimulate you?"

"Or barley wine to fortify you?"

"Have you eaten today?"

"The food sold at the depots is unpalatable."

"And unsanitary."

"Didn't Lilian Heigold serve with the Sanitary Commission during the war?"

"How is she keeping? We haven't seen her in years."

"And her husband—what was his name?"

"Fred."

"A nice man. What a shame he lost his voice!"

"He had a fine singing voice."

"A baritone."

"He was a clever mechanic, as I recall."

"He could fix anything."

"Except his vocal cords."

"A pleasant man—always a smile on his face."

"He spoke with a natural eloquence."

"Daniel Webster without the affectations."

"Daniel Webster without 'the gigantic intellect, the envious temper, the ravenous ambition, and the rotten heart,' as John Quincy Adams said of him."

"Of Webster, not Fred."

"He could have made a powerful impression on the lecture platform!"

"Fred, not Webster, the windbag."

"Pity, Elizabeth, that you fell out with Mrs. Heigold."

"I had my principles!"

"And Lilian had hers."

"I would not budge an inch from what was right!"

"Nor would she."

"Did she strike you as pigheaded, Ellen?"

"You're an obstinate woman, Mrs. Cady Stanton; there's no denying it."

"I'm a woman of strong opinions."

"You are opinionated to a fault!"

"Well, isn't that the pot calling the kettle black!"

Having talked themselves out, they subsided into their chairs.

My replies were delivered as pell-mell as their questions

had been asked: "I'm feeling better. Lilian and Fred appear to be happy. He has not regained the power of speech. Lilian has strong beliefs; some you have in common, some not. She sends her regards." I said nothing of her residence in the Tarrytown jail. Daniel Webster, alive or dead, was of no interest to me. Of the conundrum in the attic, I was determined to put it out of my mind as a thing impossible to solve.

"I'd like a glass of barley wine and a cold supper," I said. "I'm famished."

They went into the kitchen and bustled. I heard the noise of platters, plates, and cutlery. I put my feet up on the ottoman with impunity, since a suffragist dare not complain of unladylike behavior. They brought my supper on a tray, which I balanced on my knees and ate greedily.

"We're glad to have you back," said Susan. "The correspondence is piling up."

"We won't bother about that now," said Elizabeth, her maternal instinct inflamed. "What you need, young woman, is rest. We've decided that you will spend the remaining weeks of your term indoors."

"An afternoon nap and an early bedtime!" Susan decreed despotically.

"Before my lying-in, I need to visit my house."

"Then you must do so tomorrow. On Thursday, your new regimen begins."

The next day, I took a Metropolitan Elevated car to Park Row and walked the few blocks to Maiden Lane. When I opened the door, I was greeted by the smell of neglect—heavy, dank air and a faint sweetness that might have been a dead rat in the wall. The dust stung my nose, and in my fancy, my lungs turned gray with silt. Below the unwashed windowpanes, a legion of flies armored in bronze lay on the windowsills; mouse dirt peppered the pantry shelves; advertising circulars and pious tracts choked the letter box. I consigned the circulars to the rubbish and kept the tracts to make Elizabeth and Susan bristle. As I was packing a few odds and ends to take with me, an emphatic rap was heard at the front door. A man who could be no other than Mr. Dode, the tallest in the world, was standing on the step.

"Mr. Dode," I said, opening the door to him.

"Are you Mrs. Finch, wife of Franklin Finch?"

"You know very well I am. What's this all about?"

He replied to my question with one of his own: "Is your husband expected?"

"He's traveling."

"Where is he now in his travels?"

"Is this a prank? Did Mr. Barnum send you?"

"I've come on official business. I must speak to your husband."

Having become suspicious, I tried to close the door, but he put his foot—a large one—between it and the jamb. "Leave at once, or I'll shout for a policeman!" I blustered, hoping to conceal my fright. "What're you playing at, Mr. Dode?" I elbowed him aside and called out for Mr. Ashton, for the two men were, to my mind, inseparable.

The tall man smiled and opened his coat to show me a

badge. "My name is Fischer. I work for the United States Secret Service. I've come about Franklin." Fischer took off his hat and lowered his head in order to pass beneath the lintel. Once inside, he went into the front room and chose the armchair in the shadow, leaving me to sit where the strong morning light would be in my eyes.

"Suppose you tell me where he is."

"San Francisco. He's looking for work as a typesetter."

"You're lying. He's somewhere in New York City."

Fischer waved away my objection. I could have played the *Hungarian Rhapsody* on my Sholes & Glidden with such long, slender fingers.

"Your husband is an anarchist. He and his fellow conspirators—Polacks mostly, and Jews—are planning to dynamite the Brooklyn Bridge."

If words were knives, mine would have cut Fischer to ribbons: "My husband is the most peaceable of men! He would never do such a thing! He admires the bridge and has nothing but respect for Mr. Roebling! Franklin and I stood on a Park Row rooftop for an entire day and night to celebrate its opening. We waved small flags and bought souvenirs. You are mistaken, sir, and I insist that you leave my house at once!" The heat of the sun and of my indignation had caused my pores to open. I mopped my damp face with an antimacassar.

Fischer smirked. "Comrade Finch became a Marxist while typesetting Samuel Moore's translation of *The Communist Manifesto* for a pamphlet ordered by the New York Workingmen's Party. I bet he can recite it verbatim, having handled every word of that pernicious garbage. Didn't you notice the stink? Frankly, Mrs. Finch, I would like to see your husband's neck in a noose, hemp or manila. No one makes a better rope for rough or legal justice than an American. Mark my words: We'll take the Philippines and Cuba. The Spaniards are finished. It's time now for the American Empire."

His jingoism was just so much hot air, of which men have plenty. "My husband has been setting type exclusively for the *New-York Tribune* since before the war."

"Horace Greeley's red rag! Marx and Engels were on his payroll for years. Your husband's association with the *Tribune* is hardly a recommendation for leniency."

I was reeling; my head hurt; the sun stung my eyes; my mind, like a carousel, spun from light into darkness, darkness into light, to the mad skirling of a steam calliope. But Fischer was relentless.

"I see you read *Harper's,* that Republican pile of horseshit! Thomas Nast should be made to drink his own ink." Fischer picked an issue of the weekly from the table and read a couple of column inches in a voice inflected with the sneer of the philistine:

WOMAN SUFFRAGE IN MASSACHUSETTS

KEEN INTEREST IN A BILL BEFORE THE LEGISLATURE—DEBATE BEGUN.

[BY TELEGRAM TO *HARPER'S WEEKLY*]

BOSTON, SEPTEMBER 12— The House began today to debate the question of empowering women

to vote in town and municipal affairs. On this
a majority of the Committee on Woman's Suffrage has reported adversely, but a minority favor
the bill.

"We're aware of your sympathy for the militant faction
of the woman's movement. And how are Mrs. Stanton and
Miss Anthony?" asked Fischer. Stretching his gooselike
neck, he brought his face close enough to mine to bite my
nose.

Did the Secret Service consider me dangerous? Did
they know I was typing not only the movement's history on
my Sholes & Glidden, a criticism of American progress and
morality, but also the correspondence of two of its founders?
What kind of woman could be persuaded by two notorious
harridans to work for the overthrow of Christian principles? Were my politics and living arrangements considered
as dangerous as those of the immigrant families pullulating
inside their tenements or those of the Indians cultivating
lice on squalid reservations? Should I repent of the errors of
my ways and pray that Franklin will do the same when he
reads of my arrest in *The Anarchist*? I mused. I pictured him
wearing his dirty boots, on a vermin-ridden bed, above a
chamber pot where sticks of dynamite had been hidden. In
my agitation, I heard the cables of the bridge snap and its
towers splash into the river, as if Moby Dick were threshing
the water with his tail—to the consternation of the gulls.

Fischer cleaned his own dirty boots on a sheet ripped
from the *Tribune*. A headline in barbed Baskerville caught

my eye; it announced a special engagement at Madison Square Garden of Barnum's circus, when "A Human Being Will Be Shot from a Monster Cannon." I hoped Miss Etta, the contortionist, would be the projectile and not *la petite* Margaret, and then I remembered that the news was old. Taking strength in the example of that indomitable woman, I clenched my fists. "I've nothing more to say, Mr. Fischer or Mr. Dode, except to tell you to skedaddle."

"You'll regret it!"

Seeing him there—so thin and tall that he could have caught ducks with a rake—I began to laugh. He glared, and I laughed all the harder. They can hear you in the street, Ellen, I said to myself; they can hear you in Hoboken and Brooklyn. In their jail cells, Lilian and Shelby will hear you and take heart. In San Francisco, Franklin's ears will prick up, and he will know that, in far-off New York City, his wife remains undaunted. "Mr. Fischer, you are a noodle!" I said splendidly.

Speechless with fury, the tall man spluttered a wordless threat, which I inferred from a finger shaken at me in admonition. Putting on his hat with an emphatic thump on the lid, he strode out the door. Caught by the lintel, the hat fell back into the room. With a kick such as Miss Mattie would have approved, I sent it flying into Maiden Lane. A west wind summoned, perhaps, by the ghost of a Cherokee shaman fallen on the Trail of Tears carried the hat aloft. The last thing I saw of Fischer, he was running down the lane in pursuit of his beaver.

I locked the door behind me and, pleased with myself, strolled to the elevated station.

"Well, I declare! You look like a changed woman!" said Susan after I had settled on a sitting room chair and laid my hat in my lap with an expression—I could see it reflected in her face—of triumph.

"I'm feeling astonishingly well!"

"Excellent, my dear! That is the frame of mind you should cultivate from now till your parturition."

"And afterward, if you possibly can," interjected Elizabeth, wiping her floury hands on her apron. "Childbearing is nothing compared to child rearing."

"Something smells good in the kitchen!" I said happily.

"I'm making Washington Squares."

"Hooray!"

"They're her specialty," observed Susan, glancing at her corpulent friend's figure. Susan is lean and tough as jerked meat.

"I'm as renowned in the kitchen as I am on the lecture circuit."

"Yes, dear, we know of your many accomplishments."

"Speaking of accomplishments, we have news of Lilian Heigold."

"What news?" I asked, pretending to be only mildly curious.

"Susan, where is the morning paper?"

"You were lining the pantry shelves with it."

"Gracious me! Whatever was I thinking?" She hurried to the pantry.

"God packed Elizabeth's head with brains, but her mind is becoming as ragtag as my aunt Fanny's sewing basket."

"God had nothing to do with it!" said Elizabeth, returning with a copy of the *Herald*. "My superior brain is the result of the coitus of two intelligent people. And you have no Aunt Fanny." She spread the paper on the table and turned the pages. "Here it is! Shall I read it?"

"Yes, only spare us a dramatic recitative."

"How else am I to convey Mr. Bennett's sensationalist copy?" She made a start.

SUFFRAGIST CUDGELS WARDER WITH STICK!!!

"I know that stick," I remarked. "I saw her demolish shrubs and wildflowers with it."

"For the life of me, I don't know why you subscribe to the *Herald*!" said Elizabeth, ignoring my first-person account of Lilian's hickory stick. "What it lacks in intelligence and fair-mindedness, it makes up for in exclamation marks."

"I want to know what my enemies are saying about me," replied Susan airily.

"You need only step inside Flynn's barroom to be enlightened."

"Louts and drunkards!"

"Will you kindly let me finish?"

"You were the one who divagated."

"I did no such thing!"

"What of Lilian Heigold?" I asked, impatient with their bickering.

Elizabeth resumed her reading of the item. As her eyes descended the column, her voice grew breathless, as if she were being swept away by the purple prose of a Romantic novel by Mrs. Radcliffe.

MRS. L. HEIGOLD OF DOBBS FERRY ARRESTED IN TARRYTOWN FOR ASSAULT!!

[BY TELEGRAM TO THE *NEW YORK HERALD*]

TARRYTOWN, N.Y. OCTOBER 24— During a meeting of radical suffragists, crackbrained reformers, and Mugwumps held last night at the Tarrytown Lyceum, Mrs. Lilian Heigold, age sixty, of Dobbs Ferry, charged into the yard and, without provocation, beat John "Johnny" Walker insensible with a hickory stick. So grievous are his injuries that Dr. Dryback, eminent physician and raconteur, fears that Mr. Walker may be reduced to a condition of permanent imbecility, if the inflammation of his brain does not subside.

Mr. Walker, age twenty-seven, is a lifelong resident of Sing Sing and has been a guard at the penitentiary for the past two years. His father, Johnny Walker, Sr., owns the Chappaqua Cider Press, on Saw Mill River, and is the Esteemed Leading Knight of the Chappaqua Lodge of the Benevolent and Protective Order of Elks. John Walker's mother, Sarah (née Haywood) Walker, is the organist at the Sing Sing First Methodist Church.

Mrs. Heigold has been charged with assault and battery, with the intent of causing grievous bodily harm, and was released from the Tarrytown jail on her husband's recognizance, while she is awaiting trial.

"Rubbish!" exclaimed Susan. "I know for a fact that Lilian's sixty-five."

"Ellen, did you know about this?" asked Elizabeth.

"I left before any news from Tarrytown would've reached Dobbs Ferry." Having neglected to tell the truth earlier, I could hardly do so then.

"It's outrageous!" said Susan with sufficient vehemence to undo the gray bun screwed to her head.

"Did you know that the Benevolent and Protective Order of Elks was originally called the 'Jolly Corks,' an after-hours drinking club for minstrels, founded in this very city in 1868?"

"This is not the time for a history lesson!"

"History is always timely," replied Elizabeth imperturbably, heaving her bosoms into place.

The following week, I received a letter from Lilian, which I read to my suffragists:

Dobbs Ferry, N.Y.
November 1st

Dear Ellen,

By now, you will have read of my troubles during Emma Hall's lecture on the reformation of criminal girls. I want you to know that the events of that night were not presented by *The New York Herald* in their entirety. I did hit Mr. Walker, Jr., on the head—twice, in fact. But there can be no question of brain injury, because he is as thick-skulled a piece of work as God ever miscreated. As Mr. Lincoln used to say, "Thick skulls are hard to break and twice as hard to pound sense into." The Sing Sing doctor who attended to Walker, a Mr. Dryback, is an Elk, like Mr. Walker, Sr., and I suspect them of colluding.

During the lecture, the younger Walker shouted the most vile and hateful things about Miss Hall in particular and the rights of women and prisoners in general that have ever burned my ears. When I could tolerate it no longer, I went outside to upbraid him. He was too far gone in drink to listen to reason, and after having knocked me to the ground, I got up and cudgeled the few brains God gave him.

I pray for the health of your unborn child, and remain—

> Your friend,
> Lilian H.

"If only Mr. Garrison had not up and died!" lamented Susan. "He'd have made such an unholy stink over this fraudulent business that Lilian would already be exonerated."

Turning to Elizabeth, she asked, "Is there nothing we can do for her?"

"I will write a letter to the *Herald*."

"That will hardly suffice!" remonstrated Susan. "Some action is required, no matter how reckless."

"I'm too old to hurl myself upon the town. I'm too old to shake Dr. Dryback by the lapels until his brains rattle like seeds in a gourd. Nor am I up to picketing the Benevolent and Protective Order of Elks and demanding an investigation into the character of its Esteemed Leading Knight. My dear Susan, I'm afraid I can do no more than petition the Tarrytown fathers for Lilian's release."

Better that ink is spilled than blood, I thought. I'd soon have reason to think otherwise.

"If I were younger, I'd put a stick of dynamite under the Grand Exalted Ruler's chair," said Susan, her eyes alight.

"Dear old 'Thunderbolt!'" cried Elizabeth affectionately.

My suffragists joined hands and sang "The Internationale."

"Elizabeth," I said after they'd finished the anarchists' anthem.

"Well?"

"If ever men give women the vote—"

"The right to vote is not theirs to give!" she snapped indignantly. "If only Jefferson had been more explicit in his declaration!"

"Should Margaret Hardesty be enfranchised?" I asked, wanting to bedevil her.

"She deserves half a vote in consideration of her stature,"

said Elizabeth in that dogmatic way of hers, which would often vex me.

"By that reasoning, Mr. Dode should have *two* votes!" retorted Susan.

So should Elizabeth, I nearly said, by reason of her adiposity. (I owe my high-flown style to having taken Mr. James's dictation; words would run through my fingers like rosary beads.)

"Would anyone care for cake?" asked Elizabeth, lapsing into her usual cheerfulness.

And so the days leading up to my travail, as it is aptly called in recognition of its agony, passed—seesawing between high seriousness and low comedy. I awoke at eight, took dictation after breakfast and a nap after lunch. I arose at three and worked at the Sholes & Glidden till six. After dinner, we sat in the parlor and made trivial conversation. Appreciating the frayed condition of my nerves, the two women avoided political controversy and domestic bickering. Instead of reading aloud from *The Woman's Journal* or *The Woman's Tribune*, Elizabeth read to me from Mary Nichols's *Lectures to Ladies on Anatomy and Physiology* or Sylvester Graham's *Lectures on the Science of Human Life,* which she herself had consulted "in my time."

We played backgammon, Fox and Geese, charades, and the Mansion of Happiness, "an instructive and morally entertaining amusement" in which pieces are moved on a board marked with vices and virtues toward a mansion where God's own pawns are eternally glad. Elizabeth had played it with her children to teach them lessons in hypocrisy. Thus does poetry enhance an advertising circular, art grace a biscuit tin, and theology become a parlor game. At ten o'clock, we retired to our beds and slept, soundly or not, according to our state of mind and digestion.

I recall little of the days just prior to the birth. I had grown large and was uncomfortable in all but the loosest clothes, with which Elizabeth supplied me from her closet. I was often sick and feverish, despite the late-autumn chill in the air. I could no longer sit at the machine and found even stenography beyond my strength. I was desperate to have the child out, and often during the day, I called to Franklin, who was either in San Francisco, looking for work, or in New York, getting ready to blow up the Brooklyn Bridge. Believed to be unwed, I bit my tongue and waited for nature to bring to full term what man had begun—a statement that, had I voiced it, would have given Susan and Elizabeth a conniption fit.

The baby arrived in a confusion of steaming tubs and shrieking kettles, spotted clouts and bloody gouts, the midwife's hands as red and beefy as a laundress's, pain and the sharp sting of blackness in my eyes, a slap, a cry, the looming faces of the eager suffragists. Were they eager for a boy to educate in human rights or for a girl to bind to their cause?

I glanced at the raw being laid across my belly, tasted bile, smelled the reek of blood and afterbirth, and, shutting my eyes on it all, slept deeply. I recall having dreamed of a constellation shining in my mind's darkness. I took it, or the dreamer took it, as a portent of an extraordinary event:

```
2 3 4 5 6 7 8 9 - ,
Q W E . T Y I U O P
Z S D F G H J K L M
A X & C V B N ? ; R
```

I opened my eyes on a strangely familiar scene: Three clowns, dressed in silk finery, were kneeling before the infant boy I held in my arms.

"We have come to worship him," they said as one.

"Who sent you?" I asked suspiciously, fearing this was another of King Herod's tricks.

"P. T. Barnum. We bear gifts for him whose coming was foretold." Each clown offered me a Washington Square on a plate.

"On behalf of the child, I bid you welcome and give you his thanks." I laid the baby in the manger and handed out Egyptian cigars.

Dressed as though for a Nativity pageant, Margaret, wearing cardboard wings covered in chicken feathers and a halo, stood beside the manger, while, wrapped in a gaudy dressing gown, Shelby held a shepherd's crook. His head bowed beneath the stable roof, Mr. Dode was chewing on a stalk of hay.

In dots and dashes, the Dobbs Ferry telegrapher relayed the joyous news of the Greatest Show on Earth:

```
--. .-.. --- .-. -.-- / - --- /
--. --- -.. / .. -. / - .... . /
.... .. --. .... . ... - --..-- /
```

```
•— —• —•• / ——— —• / • •— •—• — ••••
/ •——• • •— —•—• • ——•••— / ——•
——— ——— —•• / •—— •• •—•• •—•• / —
——— •—— •— •—• —•• / —— • —• •—•—•—
```

Fred Heigold chalked a message on a slate: "May he grant us all, men and women of every race and kind, the scourged and pilloried, the feebleminded and the poor freaks of the circus, the right to exist."

"We are exceedingly glad!" exclaimed Elizabeth, laying a dimpled hand on my shoulder. "We are free at last!" cried an enraptured Susan.

"But a drafty stable is no place for a newborn babe!" scolded Elizabeth, who in her day had brought forth seven babes and wrapped them in swaddling clothes.

Jumbo the elephant put his head in at an open window and trumpeted a theme by Handel.

The *Herald* proclaimed in a seventy-two-point blackletter headline:

𝕳allelujah! 𝕳allelujah!! 𝕳allelujah!!!

"I must commemorate this great occasion, which henceforth shall be called the 'People's Day!'" said Jacob Riis, holding a camera. The magnesium flash filled the room with a blinding radiance. "What is the child to be called?" he asked, licking the end of a pencil.

"Martin Finch," I replied, blinking my eyes in the morning light coming in at the window.

The imagination is part pleasure ground, part nightmare. Mine had become inflamed.

"Praise him!" cried the midwife who had attended me. She was washing the baby in a flowered chamber pot.

Stepping from the shadows, Henry James wanted to hear about my "sensations," but I refused to let the mystery of childbirth be turned into literature, which is another kind of circus.

From December 1883 until the end of April, Susan and I reveled in the novelties of motherhood while Elizabeth acted the matriarch, giving us the fruits of her ample experience, whose gift neither Susan nor I resented. The two who had vowed to belong to no man vied for the boy's affection and argued whether stewed prunes or mashed sweet potatoes were better for his bowels. The Sholes & Glidden lay under its shroud, as if it were a small mammal waiting for the provocations of spring, when new ideas would break through the crust, and somnolence be cast off.

Unlikely as it seems, I stood with only a slight trembling of the knees at the podiums of several lyceums. Elizabeth and Susan stayed home with Martin while I presented myself as an unwed mother, a status I'd come to believe to be the case. I demanded that the stigma attached to a child born out of wedlock and to his mother be erased, if not from the closed mind, at least from the statute books. I was the subject of articles in the press—most of them invidious—and saw my face engraved on newsprint. (I would live to regret the publicity.)

Invariably, I would end my speeches with a passage Elizabeth had once addressed to the New York State legislature:

> Shall the frenzied mother who, to save herself and child from exposure and disgrace, ended the life that had but just begun, be dragged before such a tribunal [of men] to answer for her crime? How can man enter into the feelings of that mother? How can he be judge of the mighty agonies of soul that impelled her to such an outrage of maternal instincts? How can he weigh the mountain of sorrow that crushed that mother's heart when she wildly tossed her helpless babe into the cold waters of the midnight sea?

The public howls for the blood of a mother who puts an end to her infant's life regardless of the poverty or savagery of the life to which the child is heir. It matters not at all that she was forced to conceive or, having given birth, was maltreated, starved, humiliated, or left to her own devices, which the world calls "depraved."

I came away from my orations—given with an ardor and an eloquence that surprised me, who was always shy of public speaking—feeling triumphant, as though my words would carry the day. I'd come home to my baby boy, kiss his darling face, and tell Elizabeth and Susan of the impression I had made, although they were more interested in telling me of a new feat of strength or agility little Martin had performed while I was gone. I was becoming vain.

In this way, the weeks and months passed, as if our former lives had been adjourned and were awaiting fate to reconvene them. We were three women at peace. A sense of purpose filled my days, and I would go to my bed each night certain of untroubled dreams.

One night, however, I did not fall asleep immediately, as had been the case ever since I was delivered of little Martin by the socialist midwife. I attributed my restlessness to the oysters we'd had for dinner; at the time, I thought they were off. Since Susan and Elizabeth ate theirs without comment, I did the same. When I finally fell asleep, I was beset by a nightmare from which I struggled to awaken. When I did, the room was dark except for a beam of moonlight. I heard a rustling of clothes and watched in fascination as Mary Surratt stole out of the shadows and picked up my baby.

"What's his name?" she asked pleasantly.

"Martin."

"Such a sweet-looking picaninny!" she said, opening the bundle and peering at his face. "They usually are."

"Picaninny?" I repeated, uncomprehending.

"I wager his father is one of those prissy, high-toned negroes got up to look like a lawyer or an undertaker."

"I don't understand," I said in bewilderment. "Where are you taking him?"

"To the cross." She might have been proposing to take a favorite nephew to the circus.

"Will I see him again?"

"You will see him there," she said, climbing out the window, the small bundle cradled in her arm. "At the foot of the cross!" she called from the pavement.

"The crib's empty!" cried Susan, shaking me roughly. "Wake up!"

"Someone has taken little Martin!" wailed Elizabeth.

"Mary Surratt," I said matter-of-factly, rubbing my eyes with my knuckles.

"Nonsense! Mary Surratt was hanged twenty years ago."

Elizabeth corrected her friend: "*Eighteen* years ago, on July 7, 1865."

"I'll fetch a policeman!" said Susan, putting on her red shawl and the gray bonnet with pale blue ribbons.

"I'll put the kettle on!" said Elizabeth bravely.

"No!" I shouted. The two women turned inquiringly toward me. "Mr. Barnum will know what to do! He's just returned from his London engagement."

"Ellen, I will go with you, seeing that I have already put on my hat."

"Will you have breakfast first?" asked Elizabeth, tying her apron strings around her ample waist.

We ate it cold.

Intermission

I muse upon my country's ills—

—Herman Melville

WHOSE TEETH ARE THOSE GRITTING the spit-soaked end of a cigar, its blue fumes filling the room to take my breath away and make my eyes water? Melville, Shelby, Henry James—no, not theirs, though they do love their stogies. Franklin, too. Men smell of them and sweat that brings to mind the odor of a stable where no frankincense or myrrh perfumes Death's sour breath.

"Die easy, Camille, die easy!"

The stone of madness weighs heavily on my breast.

"Juba dis and Juba dat."

I shall perform the "Chloroform Rag" on the Sholes & Glidden. Now watch my fingers strut!

> One said it was a frog,
> But the other said nay;
> He said it was a canary bird,
> With its feathers washed away.
> Look ye there!

My name is Ellen Finch, and I am no man's wench—not even yours, dear husband, to whom in church I pledged my body and my worldly goods.

They have taken my child, and I do not know where to find him.

"Hish! God goes 'mong the worlds blackberrying."

Mr. Tambo, Mr. Bones, kindly say where my boy has gone, and I shall be forever yours.

Olio

. . . we shall go up or down together . . .

—Susan B. Anthony

Prince of Humbug, &c.

WE WERE SHOWN TO BARNUM'S WAGON by a roustabout carrying a monkey on his shoulder. No sooner had we climbed aboard than the abominable showman launched into a joke in dubious taste: "A bereaved husband kept the ashes of his beloved wife in a jar on the mantel, which he tended with the devotion of a monk for the Buddha. The next winter, this paragon of spouses sprinkled her ashes on the icy steps outside his house, so his new wife would not slip and fall!"

"Are you trying to be offensive?" rasped Susan. With her sharp face, she appeared as if she could split the incorrigible wag's skull in two.

Barnum roared and in his high-pitched barker's voice asked, "Why, Miss Anthony, don't tell me you believe in wedlock—lawful or awful as the case may be?"

"My beliefs are my own business, Mr. Barnum!" she snapped back like one of Stephen Perry's rubber bands.

"And may I inquire what position you take in the matter of free love?"

"The same as I always have: Someday women will make you men pay dearly for it."

"You are a fire-eater, Miss Anthony, and I respect your

fearlessness!" He doffed his shiny ringmaster's hat and bowed deeply.

Susan laughed in spite of herself. "You are a devil, sir!"

"I am the Prince of Humbug, madam, and am heartily glad to discover in you a sense of humor! I had been led to understand that the woman's movement was as humorless as a justice of the peace or a darning egg."

"We need your help, Mr. Barnum, not your teasing."

"Ladies, you have caught me at a bad time. The Ethnological Congress of Savage Tribes is soon to be convened in this very city, a spectacle that will set you hens clucking as if God Almighty had jumped on Washington City, wearing His biggest boots, and stomped those good-for-nothing mudfish till they cried 'Olio!' and enfranchised the entire female race! Coming soon to Madison Square Garden for a limited engagement will be . . ."

He consulted a printer's proof of a four-sheet billboard fantastically illustrated and biliously colored, on which he had been making changes with a crayon. "Attend, ladies, to Barnum's savage congressmen!" Like *The New York Herald*, Barnum couldn't state a fact or a fancy in print or conversation without at least one exclamation mark.

"'Bestial Australian Cannibals, Mysterious Aztecs, Imbruted Big-Lipped Botocudoes, Wild Nubians, Ferocious Zulus, Invincible Afghans, Pagan Burmese Priests, Ishmaelite Todars, Dusky Idolatrous Hindus, Sinuous Nautch Girls, Annamite Dwarfs, Haughty Syrians, Oriental Giants, Herculean Japanese, plus assorted Kaffirs,

Arabs, Persians, Kurds, Ethiopians, Circassians, Polyne-sians, Tasmanians, Tartars, and Patans!!!'"

Dazzled by the vision, Barnum sought our approval. Susan knew how to use a man's egotism against him, like a wrestler tossing a braggart on the hip of his braggadocio. "We will not forget your contribution to better understand-ing among the races, Mr. Barnum."

Her faint praise satisfied him. "Miss Anthony, did you happen to see, in younger days, the 'Racial Anomaly' on display at my American Museum before the 1865 fire burned it to the ground?"

He did not wait for an answer but went on "at full chisel," as Franklin liked to say. "I will never forget the handsome tribute printed in the *Times*: 'Almost in the twinkling of an eye, the dirty, ill-shaped structure, filled with specimens so full of suggestion and of merit, passed from our gaze, and its like cannot soon be seen again.' Two white whales captured off the coast of Labrador were boiled in their base-ment tank and one of my prized Numidian lions terrorized Manhattan until a fireman dispatched it with his ax. Wax-work figures of the illustrious melted, although the effigy of Jefferson Davis was saved from the flames—by a member of the Klan, no doubt. The actual Davis was arrested and later sold insurance. History is one smashup piled on top of another, the shards glued together with irony. Eventu-ally, the paraffin Davis was kicked to pieces in Ann Street by nativist hooligans." Barnum paused in his headlong flight of words and let his eyes sweep a wall covered with photographs of the famous and the freakish. "What was I going on about?"

"The Racial Anomaly," I said, opening my mouth to speak for the first time since our arrival in the stuffy, malodorous wagon.

"Thank you. My brain grows more addled by the year. The Racial Anomaly was white—as white as you ladies are in your bathtubs—but he had been born a negro. He confided in me that he'd changed his color and the complexion of his very soul by eating a particular medicinal weed, which, alas, he never identified. Had it been in use earlier in the century, the weed could have prevented civil war and accomplished what Douglass, Garrison, John Brown, and the like did not: emancipated the negroes, who would have become indistinguishable from white men. Imagine, good ladies, if a weed could be found that would turn women into men!"

I sensed Susan's exasperation as Barnum extolled the benefits of such an arrangement: "Overnight, your associations, conventions, indignation meetings, parlor debates, and hen parties would be superfluous. You could take up cussing and chewing tobacco. Think of the erstwhile women who could cast their ballots and send themselves to Congress, where they would sit and bray like the other jackasses!"

"Mr. Barnum."

"Yes, Miss Anthony."

"You talk the most awful bunkum!"

"Perhaps you're right. I can't imagine a world without sinuous Nautch girls."

Foreseeing no end to the comic overture, I launched into an aria of tears.

"What's the matter with her?" he asked.

"She has brought her troubles to you, sir, and you go on about braying asses!"

"You won't find Barnum backward when it comes to chivalry."

"Miss Finch believes you can be of help."

"I'm a friend of Margaret Hardesty," I said, drying my eyes.

"Ah, little Margaret! Had she been Eve, mankind would not have gotten itself kicked out of Eden."

"Only because she could not have reached the fruit in the tree of knowledge," said Susan. "Eve's gift to humankind was curiosity."

"A noble quality! Once again, Miss Susan, my hat is off to you." He held it in his hands. "I admire quick wittedness in man, woman, or beast." A rabbit poked its nose above the brim. "I appear to have expropriated Maxwell the Magician's partner. By such follies, America grows."

"And breeds a race of rats!" said Susan tartly.

"Speaking of rats, how fares that paragon of philandering, the Reverend Henry Ward Beecher, after the scandalous revelation of his affair with Elizabeth Tilton? To think that, in ten years, he has advanced from abolitionist to adulterer. What next? I wonder. Anarchist perhaps, since he has a proclivity for unlawful acts beginning with the letter *a*. Please give my regards to Mrs. Stanton, whose tattle dropped the reverend into the stew of juicy tidbits whose savor the public cannot do without!"

Susan sniffed in disdain of the abolitionist who had armed John Brown and his would-be army of slaves with "Beecher's Bibles," rifles shipped to Brown in crates claiming, on their lids, to hold the Word of God. "Mr. Beecher's infidelities have lighted a 'holocaust of womanhood,'" she said, quoting Elizabeth, who had reviled the self-righteous fornicator whose first dalliance had been with a young woman copyist of his sermons.

I'm grateful to you, Mr. James, for having never once tried to outrage me.

"Clowns are the pegs on which the circus is hung," said Barnum wryly.

I had been turning a shaving mug over in my hands while Susan and Barnum waged a war of wits. The mug was decorated with four cupids bearing an escutcheon dulled by dried lather. In a sudden fury, I smashed it on the floor.

Barnum flew into a rage. "Damn you, woman! That was a gift from the prince consort!"

Susan hid a smile in her glove as Barnum picked up pieces of broken china.

"If I were not inured to disaster, I'd order Stanley Carl to feed you to his lions!" He snarled like one. "It's better to be insured than inured, but the premium is exorbitant for a man of my inflammatory history." Fires had destroyed the American Museum, the Hippodrome, and Iranistan, his Moorish palace in Bridgeport, at the time the largest private home in America.

"I am very sorry, Mr. Barnum," I said abjectly. "But I'm mad with worry!"

"Young woman, what is the trouble?" His tone had changed in an instant from irascible to paternal.

"My baby has been stolen!"

Laying aside the remains of the Prince Albert mug, Barnum turned to Susan, who nodded and said, "We need your help in finding him."

Barnum scratched his cheek thoughtfully. Soap from the royal mug will never again do honor to your face, I said to myself. Susan apologized for the "wicked destruction of property," and promised to send him a tin of Mrs. Stanton's Washington Squares.

"I'd be afraid to eat them," said Barnum, clutching his neck and sticking out his tongue in a pantomime of asphyxiation.

"Elizabeth is many things, but she's not a poisoner."

"What your friend is, my good woman, is an opportunist," said the caliph of claptrap.

"You slander her, sir! And I am not your good woman!"

"Come, come, Miss Anthony! Her nose for money is almost as keen as my own." He took a gigantic handkerchief from his pocket and blew his nose with such stentorian effect that Jumbo answered him in kind from his cage. "What is the going rate for speaking engagements?" Susan made no reply. "Answer, or I won't lift a finger to help you."

He waggled his pinkie, so that we might admire the ruby ring that decorated it, a "gift from Jenny Lind."

"One hundred dollars for a mixed crowd, fifty for women, and ten on the Sabbath," I replied, though the question had not been put to me.

Susan glared; the heat of her gaze could have melted the bone buttons on my dress.

"As a statesman, she is downright greedy, but as a celebrity, she's underrating herself."

"States*woman*!" interjected Susan. "Or statesperson, if you like."

"Mr. Barnum, please!" I assumed an exaggerated attitude of abjection that Frank Ashton, the Posturing Man, would have applauded. Had Elizabeth been there to see her stenographer on her knees, she'd have sent me packing. "I beg you to help us find my baby, Martin!"

"Have you no husband to rely on that you must come to Barnum for assistance?"

"She has none to speak of," said Susan with an inscrutable, tight-lipped smile.

"Lucky for you Barnum is a man of the world. Rise, dear girl, and tell me your troubles."

After I'd related my sad tale, replete with tears and hand-wringing, he called from the window to a passing Wildman from Borneo: "Fetch Mr. Gallagher. You will find him asleep in his wagon." Barnum touched the side of his nose and winked at us. "Our Mr. Gallagher drinks. He claims it's a nerve tonic. The old soak! Barnum knows shecoonery when he smells it! He's up on all the latest dodges."

The Wildman from Borneo removed his false incisors, each one sharp as a chisel, and affably replied, "Righto, boss!" He winked at Susan and hurried to the old soak's wagon.

While we waited for Gallagher's arrival, Barnum took up a red crayon and worked on the banner headline for the Ethnological Congress billboard. Dissatisfied with one, he would write another, each attempt more bombastic than the one before.

~~Come See The Greatest Convocation Of Human Species!~~

⌒⊗⌒

~~Behold &~~ Marvel At The Biggest ~~Assembly Of~~

⌒⊗⌒

~~For The First Time Since The Confounding At Babel~~

"Whatever you do, do it ardently," he counseled, slashing yet another sentence that failed to satisfy his demand for grandiosity.

~~Witness Prodigies That Defy The Limits Of Human Nature!~~

"*Rodomontade* is my favorite word—after *money*, of course. During a long career as a huckster of high jinks, I've learned that the more fantastic the first is, the more fabulous the second will be." He scratched at the paper proof and tried again.

"*Voilà*! What do you think of this?" he asked Susan, jabbing his crayon at the product of his garish imagination's restless milling:

BEHOLD **BLOOD** CURDLING **& HEART** STOPPING
MONSTROSITIES
THAT DARE TO CALL THEMSELVES HUMAN!!!

"I hope that women will be represented," she replied with unintended drollery.

"Naturally!" declared the sultan of spectacles. "Contrary to the opinion of some of my sex, I believe that women have the same right as men to call themselves human—or monsters, if it comes to that."

"I'm pleased to hear it!" she grumbled.

"Now for the finishing touch . . ."

"Behold the finger of God commanding the people to go to Barnum's and worship a creation second only to His own!"

What folly! I thought, not daring to speak my mind. I could only guess at the thoughts seething in Susan's matriarchal brain. Fortunately, Mr. Gallagher made a timely entrance before another priceless souvenir could be dashed to pieces. Barnum folded up the press proof and put it in a drawer.

"Miss Susan B. Anthony, Miss Ellen Finch, may I present Special Officer Gallagher of the Pinkerton Agency, on permanent assignment to the Grand Traveling Museum, Menagerie, Caravan and Hippodrome."

Susan nodded warily. I shook his plump hand eagerly.

"Pleased to meet you," said the portly Irishman, whose

breath did nothing to refute the chief stereotype attached to his people.

"Mr. Gallagher! A child has been kidnapped, and we need you to find him posthaste!" The impresario of bull and bunkum used the same tone to motivate Homer Silvey and Al Cole, masters of canvas, to strike the circus tents, Miss Emma Jutau to slide down from the big top's upper reaches by her teeth, or Billy Burke to warble his budget of songs.

Gallagher took out a notebook and a pencil, licked its lead, and asked, "Name?"

"Martin Finch II," I replied.

"Age?"

"Five months."

"Last seen?"

"Mrs. Crockett's boardinghouse, Forty-second Street, Murray Hill."

"Second floor," interjected Susan.

"Any distinguishing features?"

"In the eyes of man's law, he's a bastard," said Susan, her own eyes glittering like daggers.

I dared not speak.

"Through no fault of his own," declared Susan.

"Do you suspect anyone?" His question was addressed pointedly to me.

"Mary Surratt," I replied, ignoring his snide innuendo.

Gallagher stared down his red nose at me. "She that was hanged for helping kill Mr. Lincoln?"

"I saw her take my baby!" I insisted, although I was less certain than I'd been when I saw her climb out my bedroom window. Self-doubt dogged me through that troublous time.

"Miss Finch is in shock," said Barnum, winking at the Pinkerton man.

Having wet his pencil again, Gallagher wrote "Temporarily deranged" in his book.

"But the child *was* taken!" averred Susan. "Mrs. Stanton and I can attest to the fact."

"The Mrs. Stanton who believes in free love?" asked the special officer.

"She does not believe in free love! That's a vicious lie put about by her enemies."

"Gallagher, your job is to find the child, not to pass judgment on anybody's turpitude!"

"Turpitude my eye!" shouted Susan.

I thought I would go mad!

"Right you are, Mr. Barnum, sir!"

"How will you go about it?" he asked, stroking his chin.

"By—consulting—Madame Singleton!" Officer Gallagher gasped, after having lost his breath to a string of hiccups.

Susan offered him a horehound drop.

"Excellent!" Rubbing his hands, Barnum turned to me and explained: "Second sight is twice as useful as plain sight, four times better than an oversight, and infinitely preferable to the hindsight in which we all indulge."

Overwhelmed by absurdity, I fainted. I was happily oblivious until the sting of spirits of ammonia brought me to my senses. Susan carried a bottle of smelling salts in her bag, although she hated to use them because they affirmed a woman's frailty.

"You should loosen her corset," said Gallagher, taking an interest in my welfare.

"She's not wearing one," said Susan, always a stickler for the truth.

"In that case, I recommend unbuttoning her blouse."

"That will be enough, Gallagher!" chided Barnum.

The officer shifted his gaze, which Susan later described as "prurient," and desisted from taking a further inventory of my apparel.

"A rare sympathy connects Madame Singleton and me," said the Pinkerton man, wanting to be seen in a better light and on a higher plain. "We imbibe the same spiritual atmosphere."

Barnum, a teetotaler, acknowledged the efficacy of strong drink in special cases and kept a selection of ardent spirits in his cupboard. He handed Gallagher a bottle of gin. "Give her this, but don't let her drain any more than the neck. The visions of a blind drunk are unreliable."

"Great gifts can be a burden," remarked Gallagher.

"Speaking of burdens, I'm worried about Jumbo. I think he's got the grippe. Ladies, did you ever see an elephant sneeze? It's not a pretty sight. Gallagher, have Madame Singleton consult her crystal. I paid ten thousand dollars for the animal, and if it's likely to die, I might be able to palm it off on Bill Cody before it kicks the bucket."

Jumbo survived the grippe but was struck by a locomotive in 1885. Barnum donated the skeleton to the Museum of Natural History, sold the great heart to Cornell, and had the hide stuffed by William Critchley. Jumbo continued to make money for the Prince of Humbug from customers wishing to view death on a colossal scale. I hoped that the gleam of avarice in Barnum's eyes would never light on *la petite* Margaret. Let her likeness be shaped in paraffin, I prayed, but protect her from the ravages of taxidermy! God grant that she will one day reside at Mountain Grove Cemetery, whole and self-possessed in death as she was in life, beside her beloved general.

Not to be outdone by man or pachyderm, Elizabeth later willed her brain to Cornell, whose anatomists were eager to discover evidence of derangement.

Ardent Spirits

GALLAGHER, SUSAN, AND I were whisked to Madame Singleton's in the antique phaeton Barnum used to make a spectacle of himself. Doffing his high hat to passersby as a trombonist blew a circus screamer, he would bellow greetings to the people of Manhattan or Brooklyn. Bells tied to their fetlocks, a pair of white horses pranced musically. Ersatz horns were strapped to their foreheads. That afternoon, Mr. Dode was not in the coachman's seat. Perhaps he was still chasing Fischer's hat. George Melville, bareback rider and "country innocent," held the reins in his oddly pink hands.

"In the Middle Ages, the unicorn was a symbol of virginity," said Susan pointedly. "It applies to only one of us."

"How can you be certain of theirs?" I asked, indicating the sleeping special agent and the coachman.

"Like many of the blustery sort, Gallagher is all talk. As for Mr. George Melville, I have it on good authority that he is a eunuch."

Susan was plainly enjoying herself. She smiled beneath her drab bonnet and waved her hand languidly at the crowded pavement like a queen of England. "Be glad Elizabeth isn't with us; she'd turn the carriage into a traveling pulpit from which to lambaste her enemies. I doubt you could stand the attention and embarrassment."

"How do *you* stand it?"

"I've stood it for going on thirty-five years and intend to continue till one of us is dead," she replied in a voice to match her profile. "Elizabeth Cady Stanton is the most brilliant woman I've ever known and the most combative. She speaks her mind regardless."

"Regardless of what?"

"Of the harm she sometimes does the cause."

"I can't imagine her doing anything to hurt the movement she and Miss Mott founded."

"The clergy won't stand for blasphemy, not even from Mrs. Cady Stanton." She took a letter from her reticule and unfolded it. "Last night, I found this on my pillow."

I recognized Elizabeth's scrawl.

"Shall I read it?"

"Please do."

Settling her spectacles on the bridge of her nose, Susan read: "'A book'—mind you, it is the Bible she belittles—'that curses woman in her maternity, degrades her in marriage, makes her the author of sin, and a mere afterthought in creation and baptizes all this as the Word of God cannot be said to be a great blessing to the sex.'"

Gallagher grunted in his sleep.

"I share her view of patriarchal Christianity, tyrannical marriages, and ruinous divorces, but nothing can change until we are made men's equal under the law. Woman's suffrage must come first, and for that to happen, we need the support of men as well as their wives."

Swaying in the gutter, a tipsy roadmender brandished a shovel and shouted, "Votes for women!"

"Forgive me, Ellen. My nerves are shrilling. I dare say little Martin has a lot to do with my irritability. We must find the dear lamb."

"Yes, we must!" I cried, glad that she had once more caught the tide of affairs that had taken us to Barnum and was at that moment carrying us in a fancy equipage toward the famous clairvoyant. "I won't rest till I find my son!"

"Nor will I! Nor will Elizabeth, by God!"

I suppose I looked dubious, because she went on to say, "And if you think she's too fleshy to be of much use, I can assure you that, underneath the fat, she's tough as gristle. She will roll over our enemies like a juggernaut! Krakatoa is nothing compared to Elizabeth Cady Stanton in a rage!"

In such a voice did the prophet Ezekiel foretell the destruction of Jerusalem. She grinned. "Thus do I fire the thunderbolts hot from Elizabeth's forge. So let us 'hustle our bustles,' as the vulgar say, though I would not be caught dead in one."

We arrived at Barnum's Hotel. The trombonist licked his lips and prepared to announce our arrival, but Susan hushed him. "I would rather not wake Mr. Gallagher from his detecting." She took the gin bottle from his hands and, setting her bonnet with an emphatic tug on the brim, marched into the hotel.

I followed in her boiling wake, as if she had transformed herself by the heat of her rhetoric into a stream of lava. We flowed up the staircase and to the door of the psychic phenomenon, who, sensing our presence or else the bottle of gin, bid us enter. We did and were invited with a cordial wave of Madame Singleton's hand to sit. She accepted our offering—a bribe in fact—graciously. I was delighted to see Margaret there. We exchanged pleasantries until Susan, her purposefulness bottled up like steam in a boiler, hissed, "There's no time for frivolity!"

"Mr. Barnum would disagree," said the psychic wryly. "Life is intolerable without it." She patted the gin bottle affectionately. "Honey catches more flies than vinegar, my dear, though I can't imagine why anyone would wish to catch them, unless it's to pull off their wings."

"We've come about my little boy," I said, my eyes suddenly wet with tears.

"Yes, I know," she said with a mysterious air. "He's been kidnapped."

Astonished, I asked, "How did you know? Did you see him in the crystal? Did you read of it in the cards?"

"I read it in a telegram." She fluttered a gray scrap of paper in front of me. "From Mr. Barnum himself. I am to render whatever assistance I can."

"Oh, thank you!" I cried, getting up from the chair to take her hand in gratitude. I noticed a large sapphire ring and wondered whether or not it was genuine.

Madame Singleton led me to a talking board. "Sit!" she commanded, her former gaiety in abeyance. I did, and she sat across from me, so that our knees touched. Margaret and Susan kept their places. "Madame Laveau!"

"*Oui*, Madame Singleton. What is your wish?" A woman dressed in black appeared. Piercing the veil that covered her face, I beheld the snake charmer, Mrs. Stoner, whom I had last seen sulking on the hotel porch during the spontaneous demonstration of physical culture by the artistes. After the séance, Margaret whispered to me that Napoléon, the viper, had died of indigestion. Barnum had made Mrs. Stoner, whose charms were fading, Singleton's assistant and given her the Haitian name of Laveau, because voodoo is, as every sucker knows, a specialty of that backward island nation. Since she performed in a dusky side-show tent, blacking up was considered unnecessary.

"Music, if you please."

Mrs. Stoner turned the crank on one of Mr. Edison's new machines, and eerie music welled up from its tin horn. It was not music so much as an atmosphere produced by a single mesmerizing note of a cello.

"Let there be night *s'il vous plaît*, Madame Laveau!"

The assistant pulled the heavy drapes closed and lit a candle, which she set on the table between Madame Single ton and me.

"*Merci*, Madame Laveau; that will be all."

Mrs. Stoner went into another room, or so I hoped; I didn't see her leave. I don't care for snake charmers, but I would not wish vanishing on my worst enemy, who would turn out to be a man named Ethan Dorn of Tennessee. He could go to blazes.

"Have you ever attended a séance, Miss Finch?"

"No," I replied nervously.

"There is nothing to be afraid of," she assured me. "All that is required of you is to empty your mind of distractions and maintain a respectful attitude toward the spirits."

Susan giggled. Madame Singleton silenced her with a glance, which could have frozen pond water or, if you prefer, brought it to a boil.

"I do beg your pardon!" said Susan, who was seldom humbled or apologetic. "I was recalling a joke of Mr. Barnum's. It was one of those preposterous anecdotes that men guffaw over in taprooms and barbershops. Men are such ridiculous creatures! Madame Singleton, do continue, and if I feel an urge to laugh, I shall bite my tongue."

The clairvoyant dismissed her with a shrug and turned again to me. "Place your fingers on the *planchette*, a darling French word meaning 'little plank.' I like to anchor the spiritus in a world of undeniable facts." I anchored my fingers on the heart-shaped cherrywood, as though I were about to play a thunderous rendition of "Dies Irae" on the piano. "Lightly, Ellen!" I did as I was told.

As a rule, I am skeptical of spiritualism, placing it in the same category as the Man-Eating Tree of Madagascar, Mark Twain's Petrified Man, and Joice Heth, the 161-year-old former slave alleged to have been George Washington's wet nurse. She was the making of the rascal Barnum, who exhibited her at Niblo's Garden to gawking crowds until she died, and then he packed the Saloon at New York City with fifteen hundred spectators—at fifty cents a head—to view her autopsy.

"I will now call my spirit guide, Miss Roux, who may, if she is in the mood to be helpful, tell us where your son is." Madame Singleton closed her eyes and warbled, "Eugenia, are you there? One rap for yes, two raps for no."

Rap.

"Hello, Eugenia! Is your cold any better, dear?"

Rap, rap!

"Did you try honey and arsenic?" She looked up from the board and said, "Grandfather swore by honey and arsenic. In the end, it killed him. Naturally, Eugenia is quite beyond mortal peril, although the grippe can make eternal life a misery."

Rap.

"She took the honey and arsenic," said Madame Singleton. "Did you find it efficacious?"

Rap, rap!

"I am sorry to hear it. I wish Allcott's Porous Plasters or Munyon's Grippe Remedy were available in the next world."

Rap, rap, rap, rap, rap!

"Sickness makes her peevish," said Madame Singleton. "Are you feeling well enough to help this poor woman find her child?"

Rap and then *rap, rap.*

"Won't you please try, Miss Roux? The child is very dear to me!"

"You must remember to speak through me, Miss Finch, or you will confuse Eugenia!"

I apologized and waited for Madame Singleton to put my question to Miss Roux, who this time answered with a single rap.

"Thank you, Eugenia," said Madame Singleton. "Can you tell us where little Martin is at this moment?"

Rap, rap.

I tasted the gall of bitter disappointment and sighed piteously. Madame Singleton gave me a stern glance. By it, I knew that the conversation had reached a critical phase. I held back my tears and waited for the incubus to utter an encouraging rap.

"Eugenia, can you tell us anything at all that will lead this good woman to her child?"

Rap. Yes!

I felt my own spirits, which had been cast down, lift. With a jerk, the *planchette* began to move on its short, spindly legs. It staggered across a piece of pale blue cardboard imprinted with letters of the alphabet, grammatical signs, and Arabic numbers from two through nine.

2 3 4 5 6 7 8 9 - ,

Q W E . T Y I U O P

Z S D F G H J K L M

A X & C V B N ? ; R

The little board tugged at our hands, lurching this way and that—an animate object galvanized by mesmeric currents. Madame Singleton intoned each letter at which the instrument stopped, while I held my breath in expectancy. Twice I heard muffled exclamations issue from Susan's mouth. Margaret kept quiet.

"Z—A—R—E—P— H—A —T—H."

"Do you mean Zarephath, New Jersey?" asked the oracle.

Rap!

"Excellent, Eugenia! Now tell us *where* in Zarephath?"

"M—I—L—L—S—T—O—N—E . . . R—I—V—E—R . . . G—R—I—S—T—M—I—L—L."

"And who lives there, Eugenia?"

"A—L—M—A . . . B—R—I—D—W—E—L—L . . . W—H—I—T—E."

"Is there anything else you can tell us that will help them find the child?"

"K—K—K."

"Do you mean the Klan?"

Rap!

"Those devils!" hissed Susan.

The *planchette* shot from under our fingers, as though in terrified flight from the horde of evildoers masquerading in white sheets and the conical hats that naughty schoolboys are made to wear by pitiless schoolmasters.

"It's a wonder that Eugenia, who is delicate and impressionable, could bring herself to spell the vile monogram," said Madame Singleton.

Then a voice croaked from the gramophone's horn:

> Over all the U.S.A., the fiery cross we display;
> The emblem of Klansmen's domain,
> We'll be forever true to the Red, White, and
>   Blue,
> And Americans always remain.

"You vicious brutes!" the medium shouted into the ether. She turned to us and raged, "They have pirated my séance!"

Martin is lost! I moaned.

As the voice began to croak another stanza, Madame Singleton poured gin down the gramophone's throat. The voice slurred and shortly stopped.

"What a waste!" she lamented.

"What shall we do?" I cried.

Susan drew on her gloves like iron gauntlets. "To Zarephath!"

"Madame Laveau!" shouted Madame Singleton. "Open the drapes!"

Pillar of Fire

HOW SUSAN AND I GOT TO ZAREPHATH has never been clear to me. I recall a paddleboat, a chariot manned by the Gilford Brothers dressed in gladiatorial costumes, and a steam-powered airship shaped like a cigar. Bewildered, we found ourselves at a gristmill, the picturesque Millstone River chattering behind it. Susan pounded on the oak door as if her hand were iron-gauntleted. "It could have been heard by the stokers of Hell," she later said, describing the sound to Elizabeth, who had been in Murray Hill, unaware of our assault on a bastion of prejudice and hatred. "If only I'd had my temperance ax!"

"Well?" asked a formidable woman, glowering in the doorway.

"Mary Surratt!" I exclaimed.

"I hope to serve the cause as bravely as that great martyr of the South did!"

"Are you Alma Bridwell White?" asked Susan, who had given me a look such as one bestows on the insane.

"I am! What business do you have here?" She stood like a bulwark not even a storm surge could topple. She would not have given way to the battering ram that had splintered the engine-house door at Harper's Ferry, where John Brown had taken refuge. She snickered at our puniness.

She terrified me but not Susan, who, for all her age and seeming frailty, was hard-bitten and iron-backboned. "We have come for the child!" she demanded in a tone of voice useful for pronouncing doom or announcing the end of days—a voice that could rattle spoons in a drawer, crack lath and plastered walls, and set a dog's teeth on edge. In such a voice did Antony "Cry 'Havoc!' and let slip the dogs of war."

The sheer force of breath expelled by the suffragist's powerful lungs had driven White backward, according to Newton's Third Law of Motion. In an instant, Susan had sprung across the threshold, hissing like an outraged goose for me to follow. "Bolt the door behind you!"

I did as I was told and felt a shiver down my back, which was part fear and part violent joy. Susan had her strong hands around the enemy's neck.

"Strangle her! Choke her to death!" I wished for Lilian Heigold's stick, so that I might split White's skull and examine the brain for a sign that she belonged to Satan's legion or for a lesion that might explain her malice.

Mouth pursed in contempt, she neither begged for mercy nor cried out in fear. Her eyes shone with an indecent hatred.

"Ellen, find something to tie her with." So calmly had Susan spoken, she might have been asking for a string to do up a parcel.

I found a ball of jute and bound White's wrists and ankles while Susan kept her thumbs pressed to the woman's throat. Those gnarled hands could have squeezed her Adam's apple to a pulp. The red tip of her tongue clenched between her teeth, Susan had borrowed a mother's fury and resolve. Only when White was trussed did the suffragist relax her grip. The effort had cost her; her arms began to tremble and her hands to shake. White laughed, and then it was my turn to be possessed by rage. I picked up the first thing that came to hand—a laundry paddle—and would have bludgeoned her had Susan not intervened.

"We'll never find Martin if you knock her senseless." She glared at White and asked, "What have you done with the child you stole from us?"

Again, White smiled. Then she brazenly sang:

> So, I'll cherish the Bright Fiery Cross,
> Till from my duties at last I lay down;
> Then burn for me a Bright Fiery Cross,
> The day I am laid in the ground.

Susan put her foot on the woman's chest. Unable to sing it, White wheezed the obnoxious refrain.

"Ellen, help me get her into a chair."

Grabbing her by the hair, we persuaded the woman into a ladder-back and secured her. Maintaining an icy composure, she would not give us the satisfaction of watching her squirm.

"What did you do with the boy?" Susan's sharp voice could have drawn blood.

"Your friend Mrs. Stanton and I want the same thing. Yes, Miss Anthony, I know who you are. I've seen your sour face on enough placards and pamphlets. After your arrest, I saw an engraved likeness of your face and recognized the resentment and stubborn devotion to a cause I see in my own."

The woman had a face that could make cakes fall.

In 1872, Susan was arrested by "a young man in beaver hat and kid gloves (paid for by taxes gathered from women)" for having dared to cast her ballot in a congressional election. The twelve men who sat in judgment found her guilty of voting "while female." In a typeface suitable to the boldness of the unlawful act and the spluttering outrage it caused among men, *The Union and Advertiser* declared, "Citizenship no more carries the right to vote than it carries the power to fly to the moon." In a letter to the editor that he did not print, Susan countered, "If, as Jules Verne imagines, mankind will one day occupy the moon, women will dust, bake moon pies, suffer their wombs to be tugged by lunar tides, and be as disenfranchised there as they are on Earth."

"I despise you and your hateful cause!" said Susan, baring her teeth.

"Ferocity becomes you, Miss Anthony. It brings out the color in your cheeks."

Beside myself, I shouted, "Where is my son?" But she ignored me.

"It's to Mrs. Stanton, I should be talking. She also believes in white supremacy and is offended by laws that would let ignorant niggers vote when educated women like us can't." She jumped over Susan's objection. "Didn't she say, 'If a woman finds it hard to bear the oppressive laws of a few Saxon Fathers, what may she not be called to endure when all the lower orders, native and foreigners,

Dutch, Irish, Chinese, and African, legislate for her and her daughters?'"

White's claim was true; Susan couldn't deny it. "What do you want with the child?"

"To use it as a symbol."

"A symbol of what?"

White ignored the question and continued: "We want to restore the values and principles of the Founding Fathers, many of whom belonged to the Klan."

"Nonsense!"

"History speaks in many tongues. It burns in me. My church is the Pillar of Fire and the Bright Fiery Cross."

"Where is Martin Finch?" Susan could have burned a hole through White, so hotly did she glare.

"At the foot of the cross."

Instantly, I recalled that Mary Surratt had foretold that I would meet my infant son there.

"And where might that be?" asked Susan with plenty of vinegar and nary an atom of honey. Nevertheless, we had caught the pest, and if she'd been a fly, Susan would have pulled off its wings.

"That, you will never find out!"

"Ellen, go find a bar of lye soap." And to White, she said, "Prepare to be purified of your sanctimonious flapdoodle." I found it in the kitchen. "Now put it in the serpent's mouth." I did, and the serpent spat it out. "Again!" ordered Susan. "This time, shove it halfway down her throat." I did, and White began to choke as her saliva turned to suds. "Now she looks the rabid dog she is."

Had I had a mirror, I would surely have seen my eyes glitter. Hatred casts its own lurid light—the hellish one that Milton in his blindness saw flickering on the lake of fire.

Susan yanked the soap from White's mouth. The bigot choked on her foaming curses.

"Where is the child!" shouted Susan.

With little else but her tongue to show her disdain, she stuck it out at us.

We left her to stew in her own juices. Standing at the open back door, we listened to the water falling down the wheel and the creaking wooden gears and savored the odors of cornmeal, burlap sacks, and river. A cat sidled against my leg, sat a moment on my shoes to wash its face, and then flattened its belly on the ground in readiness to break its fast on a plump sparrow.

"I don't know how to make the damned woman speak!" cried Susan.

We went into the room below the grain bin. Amid the noise of corn pouring through the tin spout, I heard the shower bath at Sing Sing. I described its construction and torments to Susan. She shut the spout and wrenched it from the hopper.

We carried White, still tied to the chair, and placed her below the spout. I opened it and watched as grain rained down on her.

"What now?" asked Susan.

"We wait for her skull to crack." A falling kernel of dried corn does less harm than a biting fly, but a torrent of them can bring an elephant to its knees.

It wasn't long before White began to fidget.

"Where is Martin?" asked Susan, having closed the spout.

She shook her head as a dog does to rid itself of fleas, but wouldn't answer.

Once again, Susan let the grain fall, until White began to moan.

"Where is Martin?" I shouted above the clatter of pelting kernels.

And still she wouldn't say!

I leaned the chair against the wall. The grain got up White's nose; she gasped for air. She opened her mouth and gulped what would have seemed like cherry pits or gravel.

Close to raving, she shrieked, "Enough!"

Susan shut the spout. "Where is he?" And when she hesitated to answer, Susan had only to touch the lever to make White talk.

"In Memphis!" she cried, the Pillar of Fire all but extinguished in her mind. "Ethan Dorn's house, on the corner of Second and Poplar!"

"Who's Ethan Dorn?"

"Grand Cyclops of Tennessee."

"Why did you take the boy?"

"To punish Stanton for championing miscegenation and free love. And to punish you"—she thrust her chin at me—"for having practiced it and given the world another bastard, and a black one at that."

"Martin's father is not a negro!" I shouted in a voice so forceful, a distant cobweb shook.

"Then how did the baby come to be a mulatto?"

I recalled the duskiness of the baby's skin when Mary Surratt had unfolded the blanket and looked at his face. But surely night, which engulfed both the child and the woman, had lent its color to the scene!

"What does Dorn intend to do with him?" asked Susan, who dismissed the question of little Martin's inheritance as a thing of no consequence.

"Sacrifice him at the foot of the fiery cross!"

She started to sing the racist anthem but got no further than "So, I'll cherish the Bright Fiery Cr—" before Susan muzzled her.

"Could it be possible that I *am* the mother of a black child?" I asked.

"For God, as for Barnum, anything is possible."

"But how?"

"Perhaps He is a negro and engendered in you a black Jesus to save His people from the lynch mob, Jim Crow, and the Klan," replied Susan earnestly.

A wasp had crawled into my nose—two wasps, one in each nostril. Oh, how they stung! I opened my eyes and peered into the dusty gray light moiling above the rafters.

"You fainted again, poor child," said Susan, stoppering the glass bottle of smelling salts.

When I call to mind that afternoon at the gristmill, I see the Pillar of Fire as it has come to be in my fancy, with its foot in Hell and its capital underneath the pediment of the Mansion of Happiness. A host of fiery angels are going up and down inside it like fireflies trapped in a glass bottle. They make a noise that might be hymning or gibbering. Who knows how time deforms the truth.

Turkish Pantaloons

BEFORE WE KNEW IT, SUSAN AND I had returned to Mrs. Crockett's boardinghouse. What is *it*? Everything we do not know, everything that was not in Barnum's American Museum nor ever could have been. I'm no more certain today of how we traveled home to Forty-second Street than I am of the means of our arrival in Zarephath. Glimpses of the world that memory draws from the well of forgetfulness are never entirely our own. They are a rich stock of pictures seen, conversations overheard, or books read, stirred together with the bare bones of fact. I had been reading Verne's *Five Weeks in a Balloon* shortly before I went to live at Murray Hill, and thus could have had airships on the brain.

Margaret was in the sitting room when Susan and I got home. She had told Elizabeth of our meeting with Barnum and the oracle of Broadway.

"Well?" asked Elizabeth brusquely. "Did you accomplish anything?" I could see she was feeling put out for having been left out of our travels in the hinterland.

"Pish, Lizzie! It was no picnic."

"Forgive me," she said with a blush that might have been of shame or the effect of choler. (She looked like a child who'd gotten into mother's rouge pot.) "I forgot myself and the reason for your journey."

"What happened?" asked Margaret impatiently.

Susan sketched an account of our foray, omitting the sensational bits.

"Then little Martin is in Memphis?" asked Elizabeth, looking to me for confirmation.

"Yes," I replied. "At the home of the Grand Cyclops."

Elizabeth shivered as Odysseus might have when he beheld the Cyclops on the island of Hypereia. Composing herself, she showed her legendary backbone in the presence of an enemy—be it one-eyed or possessed of a pair of them, hate-inflamed and peeping through two holes cut into a sheet. "Who will go with me to Memphis and rescue our boy?"

"I will!" I shouted with a mother's fervor.

"I will!" exclaimed Susan, incited by her friend's zeal.

"I will!" cried Margaret with an enthusiasm disproportionate to her size.

Elizabeth appeared doubtful. "Can you manage so harrowing a trip, my girl?"

"I'm not your girl!" snapped Margaret. "And I can!"

"Yes," said Elizabeth, impressed by her pluck. "I believe you can."

"Susan?"

"Yes, Elizabeth?"

"Get me my bloomers!"

Susan hesitated. "I don't think they are quite the thing."

"They are *just* the thing! They will show those nasty

swine who have the gall to call themselves Christians and Americans that I mean business."

Elizabeth turned to me and explained, "A woman looks Amazonian in bloomers as she strides about the town and countryside unimpeded by lengthy skirts. They are de rigueur for a woman on the barricades—I will not say 'manning' them." She turned again to Susan. "You ought to wear yours, as well."

"I cut mine up for rags years ago." A Quaker, Susan had refused to exchange her delaine dress, relieved with pale blue ribbons, for the short jacket and Turkish pantaloons whose patterns Amelia Bloomer had published in her temperance magazine, *The Lily*.

Elizabeth had worn them, to her husband's dismay and the irritation of her father, Judge Cady, until she grew tired of being teased.

> Heigh-ho! the carrion crow
> Mrs. Stanton's all the go
> Twenty tailors take the stitches
> Mrs. Stanton wears the breeches.

"They give one a marvelous sense of freedom!" said Elizabeth as Susan went to get them.

We could hear her rooting in the trunk room before she returned with the martial apparel and handed it to her friend.

"I'll put them on at once!" announced Elizabeth, who marched into her bedroom to the rustling of the black silk dress she often wore during her emeritus years.

"She'll never get them on," said Susan with enough vinegar to pickle an egg.

Elizabeth returned, chagrined. "I've decided not to wear them. If I happen to be lynched, I don't want to be wearing pants. Unashamed of my sex, I will flaunt it for all to see!"

At that moment, Gallagher, the Pinkerton man, entered the room without knocking.

Elizabeth rebuked him, "Decent people do not barge, uninvited, into another person's sitting room!"

"I'm a special officer and used to unlawful entry," he said placidly.

"Elizabeth, allow me to introduce Mr. Gallagher, Mr. Barnum's private detective," said Susan. She'd spoken smugly, as though to gloat over her companion's ignorance of the fact.

"I hope he wiped his big boots outside. Mrs. McGinty isn't due till Tuesday."

"What brings you here, Mr. Gallagher?" asked Susan, assuming authority for the special officer in Barnum's absence.

"The boss has a private train ready to take you to Memphis."

"How the devil did he know we'd be going to Memphis?" demanded Susan. "We just this minute made up our minds."

"As to that, there are three possibilities. I detected it."

"In your dreams!" jeered Susan.

"Madame Singleton divined it."

"And the third?"

"I followed you and Miss Finch to Alma Bridwell White's house and watched through the window as you tortured her. I needed no crystal ball to foresee your immediate descent on Memphis."

"Susan, did you torture the bigot?" asked Elizabeth.

"I did."

Elizabeth nodded her stately head in approval.

"I did, too," I said, wanting to be praised. In that pandemonium, I forgot you, Martin.

"I commended you both to Mr. Pinkerton, who wishes you to know that he will hire you as special agents, if you've acquired a taste for the business. Ladies, the train is waiting. Mr. Barnum has ordered me to accompany you. My carriage is outside, a horse between the shafts that Alexander the Great would have envied. The horse, I was assured by the master of stables, is unadulterated Arabian and flies like Aladdin's own carpet."

"Wait till we change and pack our cases," said Susan, whose clothes, like mine, needed to be brushed and aired. Gristmills are dusty and musty.

"We have no room for cases, ladies. Dress if you must, but the train can't wait. Mr. Barnum's influence is great, but that of Mr. Vanderbilt, who owns the railroad tracks, is greater. Margaret, I took the liberty of packing a few of your things. You'll find them in the Pullman car. Now *chop-chop*, which is Malay for 'vamoose!'"

Like the Almighty, I moved in mysterious ways at that time in my life. And so it was I seemed to awaken in Grand

Central Depot, surrounded by—does one say a "clutter of clowns"? There were a dozen of them, including Billy Burke, Joe Kibble, and Charles Bliss. They fussed and frolicked, waiting to pile inside the car at the rear of the train, which they were to share. In addition, a caboose, a Pullman, and a parlor car made up the "Barnum Special," which followed three freight wagons belonging to the railway.

"In Mr. Barnum's opinion, twelve clowns should be sufficient to fluster a Grand Cyclops and turn a meeting of the Ku Klux Klan inside out and upside down," remarked Gallagher, who had exchanged his derby for a cowboy's Stetson and his Pinkerton badge for a sheriff's tin star. "Personally, I'd have brought a pair of hungry tigers—and imagine what Jumbo could do to a picnic of snakes with his big feet! But Barnum knows best because Barnum is boss."

"All aboard!" shouted the conductor, waving a flag to the engineer, who answered with three shrill blasts of the locomotive's whistle.

Elizabeth, Susan, Margaret, Gallagher, and I hurried aboard as the clowns climbed into the "clown car." At the last minute, a man stepped from a billow of coal smoke and jumped aboard the caboose.

Had God not gone silently about His creation, having no one to hear Him but the angels, who shrink at disharmony, the commotion could not have been any noisier than that inside the depot's vast balloon shed: clattering trolleys, the clunk and clutch of machinery, the powerful exhalations of Baldwin locomotives, the thunder as their iron wheels fought for purchase on the tracks, the ratcheting of cars across rail ends, the hawking of newspapers and patent medicines on the smoky platforms, the shouting of fare-wells, cautions, and reminders, and the thud of a steam derrick digging yet another track bed. For always the great city must build and rebuild itself in reply to its manifest destiny.

The Ditch

"WE STOP IN CHARLESTOWN, where the freight cars will be shunted onto a siding," said Gallagher, perusing a map. "From there, we go west on the Memphis and Charlestown tracks to the Grand Cyclops's front porch."

"How long will it take?" asked Susan, who ran her affairs according to schedules and itineraries, unlike Elizabeth, who since she'd stopped having babies ignored clocks and calendars.

"About eighty hours, barring the unforeseen."

"Never neglect the unforeseen," said Susan. "It's one thing in life we can depend on."

"Three days," I said, dispirited.

"And nights," said Gallagher cheerfully. "But thanks to Mr. Barnum's generosity, you ladies will pass the unconscious hours inside a Pullman Palace car. I'll sleep here in the parlor car, as is right and proper."

"What about breakfast, lunch, and dinner?" asked Elizabeth.

"The boss has laid on a 'plethora of comestibles,' from

oysters to strawberries, together with champagne for the tipplers and small beer for the Temperance Party."

"Hooray!" crowed Elizabeth, patting her belly

"Mr. B. has managed the affair quite well," said Gallagher. "The tyke is as good as saved."

"You're an ignoramus!" said Susan tartly.

"*Tsk, tsk*, your temper is showing, Miss Anthony. It's turned your face red as your shawl."

Susan glared and bared her teeth at Gallagher. "To rescue baby Martin from those devils will take more than four women and a *s*—"

"Pinkerton man," said Gallagher, finishing her sentence for her as he polished a bottle of Old Hickory with his Wild West neckerchief.

"Souse!"

"I do my best ratiocinating when staring into a glass of spirits," he said amiably. "Clear or amber, it's all the same to me. And do not forget the clowns, madam! They are formidable."

"Twelve loons dressed in silly clothes!" When pressed, Susan was as hot and quick as a lighted fuse.

"George Bliss has wreaked havoc with his leaping."

"Pish!" hissed Susan.

"Grandees and royal highnesses have lost their heads to Billy Burke's songs."

"Posh!" scoffed Elizabeth.

"In 1871, a dozen Carthaginians of New York died laughing at Joe Kibble's comic capering."

"Piffle!" jeered the pair of suffragists.

Undismayed by their skepticism, Gallagher asserted that the clowns would, in the words of the boss, "exfluncticate the vermin."

Grave outcomes teeter between outrageous farce and appalling tragedy. What could be more preposterous than a mob of men dressed as hobgoblins, or more dangerous? What is more fabulous than the cross and more harrowing than to see it burning in a black man's yard? Can you imagine a better subject for a tragicomedy than four women, a drunk, and a parcel of circus clowns confronting an invisible empire of bloodthirsty hellions? Hippocrates may have been right, and humankind does act according to the four humors. If that is true, then the lessons of the Sunday school, the homilies delivered from the pulpit, the transubstantiated bread and wine supped adoringly at the altar rail cannot soften the hearts of those with a disproportion of blood and bile in their natures any more than I can command my eyes to glitter in mirth or weep at the brutalities that one kind of being inflicts on another. Shall we pray for the fire that consumed the wicked of Gomorrah? Will He send it or a brigade of firemen?

"They'll eviscerate and annihilate the 'crackers!'" said Gallagher, pleased with himself.

We will succeed; we will not succeed; we will s— In time to the train wheels' clicking over the rail ends, I intoned the hope of a happy outcome, followed by its negation. I might have been picking petals from a daisy to find out whether someone loved me or not. My mind, which had been rational and enlightened, was fuddled by superstitious notions.

If I'd had a voodoo doll of Grand Cyclops Dorn, I'd have pierced its heart with a hat pin and then thrown it on the fire, as, once in a nightmare, I had fed mummified cats into a locomotive's firebox.

Silence descended on the parlor car. Elizabeth was asleep; her chin rested on her bosom. I noticed dribble at her lip and felt ashamed for her and of myself for having stared. Susan was gazing intently into her palms, as if she could read her fortune there or discover the stigmata of a martyrdom she both feared and wanted. Margaret was drawing figure eights—or if you prefer, the symbol of eternity—on the plush seat with a fingernail. I felt the inertia of a limed bird after its surrender to the bird catcher's stratagem, when it realizes in its tiny brain, flustered heart, and hollow bones that its life is no longer its own. I turned my tired eyes to the window.

I was mostly unaware of the scenery, though I can tell you about the ditch. It seemed an unending ribbon running parallel to the tracks just beyond the ballast stones. It flickered like a moving picture showing images of sky blue water fleeced with clouds and a stagnant fen green with scum. Hardscrabble trees grew beside it—blackthorn, willow, swamp ash, scrub pine, and sumac. Finding little nourishment in the stony ground, they were stunted, their leaves dusty or sooty from locomotive smoke. I don't recall having seen a man or a woman along the way. I lie—I remember a tramp holding a pot, his arm thrust out at an impossible angle. I guessed it had been broken by a minié ball or an accident and left to mend on its own. What else? An old boot. Where, I wondered, is its fellow? And where is the man or woman who wore it? I remember a muskrat slinking into the weeds as the train thundered past, a cat and its empty eye socket, a dead dog lying half in, half out of the ditch water, and an egret standing on one leg, its white plumage miraculously unsoiled.

The land itself was beyond my ken. By *land*, I mean the America that had not yet been deeded to Cornelius Vanderbilt and his fellow barons. From my window, I could see nothing that didn't belong to them. In my mind's eye, which has the power to roam the farthest stars, I could picture nothing that they had not papered over with documents of ownership, bonds, and shares to keep them fat. Sitting in that railroad car, I felt detached from the wide world and blind to its beauty. I was a carrot waiting to be pulled up from the dirt into the light of day, to strike a mad figure. I *was* mad! I could say that my journey was an inward one; moreover, there might have been something in it touching on the theme beloved by writers of bildungsromans. This much I knew: I was riding on the Barnum Special, heading west to a place that existed, for me, only as a thought, an unpleasant one at that. And you were waiting for me there, dear son.

We marked time as people do who find themselves between events—great or not, it doesn't matter. They occupy themselves with the same vapid amusements whether they're waiting for the rain to stop or a battle to begin that is likely to deliver them into a surgeon's hands, or an undertaker's. We played cinch and jubilee in the desultory way of the bored. Our wits and appetites were dull. We played cards, ate and drank of Barnum's plenty while savoring nothing, and read the newspapers that greeted us each morning with news of the towns we had passed in our sleep. (Did Gallagher say the journey would take three days and nights? Surely it took twice as long.) The clowns caught the papers on the fly, using the catcher crane arm attached to the side of their car. I would close my eyes and pretend to be asleep, but I could not shut out the sound a train makes rolling over tracks, the slap of pasteboard cards, the rustle of newsprint, and the music of Margaret's small fingers wandering over the keys of a melodeon furnished by our benefactor. I overheard conversations that went by fits and starts and seemed of little import to the speakers. I mean, they had no stake in what was said, as if they were acting in a play—and not a well-made one.

"I bid hearts!"

"Did you? I had no idea!"

"Your mind is not on the game, Elizabeth."

"My thoughts are scattered today. It is today, is it not?"

"It could not be otherwise."

"Wonderful thing, a Pullman car."

"Margaret, that note was sour."

"I beg your pardon."

"I dislike the melodeon. The word promises a sweetness the music betrays. It can sound like a man at his last gasp."

"Or a woman, to be fair to our sex."

"The bid was spades!"

"You're unusually peevish today, Susan."

"My corn kept me awake all night."

"That reminds me of 'The Princess and the Pea.'"

"I hated fairy tales as a child."

"My father resented me for having been born a girl."

"Oh!"

"Does your corn pain you?"

"My corn? Elizabeth, I have a toothache! I never said a word about corns."

"Oil of clove is just the thing for a toothache, but, alas, I have none."

"I'll ask Gallagher next time he's awake."

"Strange people, the Irish. My father detested them. The Cadys were finicky."

"The notes are all wrong, Margaret!"

"I beg your pardon."

"The Daughters of Lost Causes is hosting a costume ball at the Abbeville grange."

"I would rather hear a kazoo played by a monkey than a melodeon!"

"Margaret, do you know 'Watchman, Tell Us of the Night'? In younger days, I was an Episcopalian, for the sake of the children."

"Organized religion is bosh."

"Men say 'bollocks.'"

"They call the place where we piddle a 'cunt.'"

"Equally vulgar are *twat* and *quim*, although the latter could be the name of a fruit preserve."

"*Twat* has an ugly sound."

"Susan, never before have we uttered such indecencies! What is wrong with us?"

"The train is cursed. Margaret, will you never get it right?"

"I beg your pardon."

"What are you thinking, Elizabeth? The last bid was hearts!"

"I feel giddy. I hope I'm not about to have a fit."

"A rapture would be just the thing to help us pass the time."

"What game are we playing?"

"Cinch! We've been at it for days."

"Will this infernal ride never end?"

"How many days, do you think, from Heaven to Hell?"

"Does Sir Isaac have anything to say on the subject?"

"If it weren't for the newspapers beside our plates each morning, I couldn't say with any certainty that we were making progress."

"I read this morning that Lilian Heigold was hanged for striking a man."

"Whatever will poor Fred do now?"

"Become a widower, drink too much, and go fishing."

"I wish I knew a few feminine arts."

"Such as?"

"Knitting. I could watch the purl stitches growing under the needles and know for a fact that I was making headway."

"Sometimes I wonder if the train is moving. One feels motion in the spine, the back of the neck, and on the posterior, which coarse people call 'buttocks' and butchers 'hams.' I feel no such pressure."

"We must not forget the child!"

"There is nothing we can do until the journey ends. Then you will see me act!"

"Elizabeth is an accomplished actor, or should I say 'actress'?"

"I'll make the dust fly and short work of our enemies!"

"That fly sitting on the plate of mackerel bones, does it feel movement?"

"There are more important questions to be asked."

"Gallagher! Will the man never wake?"

"When he does, it will be with a regular katzenjammer."

"I'm at your service, ladies. I was saving my energies for our assault on the capital of hatred and intolerance. And for your information, Mrs. S., I've not touched a drop since yesterday, when Phineas T. Barnum's magical spring did the unthinkable and dried up."

"Yesterday was when, exactly?"

"Why, *yesterday*, naturally!"

"How long until we reach Charlestown?"

"Charlestown came and went."

"Nonsense! I would have noticed."

"Mr. Barnum arranged things to minimize distractions."

"Who is the man in the caboose?"

"There's no one in the caboose, Miss Anthony."

"When the train rounded a horseshoe curve this morning, the caboose came alongside us, and I saw a man sitting by the window."

"I expect you imagined him."

"He waved to me!"

"A trick of the eye caused by sunlight on dirty glass."

"The sky was overcast."

"All the more reason to disbelieve your eyes."

"I declare there is no making sense of it!"

I shook off my drowsiness and spoke for the first time since breakfast, "How did my baby get from Zarephath to Memphis?"

"After the Thirteenth Amendment abolished slavery, the blacks no longer needed the Underground Railroad. The Klan took it over and uses it to send agents north and smuggle contraband south. Martin was sent to Memphis in a crate of incendiary pamphlets printed by your husband to incite white violence against the negroes."

"Franklin would never do such a thing!" Furious with Gallagher, I could have brained him with one of his empty bottles.

"Anarchists will do anything to achieve their ends."

"I suppose Mr. Dode is at the center of this plot against Franklin," I countered, as though wringing vinegar from a rag.

"If you're referring to Mr. Fischer, he has uncovered a number of your husband's un-American activities. He'll swing for them, I assure you. For your information, madam, the Secret Service does not plot nor seek to harm innocent men."

"And women?" asked Susan, incredulity ironing some of the wrinkles from her face.

Gallagher shrugged. "Show me an innocent woman."

"Dreadful man!"

Gallagher picked his teeth with his sheriff's star. Elizabeth, Susan, and Margaret fell to musing. I set aside the lies told about Franklin as unworthy of consideration and thought instead of the man in the caboose: So Susan saw him, too! Lulled by the lullaby of the rails, the party of malcontents shortly closed their eyes. I left them to their dreams or reveries and walked back to the clown car. Standing on its little porch, I put my ear to the door and heard not so much as the dying echo of a pratfall, a laugh, or the weeping in which clowns sometimes indulge when they think they're alone. I opened the door. The car was empty. Only pots of greasepaint remained to prove that clowns had once been there. Where had they gone? I asked myself. Did they get off the train at Charlestown as we slept inside the enchanted space Barnum had created for us? Without their assistance—feeble as it would have been—what chance have we against the Klan?

I started for the parlor car, when I remembered the reason I had left it. I went to the door of the caboose and knocked. No one answered, yet I was aware of a presence on the other side.

"Who's there?" I asked.

I could hear someone faintly breathing.

"Is it you, Mr. James?"

Whatever reply there may have been, it was drowned by the roaring in my ears.

Afraid, I rejoined the others. Their eyes were closed,

their chins nesting in their collars. I would say nothing about the vanished clowns or the person whose labored breathing I had heard.

We pressed on to Memphis!

No Country for Circuses

ON THE EASTERN BANK of the Wolf River, ten miles shy of Memphis, the train balked. It had come to a gradual stop, as though the last lump of coal had given up the ghost in the firebox, its gritty atoms rising into the noonday air. Beneath the trees, a dusky light seemed to sway.

"What the devil is the matter?" demanded Gallagher, his red nose out of joint.

"Won't budge," replied the engineer, who hailed from New Hampshire, where words are not wasted on the obvious.

"Why not?"

"Don't know."

"Try again."

The engineer shrugged in despite of all fools who refused to accept the vagaries of the mechanical world. He reengaged the valve gear, but the iron wheels spun help-lessly, unable to get a grip on the rails, which might have been greased, for all the progress the leviathan made.

"Like I said, she won't budge. She'll go backward right

enough." He demonstrated, and the train rolled a few yards in the direction of Charleston.

"How very odd!" exclaimed both Elizabeth and Susan. "Why in blazes won't it go forward?"

"Don't want to," said the engineer. Years of locomotion had made him indifferent to the affairs of a universe governed by machinery and timetables. His attitude toward them was one of resignation, like that of a cowboy unsurprised by a cow's-plat on his heel.

Exasperated, Gallagher kicked one of the ponderous wheels and then hopped on one foot while he held the other, like a man in a music hall sketch who has stubbed a toe. (What a funny piece of business Mr. Ashton, the Posturing Man, could have made of it!) "Damn it to Hell!"

The engineer chortled. He took out a bandanna and placed it daintily on the iron seat of the cab and, opening his lunch kettle, took out an apple and a turkey leg.

"This is no time to eat!" shouted Gallagher.

The engineer consulted his pocket watch, said that it was indeed time, wiped his greasy hands on an oily rag, and went about his lunch.

"What're we to do?" asked Susan.

"We will go on!" said Elizabeth firmly.

"Don't expect me to carry you when you can't take another step!" said Susan irritably.

Elizabeth glowered and would have pounced had Gallagher not said, "In their big shoes, the clowns will never make it through these woods."

"The clowns are gone," I said.

"That settles it! We go back to New York." He turned to the engineer. "When you are done stuffing your tripes, locomote us to Grand Central."

The engineer began to reply, choked on a bit of apple skin, spat, and said, "Okay."

"I hope you choke, you miserable son of Adam!" said Susan. If her words had been a razor, they would have shaved the engineer's cheeks in a trice and then lingered deliciously at the bristles on his throat.

Gallagher spun round on his boot heels, which made a pleasant gravelly sound, and started toward the parlor car. "Ladies, shall we go?"

"Not without the baby!" thundered Susan.

"You can't leave us here!" fulminated Elizabeth, as she had done for our sex since Seneca Falls, when she declared, "The history of mankind is a history of repeated injuries and usurpation on the part of man toward woman."

"As Mr. Barnum's agent, my obligation is to his property. In that you both insist that you are no man's property, you are on your own." He doffed his Stetson and then, smirking, settled it back on his head with an insolent snap of the brim.

"We won't go back without the child!" vowed the suffragists. My heart in my mouth left no room for words. I could do nothing but nod vigorously in assent.

"Margaret, will *you* come?" asked Gallagher. "You're a circus employee. Your duty is to Mr. Barnum."

"No, I won't!" She was standing on a hill of clinkers, an elevation that increased her physical stature, if not her moral one, which, being superlative, would not admit of enlargement.

"What can a midget accomplish against a Grand Cyclops?" Having drunk his courage dry, Gallagher was a man without gumption.

"What did David do to Goliath?" asked Margaret as she picked up a stone and threw it at the special agent. A red wound blossomed on his forehead.

"Mr. Barnum shall hear of this!" he cried, waving his fist. Then without another word, he climbed aboard the parlor car. The locomotive let off steam, jolted into reverse, and headed east—the caboose in the vanguard, carrying its mysterious passenger.

Can it be Franklin? I wondered. Did he become a fugitive from the law after committing some outrage against capitalism? I tried to imagine my husband on the run. No, Franklin is not the stuff of which anarchists are made. He's in San Francisco, looking for a job.

We walked on beside the tracks, Margaret with a difficulty that the shortness of her stride and the sharp stones underfoot could not entirely explain. She seemed to droop the closer we got to Memphis. Elizabeth noticed her weariness and brought our little sorority to a halt.

"We should rest," she said, obedient to the maternal instinct with which she was amply provided.

We sat on a sandstone column that had fallen into a field of jimsonweed, called "the Devil's snare," circled by thorn bushes, dark and bristling.

"Margaret, maybe you should have gone with Gallagher," said Elizabeth gently.

Susan gave her no chance to respond. "I don't trust him, and I don't much care for Barnum or anybody else who employs one of Pinkerton's men, who are nothing but thugs for hire!"

"I belong with my friends," said Margaret simply. "Though I'm so tired, I could shut my eyes and sleep for days and days."

"We're not wanted here, especially you, Margaret, for the same reason the train balked," I said. "With the suddenness of a revelation, I understood the cause of both her weakness and the locomotive's recalcitrance. "This is no country for circuses."

"You may be right," said Elizabeth thoughtfully. "Margaret, perhaps you should wait here until we return with the child."

"If I go on awhile longer, I'll shake off this listlessness." But she did not shake it off; we had not taken fifty paces before she had to stop. "I can't take another step. Forgive me." She closed her eyes and crumpled onto the ground like a half-empty sack.

Just then, a black man called to us from an opening in a dense woods of honey locust trees. He was tending a fire. A pot was hung from a notched stick above the flames. He was beckoning us with his hand. We helped Margaret to her feet and to his fire as her head bobbed back and forth.

"The little lady appears all in," he said kindly. He was one of those negroes who could have been any age from sixty to one hundred. His bald head was as polished as a lucky chestnut. The veins on the backs of his hands reminded me of roots. His eyes were overcast by cataracts.

"Can you help her?" I asked, sensing that he could. He saw the trust in my eyes, which Shelby Ross had once called "pretty," and smiled warmly.

"I came a long way for just that reason," he said. He lifted the rattling lid from the pot, brought his face close to the potion—for such I knew it to be—and sniffed. "Almost done," he said, covering the boiling mixture. "You ladies are crazy to have started on this undertaking." He fingered the loose flesh at his throat. I noticed a scar that could only have been left by a rope. "You see plain enough I am old, but if I was to tell you that I'm the same age as Abraham was when he died, you would think *I* was crazy. It's one thing to read about the old begetters in the Book of Genesis, but to sit next to a hundred-and-seventy-five-year-old black man waiting for a pot to boil has got to be dumbfounding."

Elizabeth giggled—nervously, I thought.

The negro examined the contents of the pot, spooned some, blew on it, and, having tasted it, declared it done. He stirred the pot, filled a tin cup, and handed it to me. "Now you get this medicine down her before she dies of spite, for you all have come to the land of the spiteful, who are waiting at the end of the tracks to do the Devil's work."

"What is it?" I asked curiously. It smelled like something I—well, I could not have said what exactly, but it brought to mind an afternoon when I was a girl no taller than Margaret. My mother had taken me to visit an old woman living at Carroll Gardens, beside Gowanus Creek. An ancient negro, his trouser legs rolled up, was tonging for oysters. Sniffing the liquid in the tin cup, I smelled the creek, the mud bank, and the man when he came out of the brackish water and showed me the oysters in his sack, their rough shells the size of supper plates.

"It's a remedy for an evil juju," replied the healer and herbalist. "Slaves made their own medicines: red oak bark tea for purging, bloodroot for croup, foxglove for dropsy, chokeberry for bloody flux, jimsonweed for rheumatism, chestnut leaf for the lungs, rosemary for the blues, sassafras for bad blood, snakeroot for snakebite, boneset for fevers. There is a root can turn a black man white, though I never saw it done. A cup of this will get rid of the vapors that got into your friend's heart. They sicken childlike folk whose hearts are gay."

"How did you know Margaret would be here?"

"I know lots of things I have no reason knowing."

"Do you know anything about locomotives?" asked Elizabeth, changing the subject from arcane matters to pragmatic ones.

"What in particular?"

"Why one would stop and refuse to go any farther?"

"Might not have been a real locomotive."

"Nonsense!" said Susan waspishly.

"Might have been the *idea* of one. Somebody might have gotten tired of lugging it around in his head and just stopped thinking about it. Even an imaginary locomotive's a heavy load. Did it disappear?"

"It rode off out of sight."

"Yessir, it was a weight got off somebody's mind. Now get the potion in her before it loses its goodness."

I rested Margaret's head in my lap and fed her a spoon-ful. Since she was fast asleep, the reddish liquid drained from between her lips. "Margaret, wake up!" I shook her, but she would not wake. Susan slapped her hard, leaving a red mark on her cheek. Stung into consciousness, Marga-ret swallowed most of the liquid before she closed her eyes again.

"She'll sleep while the vapors come out." The black man pointed a gnarled finger at Margaret's breast. He covered her with a piece of sacking, felt her forehead tenderly, and said, "In a little while, she'll be right again. But you ladies take care. You are walking into the lion's den, like Daniel, and I have no root to brew to keep you safe from the hatred of men. Unless the Lord sees fit to close the lion's mouth, I fear for you."

Elizabeth laid her hand on the black man's sleeve. "You've done a good deed today, my friend, and we're beholden to you. I hope you, too, will be well and go well."

"I go where I need to go," he replied cryptically. He smiled and, having gathered up his few belongings, walked into the forest, until he disappeared from view. In my fanci-ful state of mind, it was a ghost I saw growing pale among the watchful trees.

Catawamptious

WE SAW NO ONE ELSE UNTIL we came to a field of okra, indigenous to West Africa, like the blacks who were picking it, watched by an overseer who glared at us as at a quartet of freaks. After an hour's trudge, we reached the outskirts of Spottswood.

To have read one of Ned Buntline's dime novels is to know Spottswood, since one half-dead hard-luck town is like another. Spottswood was dirt streets planted with a scraggle of "concerns," few of which looked likely to take root. The men favored the saloon, the barber's, the stable, and the hardware store. The women patronized Gould's Emporium and the Baptist church, whose steeple had been blasted by lightning. Inside, someone was picking at a hymn tune as at a worrying scab. We went into a lunchroom next to the hotel, where strips of fly-beaded sticky paper hung from the ceiling. We were arrested while eating strawberry buckle. Susan and Elizabeth would not go quietly; they tongue-lashed the sheriff, who "took off the kid gloves—women be damned!" If Lilian Heigold had been there, she'd have split the dullard's skull with her stick.

"I won't be interfered with!" protested Elizabeth through the bars of our cell.

Susan, on the other hand, having had previous experience as a jailbird, was outwardly calm. "What charges do you have to bring against us?"

The sheriff took off his dented Stetson and mopped the

sweatband and his bald head with an unsavory handkerchief. Having satisfied the demands of frontier hygiene, he put his hat back on and squinted down the barrel of his gun at four wanted posters that its butt end had tacked to the jailhouse wall. We saw our faces reflected in four crudely engraved portraits.

"We've no use for your kind in Shelby County!" he growled. "They may tolerate your shenanigans back east, but in Tennessee women know their place." He sat in a chair and spun his spur with menace.

"I suppose you object to a woman's right to vote," said Susan with a prideful sniff.

"And of her right to a fair wage!" declaimed Elizabeth, as if she were in Philadelphia at the Athenaeum, instead of in the land of lynching.

"And to be protected from a husband who bullies and dishonors her!"

"And to divorce him!"

"And should she divorce him, to keep her property and her children!"

"And to marry whom she pleases, even if the man happens to be a negro!" A skillful orator, Elizabeth saved the most inflammatory issue for last.

Infuriated, the sheriff spat tobacco juice through the bars. Margaret had to jump to save her shoes. "We won't put up with any of your New York City horseshit!"

"What do you intend to do with us?" asked Susan, giving another sniff of disdain, which her pinched nose amplified.

"Keep you here till the circuit judge gets around to visiting. In the meantime, I hope the good citizens of this town will overpower me tonight and drag you four to the nearest tree. I would pay to see it properly done."

"Why have you arrested *them*?" asked Elizabeth, indicating Margaret and me.

He raised his fist to me and snarled, "This bitch whelped a black bastard, and in Shelby County, fornication and miscegenation are against the law." He jabbed a finger rudely toward Margaret. "And that one there ran away from the Arkansas Asylum for Wayward Girls, where she was locked up on account of immorality and arson."

"I am not a girl, nor am I immoral!" said Margaret grandly. "And I am certainly not an arsonist! I'm an attraction of P. T. Barnum's Grand Traveling Museum, Menagerie, Caravan and Hippodrome. Having lost nearly everything five times to fire, he wouldn't have hired me had I shown the least tendency toward pyromania."

"If I were you, I wouldn't mention that trickster's name in Shelby County. We don't take kindly to flimflam and bunkum." The brute spat again. "For your information, midget, an agent of the Confederate Secret Service set fire to the American Museum to punish Barnum for being a bigmouthed nigger-lover and a Jew." The sheriff put his face against the bars and hissed, "Let me tell you something: I believe in Hell, and you four bitches have stumbled into a place seven times hotter. So keep your puke holes shut while I go home and stuff mine with pork chops and hominy. And if I get a bellyache 'cause of you, I'll personally see that you're catawamptiously chewed up, as we say in Shelby County!" He grimaced, as though he'd taken a bite of Susan, whose sour face promised indigestion. He turned and went to his supper, locking the jailhouse door behind him.

The sheriff's talk of Hell brought to mind the story of Nebuchadnezzar, king of Babylon, and Shadrach, Meshach, and Abednego. The king commanded that they be bound and thrown into a fiery furnace, which was stoked for their cremation to burn seven times hotter than usual. When he looked inside it, he saw the three Hebrews walking unbound amid the flames and, with them, a fourth man who resembled the son of God. Which of us, I wondered, would be the most likely child of the Almighty? Margaret, I guessed, because it would be just like Him to embody Himself in the most unlikely piece of creation, the better to astonish. (Try as I may, I can't imagine any other god but Barnum.)

"The sheriff would make a dramatic illustration for the lecture platform," said Elizabeth. "We could call him 'Man at His Most Evolved.'"

"I'd rather see the so-and-so stuffed in a taxidermist's window," countered Susan acidly.

"What now?" asked Margaret.

"Time will tell," replied Susan.

"If we can escape, should we go back or press on?" asked Elizabeth.

"Let's put it to a vote." Not even the threat of being chewed catawamptiously could weaken Susan's devotion to woman's suffrage. We were a democracy of four and would respect the wishes of the majority. Trembling, I awaited the result that would determine Martin's fate.

We voted by acclamation: "On to Memphis!"

"Thank you, dear friends!" I cried. "And should it be the case that my son is a negro—"

"He could be a Tartar, for all I care," said Elizabeth grandly.

Like a special envoy of the Omnipotent, the sheriff's wife entered. Seeing bedclothes in her arms, we thought she had come to make up our cots. "Hurry!" she said, unlocking the cell door. "You might not get another chance!"

We were astounded by this turn of events.

"Why are you helping us?"

"I'm a suffragist—or I would be if I lived up north and weren't married to a lout."

"Does he beat you?" asked Elizabeth, who habitually canvassed women on their treatment by men.

"Yes, but there's no time to show you my bruises. You must hurry, before he whistles for his pie."

"He'll suspect you," said Susan worriedly.

"He'll blame your escape on the negroes."

"Come with us!" urged Elizabeth, taking the sheriff's wife by the hand.

"I can't leave my children. Now you really must go!"

We followed her out the back door. "Take these." She gave us each a bedsheet and a pillowcase. "When you get to Memphis, put these on." She gave me a pair of shears and said, "Tonight, they intend to sacrifice your son to the

Imperial Wizard. Everyone will be dressed in Klan costumes. You'll be able to pass unnoticed among the crowd. *Look*!" She pointed west, where night had begun to fall. The sky seemed on fire, as if the remnant light of Krakatoa shone. The evening sky had looked like this when Barnum's museum, his Hippotheatron, and Iranistan, his mogul palace in Connecticut, were consumed. On such a night an age and more ago, Caesar's centurions had set alight the Great Library of Alexandria, where *catawamptious* did not appear on the scrolls and codices written in all the languages of the literate world.

"Godspeed!" said Susan.

"We're grateful!" said Elizabeth.

"Thank you, you dear good woman!" cried Margaret, close to tears.

I threw my arms around the sheriff's wife and let my eyes rain. She shook herself free and pushed me toward the burning sky.

The Invisible Empire

I'LL NEVER FORGET THE FLOURY CHEEK of our jailor's wife, who was, I suppose, making a pie as she struggled with her conscience. That courage can rise like dough in a bowl is heartening. I'm glad whenever I recall an atom of kindness from the oblivion that swathes our little lives as a bandage does tender flesh. I would not thank God to be reborn if

His grant meant that I must relive that painful time. One does not care to be mauled twice by a tiger—not even in exchange for immortality.

On the outskirts of Memphis, we came upon a disused railroad shed. We went inside and, with the shears, cut eye-holes in the pillowslips and roughly tailored the sheets to fit our different forms. Margaret needed half a sheet; Elizabeth had to make do with one, an accommodation that exposed her lower extremities.

"Praise God you didn't wear your bloomers!" remarked Susan, casting a critical eye on her friend encased in a linen shroud.

"You look like a malnourished ghost!" retorted Elizabeth, stung by the affront.

"This is not a beauty contest!" objected Susan, rearranging her sheet.

To hear them fuss, you would have thought we were in Mrs. Crockett's boardinghouse and not in a tar-paper shack stinking of oil and creosote, surrounded by Klansmen awaiting the Holy Terrors to put an innocent mulatto child to the stake.

I accepted Susan's idea that little Martin had been begotten by God's special agent, an angel of color that the prophet Ezekiel had glimpsed in a dream, "whose appearance [was] like the appearance of brass." But I struggled to answer the question, If I had the fabulous root that could turn black to white, would I brew a potion and give it to my child to drink, or would I let him be as God or accident had made him? To save the skin of one we love, what principle will we not betray, what treason not commit?

Disguised, we walked toward the heights overlooking the Mississippi River, where the city had fallen to Union gunboats during the War of the Rebellion. No sooner had it ended than Nathan Bedford Forrest, a Memphis man, founded the Invisible Empire. (Too late, he would repudiate it.) On the bluffs stood three tall crosses slathered with tar to make them flammable. The flanking pair had been set alight; flames rose into that region of the air where night birds fly. On one, Elizabeth's straw-filled effigy hung; on the other, Susan's. I could hear them crackle. The central cross had not yet been lighted. I knew that it was intended for my child. Holding flaming torches aloft, a satanic host of robed and hooded men waited expectantly for the appointed hour.

"They've made my effigy three times larger than yours!" complained Elizabeth.

Susan snorted and said, "Keep your mind on the business at hand, Lizzie."

We passed fearfully through the mob, in spite of the anonymity conferred by our costume. Their eyes fixed on the crosses, none noticed Elizabeth's shins. Not even Margaret stood out in the crowd, since the Klansmen had dressed their children as smaller versions of themselves. For all her fortitude, however, Margaret began to whimper. A Klanswoman stopped and spoke to her, "There's no reason to cry, child. You're among the chosen people. No harm can come to you." She patted Margaret's covered head and walked away, pulling a miniature Klansman sucking his thumb after her. I wished I had a gun, so that I could deflate her smugness with a bullet. Thus does hatred beget hatred, from age to everlasting age.

Night was falling fast, and the mob moved restlessly toward the hill. As we drew near, we saw that a platform had been raised in front of the central cross. With its row of chairs and a potted plant, it was like any other stage from which a harangue or a homily would be delivered (except that the plant was the highly toxic Heart of Jesus). At the center of the platform squatted a bulky object covered by a sheet. (The sheet was *ensanguined*—a word meaning "bloody," I'd learned from Mr. James.)

Six men climbed the wooden stairs; five sat and the sixth, Ethan Dorn, the Grand Cyclops of the Memphis Klan, tore off the bloody sheet to reveal an altar. Arranged before him lay the symbolic instruments of his priesthood: a bucket of tar, a sack of feathers, a knife, and a noose.

"The frightful hour of the dreadful day, in the weeping week of the furious month, has come," he intoned solemnly. "Goblins and ghouls from all over the realm—its dominions and provinces—have assembled tonight on this shining hill where Nathan Bedford Forrest laid the foundation for the Invisible Empire. He later fell into error, as prophets sometimes will, but we honor him as the founder of our holy order.

"Along with Grand Turk Butterfield, Grand Sentinel Wallace, Grand Ensign Rollins, Grand Magi Ford, and the venerable Grand Giant Collins, Grand Cyclops emeritus, I welcome you to this special wrecking, in which the gross product of an intermarriage—detestable in the sight of God and His Klan—will be cleansed at the foot of the fiery cross."

A thousand ghouls and goblins began to sing the hymn whose refrain I'd first heard from Alma Bridwell White's pukehole in Zarephath:

> To the Bright Fiery Cross, I will ever be true;
> All blame and reproach gladly bear,
> And friendship will show to each Klansman
> I know;
> Its glory forever we'll share.
>
> So, I'll cherish the Bright Fiery Cross
> Till from my duties at last I lay down;
> Then burn for me a Bright Fiery Cross;
> The day I am laid in the ground.

So mighty was the voice that rose from a thousand blasted hearts, it could have raised the dead negroes who'd been lynched, burned, or beaten from the shallow graves into which they'd been shoveled. The ghouls, hydras, furies, and terrors were in ecstasy, because there's no sport like a blood sport and no living creature—not a fox or a wolf, a lion or an elephant—is more gratifying to slaughter than a man, preferably a black, yellow, or red one. With each new stanza, the hymn grew louder; each time the refrain was bellowed, the frenzy of the mob increased, and so did our terror. Shivers ran through us like electric shocks, but they were identical to the fits of rapture of the beings around us—I cannot call them "human."

Grand Cyclops Dorn returned to his theme; his words came faster and more trenchantly. He was inflaming the mob as the Klan's fallen idol Nathan Bedford Forrest had done when he incited the men of Fort Pillow to massacre five hundred surrendering black Union soldiers. "Behind me, you see the charred likenesses of two of the North's most repulsive women. They promote the amalgamation of the races. They would corrupt the purity of our offspring with the tainted blood of Jews, coons, Polacks, papists, and dagoes."

The mob sang lustily:

> We're busy working for our race,
> Our families, and our homes;
> We keep the niggers in their place
> And the dago pope in Rome.

"I can tell you all with absolute certainty that we are doing the Lord's work," said Dorn.

The multitude answered its high priest in a single unmusical voice:

> Oh, I'd rather be a Klansman
> In a robe of snowy white
> Than be a Roman Catholic priest
> In a robe as dark as night.

"Do you think God would have allowed Africans to become enslaved if he had the least regard for them?"

"No, God be praised!"

"Do you think the Almighty has the least little bit of love for the negro race?"

"None at all!"

"Do you think He intended that there be a place called Orange Mound in the State of Tennessee, where negroes can live on land only white men know how to work?"

"No, *suh*, He most surely did not!" The infernal congregation had fallen into the call-and-response patter—the shouts of praise and indignation—heard in a black church.

"Do you think He's pleased with His white children for allowing such a travesty?"

"Stick 'em in the ground and leave 'em to rot!"

His forearms resting on the altar, Dorn went on in a confidential tone: "Now if anyone from up North was to hear me . . ." Elizabeth went rigid inside her sheet and, I imagined, turned as white as it. "They would think me full up with braggadocio, which is what we country folk call 'bullshit,' having no use for dago words, French ones, or the *palabras* of the darkies who live on the wrong side of the Río Grande."

"Burn the greasers!" screamed the crowd. "Turn them into human torches!"

"I would love to send the Twelve Terrors and a wrecking crew to lay waste to the nigger Mexicans who have the temerity to live smack up against our southern border!"

"Build a wall! Build a wall to keep them out!"

"I would personally set fire to anybody living within the sacred Realm of Tennessee who has the gall to talk spiggoty or any other ignorant lingo!" shouted Dorn. The mob's thundering applause could have pulverized gallstones. "But we are here tonight to set another fire—"

"Hallelujah!"

"A fire of purgation that will show the Lord God that His chosen race won't stand for miscegenation, won't sit quietly by while the sacred blood of the white race is polluted by the black blood of the negro or negress, and will never tolerate bastardy!"

"Lord, show no mercy!"

He took the ceremonial knife and pointed it at Elizabeth's burnt effigy. "If I had this perversity of nature in front of me, I would gut her and fill all the lamps in Memphis with her lard and have enough left over to waterproof a revival tent." I could almost see Elizabeth's hackles rise. "Elizabeth—Cady—Stanton!" He spat out her name like something vile on the tongue. "Elizabeth Cady Stanton is the author of all women's mischief in this country. She is a godless, unwholesome demagogue who preaches a woman's rights: her right to have an opinion and speak it publicly no matter how ridiculous, the right to vote for a president or a governor when her only experience with a ballot is casting it at the county fair for the best apple pie or homemade hat, the right to leave her husband on a whim and take his money, his property, and his children with her, and the right to sleep with negroes anytime she feels her loins itch!"

"God pour His holy fire on the whore!"

He pointed his knife at Susan's effigy. "Now this person—I do not dare call her a woman—Miss Susan B. Anthony—the *B* stands for bitch!—is Stanton's battleax, who graduated from loving negroes to women." He spat again. (Southern men must get dry as sticks by the end of the day.)

"Please, God, throw her into the lake of everlasting fire!"

"Of the two, Susan [*spit*] B. [*spit*] Anthony [*spit*] is far worse because—all you ghouls, goblins, furies, dragons, and genii—she is unnatural."

"Oh, Lord of Heaven and Hell, skin her, tan her, and turn her into leather pouches to keep our chaw in!"

"Susan B. Anthony is worse than any fallen lily, soiled dove, strumpet, or succubus. I can forgive the wayward girl who lets herself become some man's creature; I could, like Jesus, forgive a woman taken in adultery so long as she is not my wife, but I will never countenance sodomy!"

"Burn the witch! Burn the witch! Burn the witch!"

"Unfortunately, these two abominations are far away from the pure hands of the righteous who would tear them limb from limb. They are living in the infamous American Babylon of the Hebrews and the Irish—New York City! But tonight we have the rotten fruit of their philosophy: the mulatto bastard of a woman who serves the high priestesses of the cult of emasculation, the woman who typewrites their obscene blasphemies and who learned her unfeminine skill at the so-called Young Women's Christian Association, which is a coven for modern-day witches."

My tongue tasted like a sour pickle, and I bit it to keep from crying out in indignation. One word—one syllable of disapproval—and I'd have been ripped apart by the ravening beast that is a mob. I'd have been catawamptiously eaten.

"Burn the bastard!" it chanted. "Burn the nigger brat!"

"Grand Guard, it is time. Bring forth the sacrifice!" commanded Grand Cyclops Dorn in the voice of doom.

"Burn, baby, burn!"

Six men dressed like the rest marched out the back door of a nearby house. Behind them, a Klanswoman carried Martin in her arms. He appeared to be asleep. She must have given him laudanum or gin, I told myself, for him to sleep through such a commotion. She and her escort brought my baby to the altar as the zealots sang:

> Rally round the sacred altar
> Purged of sin and baseless fear;
> Ne'er shall Knights in armor falter,
> Nor shall Craven enter in.

The Grand Cyclops put the child on the rough-hewn altar and, with a finger dipped in pine tar, drew the sign of the cross on his small brow. Next, he sprinkled feathers over him, and around his neck, he tied a noose fashioned from butcher's twine instead of the hemp reserved for the fully grown. The ritual at an end, Dorn held the baby on high for the people to see. They roared their disapproval and shrieked their enmity. By the infernal blaze of their torches, they stamped their feet as one. Thunder rolled across the river into Arkansas. Joshua's army of forty thousand Israelites had made such a noise on the Plain of Jericho. The ground shook as it had in 1812, when the earth buckled at the New Madrid fault line in Missouri and people trembled as far north as Cairo and as far south as Memphis—cities of the New World, visited by the ruthless gods of the old. Yes, hyperbole is necessary! How else am I to capture an experience that was out of all proportion to ordinary life?

Mark Twain would have said, "By exaggeration!"

Gallagher would have sneered, "By prevarication!"

Henry James would have asserted, "By convolution!"

Barnum would have boasted, "By mystification!"

Dorn raised his hand, and the crowd grew silent. "I now call upon the Imperial Wizard to make his presence known!" The crowd parted, and a large man astride an enormous white horse decked with flowers ambled toward the platform. His conical hat was twice as tall as any other, and his robes were scarlet. The ghouls and other lesser folk fell back at his approach, many of them trembling in awe. "Bow down to the Imperial Wizard!" shouted Dorn, who made his obeisance to the leader of the Klan.

Sitting his horse lightly, the Imperial Wizard nodded his noble head to his worshipful followers, from whom not a peep was heard. Not even the little Klan boys and girls dared to make a sound, for fear of incurring the Wizard's high displeasure.

Dorn turned to the five dignitaries on the platform. "Light the sacred fire!"

They rose from their chairs and went to the central cross,

which was also painted black with tar. No sooner had their torches touched the wood than it caught fire. The flames spread upward in a *whoosh* until the cross was engulfed. People as far away as Fulton could've seen the ghastly light in the sky and would have wondered at its meaning. The shrouded assembly kept a religious silence as the Imperial Wizard on his horse drew as near to the fiery cross as he could without scorching his canonicals.

"The Grand Council of Yahoos has tried this abomination," blustered Dorn. "And it has found him guilty of the grievous sin of having been born black. Accordingly, the Grand Council sentenced Martin Finch, by the 'one-drop rule' of blood, to be given to the fires of retribution and be consumed therein. If his mother were here, she would be put to death, as well, for conceiving him in her white woman's belly."

Dorn took my darling babe from the altar and carried him to the cross, where a manger packed with straw awaited him. Meanwhile, the five potentates had assembled into a tableau in mockery of the shepherds who, in Bible times, had left their flocks and gone to glorify the baby Jesus in Bethlehem.

"Before you all and in the name of the Imperial Wizard of the Invisible Empire and of the white race, which God made in His image, I sacrifice this creature! *Non Silba Sed Anthar*: Not for Self, but for Others."

"Not for self, but for others!"

Fists clenched, I rushed toward the monstrous Nativity. Elizabeth gasped, Susan moaned, and Margaret's voice caught in her throat. Entranced by the flames, no one else saw me. Dorn was about to toss the child, like a stick of firewood, into the burning manger. I took the shears from underneath my robe and would have plunged them into his wicked heart had a Voice (the common noun is too paltry for so uncommon an utterance) not cracked the awful silence into splinters, like a window shattered by a stone.

"Let My Son Go!"

I don't know how to convey the quality of that voice, which seemed to have no source other than the sky. It was loud—what a feeble word to say how it boomed and resounded round about us! In such a voice, God had called into being the firmaments, Earth, and all living things. With it, He had plundered Adam of a rib and made Eve, whose moist earth would bring forth all the generations of our kind, which must end in the cold earth of the grave. In such a voice, God had sent plagues against the stiff-backed Egyptians and charged the angel of death to visit them in their houses to break them of stubbornness. At its dread command, the Red Sea had parted, the tablets of the law cracked, and fire poured onto the heads of the Sodomites. In a voice like that which thundered above Memphis at the frightful hour of the dreadful day, in the weeping week of the furious month, Ahab had shouted his defiance at Moby Dick.

The stentorian Voice continued: "If Any Harm Befalls Him, I Will Destroy Your Houses, Slay Your Children, Sow Your Bodies with Corruption and Your Fields with

Salt, Turn Your Wits with Fevers, and Damn Your Souls to Everlasting Pain!"

Dorn dropped the baby in the grass and ran. The white horse decked with flowers reared and threw the Imperial Wizard to the ground, which opened to receive him. The grand army of the Invisible Empire skedaddled into the forest.

I was about to scoop Martin up in my arms, when the Klanswoman who'd carried him from the house and given him to Dorn knocked me to the ground. Tearing off my hood, she cried out in recognition, "You!" I knew the voice and the eyes behind the mask; they belonged to Alma Bridwell White. She took the child and ran toward the burning cross, the tar snapping and the scorched wood swelling in the heat. She'd have given him to the fire had Margaret not snatched him from her grasp. White turned in fury; as she did, a fountain of sparks fell onto her robe, setting it alight. She spun crazily, as though a swarm of bees had settled on her; she swatted the flames and screamed. In a moment, she'd exchanged her white robe for one of fire, like the golden one Medea gave Jason. As Margaret, Susan, Elizabeth, and I watched, White ran to the bluff and jumped into the Mississippi. Once, I'd watched as boys poured coal oil on a crow and lighted it. White reminded me of that terrible sight, though I didn't pity her as I had the blazing bird plummeting from the bridge into New-town Creek.

"Let's go before they come back!" urged Susan.

We hurried along the heights and didn't stop until we reached French Fort, lower down the river.

By the wall of the deserted garrison, we caught our breath and collected our wits like scattered parcels. Martin fretted in a sleep nourished by a potent distillation while we marveled at events and, in particular, the Voice, which had delivered us from evil.

"It could only have been God's, for none other could have routed a multitude of hardened men and scarcely less hardened women," reasoned Susan. "Only He is capable of so mighty an effect."

Although Elizabeth was loath to surrender her religious skepticism, she couldn't explain the "effect" by adducing either natural or mechanical causes to anyone's satisfaction, including her own.

"I've heard it before, though not so hugely amplified," said Margaret.

We looked at her dubiously.

"When?" asked Susan.

"From whose mouth?" asked Elizabeth.

"Mr. Barnum's speaking through a megaphone when he addressed spectators in the seats farthest from the center ring; in barrel-vaulted train sheds amid the thunderous noise of departure when he bid farewell to onlookers; and in Gotham, Chicago, San Francisco, and London when he shouted greetings to passersby above the din of traffic, circus screamers, and excited elephants."

Elizabeth and Susan were not convinced. They could believe in a god who can crack the foundations of the universe with a shout, but a mere man or woman—no. True, some can shatter glass with a long-held operatic note, but a party trick is hardly comparable to an admonition that can disperse a thousand fools.

I accepted Margaret's explanation because it solved the mystery surrounding the person Susan had glimpsed and I had heard softly breathing inside the caboose. Human beings can't tolerate a mystery and, in trying to solve it, will many times beget a greater one. Just so do we move from question to question while the world becomes more complicated instead of less, and we ourselves grow more puzzled and alone.

Little Martin opened his eyes and looked into mine with an intelligence and a frankness I had not seen there before. I thought I saw him wink, as if he knew a secret I did not, such as the mystery of his birth. There was no doubt about it: He was a negro boy.

Minstrelsy

A MILE OR SO BELOW FRENCH FORT, we came upon the ramshackle abode of Mr. Brister Warwick, a former slave. He greeted us with a shotgun aimed unequivocally at Elizabeth, who appeared to be our leader and was the surer target.

"Get your hands up!" he said with the meanness you

sometimes find in people who've had all they can stand of cruelty and terror.

You see, we'd neglected to take off our improvised goblin suits.

"We're not Klanswomen!" spluttered Elizabeth. With a gun barrel poking at her ribs, she could be forgiven her petulance. "We are northern suffragists traveling incognito."

The man appeared suspicious. Who could blame him? In Shelby County, a night visit from folks dressed like ghosts did not bode well for a negro. To be fair, Shelby was not the only county in America where black people could be dragged from their homes in the middle of the night. Some folks think lynching is more fun than a circus, and admission is free.

"The Klan is after us," said Susan, calmly disrobing. The rest of us quickly followed suit.

Facing two old women, a "slip of a girl," as Franklin liked to say of me, a tiny woman, and a baby, Brister relaxed his grip on the rifle's business end. "This have something to do with the ruckus I heard from upriver?"

"It does indeed," said Elizabeth, who related the story of our anabasis and explained the reason we had come—a story that would have been smoother in the telling had it not been for Susan's interjections. Margaret and I forbore to contribute to the babel. Little by little, Brister became convinced of our innocence. Whether he believed in the Voice is another matter. He offered to help us get out of Tennessee.

"Just before first light, I'll row you across to Arkansas. Not that Arkansas is friendlier to northern busybodies than

Tennessee, but any dogs they've set on you will lose your scent in the river."

"We're grateful to you, Mr. Warwick," we said in our several ways, all of them sincere.

"You folks hungry?" We were. "I have salt meat and bread and some goat's milk for the child." He went into his kitchen shed and returned with our meager supper. Before we ate, he blessed it and commended us into God's safekeeping.

"Get some rest," he said. "I'll give you some blankets to sleep on."

"We brought our own bedsheets!" quipped Elizabeth, whose native cheerfulness supper had restored.

I made a nest for Martin in an empty apple crate and watched as he tumbled back into sleep. You're better there, I told him in my thoughts. I couldn't sleep, or maybe I did. Sleep or wakefulness, Tennessee or Arkansas were one and the same to me then. That night, I clung to certain facts: the child, the sour smell of goat's milk on his breath, a blister on my thumb raised in cutting bedsheets, Elizabeth's snores, Susan's slumberous harrumphs, the glint of light on the barrel of the old negro's gun, which he held in his arms as he dozed by the iron stove, and my memory of the Sholes & Glidden, which was fading.

6 - ,

Q W   I U O P

Z

A X &   N ? ;

Brister took my hand. His felt like bark. Outside, the sky was dark, but I saw in his face and in Elizabeth's as she held the candle to her watch that it was not to row us across the river that he'd disturbed our rest. He put his finger to his lips and whispered, "Listen!" I did and, in the distance, heard the baying of hounds that had been loosed on us. "Get your things! Hurry now!"

He went into the shed and returned with an empty feed sack containing bread, pears, and a jar of milk. He gave me a clean cloth. "If the baby starts to fuss, soak some milk with this rag and let him suckle it."

He blew out the candles and led us quietly to the riverbank, where a skiff was tied to the branch of a cottonwood. "Hurry!" he said again. We got into the boat and made for the channel where the current flowed swiftly toward the Gulf. The only sounds were the softly groaning tholes, disgruntled bullfrogs stirred up by Brister's oars, and the light slap of water against the prow. The crying of the dogs grew faint.

"An idea came to me in the night," he said. "The *Rufus J. Lackland* tied up at Wyanock Landing yesterday, five miles downriver. She'll be on her way again sometime this evening. If you manage to get aboard, you can get to New Orleans and then catch a train to New York."

We took heart.

"I pray no harm will come to you, Mr. Warwick, for helping us," said Susan earnestly.

Elizabeth muttered words I didn't catch. Margaret grabbed his hand and kissed it. He pulled it away and went on rowing. Had there been light enough to see his face, doubtless I'd have seen his embarrassment—his black skin notwithstanding.

"Before we get to the landing, I mean to row ashore and get you two blacked up." He pointed to Elizabeth and Susan.

"Whatever do you mean?" asked Elizabeth.

I couldn't tell if she was dismayed, horrified, or thrilled.

"Klansmen are everywhere in these parts. At Wyanock, they could be on the lookout for you all. If I black up Mrs. Stanton and Miss Susan, you can pass for colored servants of Miss Finch and her little sister." He turned to Elizabeth. "If you carry the boy, folks will think he's yours." What further confirmation of my son's negritude could I ask for? Little Martin was black—but he was not a bastard.

"I bore seven children, and I don't think it's fair to be burdened with an eighth at my time of life!" she complained.

"*I* will play mother," said Susan with the air of a martyr who plainly enjoys the role.

Brister bit the water with his oars, and the boat jumped toward New Orleans (as if four hundred miles of river weren't in the way). A mile or so above the landing, he slewed the boat to shore. He led us into a stand of pines and made a fire. With a piece of char, he blackened Susan's and Elizabeth's faces, necks, and wrists. "Lucky for you two, your hair lost its color." Susan's was gray, Elizabeth's white. He gave them each a bright rag to tie around their heads. Squinting at the result, he said, "Sisters, you look fine!" He reached into his sack and took out a shiny red dress. "Mrs.

Stanton, put this on—and don't pother! It belonged to my wife, who was taken in December. She was a big woman, like you."

Elizabeth held the dress at arm's length, as if expecting an uprising of moths. "Is this really necessary?"

"My Ida got married in that dress. She always said she wanted to be buried in it. I didn't see her sister—a slack-jawed, lopsided Louisiana cane cutter—switch it for a calico shift. Poor Ida was already in the ground when I caught Beulah wearing it. I made her take it off in the yard to shame her." Sensing Elizabeth's reluctance, he said, "Ida didn't die of something catching."

"Oh, give it to me!" Elizabeth took the dress and walked a short way into the woods in search of privacy. I could tell she was annoyed. To be at the mercy of a man's cunning, a negro man's at that, or to be eyed up and down like a heifer at a cattle show—I couldn't say which of the two she considered more humiliating.

"How do I look?" asked Elizabeth, coming out from behind a tree.

"Like the Whore of Babylon in blackface," crowed Susan.

"So long as no one can recognize me."

Brister gave each of the suffragists a pair of Ida's Sunday gloves to hide her white hands.

We started walking toward the skiff.

"Hold on, ladies!" said Brister. "This is as far as I dare. The landing's a mile off. Just stay on the towpath, and it will take you right to it. Get aboard the steamer soon as you can and keep out of sight till she gets under way."

We said our good-byes. Margaret wept—circus people are sentimental. Susan shook the old man's bony hand. Beguiled by Ida's dress, Elizabeth kissed the old man's grizzled cheek. Brister cleared his throat, climbed into his skiff, hoisted the patched and mended sail, and started back to French Fort.

"I feel like a croquet ball that is made to roll across the lawn by the tap of a mallet."

"Lizzie, you do talk nonsense sometimes!" said Susan with enough bite to core an apple.

"I'm most myself in my black silk dress; in blackface and red sateen, who knows what I shall become?"

"And who were you in your famous bloomers?"

"I've outgrown them as one does the mistaken ideals of her youth."

"Or for being overly fond of custard pies."

"Plump women are more admired than sticks like you!"

"Admired by whom?" Susan had treed her as a hound dog does a raccoon. To answer with the word *men* would have betrayed woman's sovereignty; *other women* could have made her seem reliant on the good opinion of her sex. To reply *myself* to Susan's question would have revealed her vanity.

Like a coon up a tree, Elizabeth hid behind her black mask. "By the time we get home to Mrs. Crockett's, I will be some other woman." She sighed.

"Well, I hope she doesn't snore!"

A steam whistle hooted in derision.

The towpath turned sharply toward the river, and the *Rufus J. Lackland* stood before us. During the war, she'd been a Confederate "cotton-clad." With battering rams of railroad iron and her bow packed with cotton bales to absorb the shock, she'd sunk Union gunboats on the Lower Mississippi.

Notice of her departure was tacked onto a board:

Leaves on SUNDAY, 13th inst., at 6 P.M.
MEMPHIS & NEW ORLEANS
PACKET BOAT

The first-class passenger packet RUFUS J. LACKLAND, S. PHILLIPS, master, is now receiving freight & will leave as above. For freight or passage, apply on board. This boat connects at Napoléon with regular packets for the Arkansas and White rivers & stops at Greenville, Vicksburg & Natchez. Bills of lading signed at office of the agents up to 4 o'clock the day of departure.

Margaret and I walked up the steamer's gangway. Elizabeth and Susan, who carried little Martin, followed at a respectful distance. Brister had warned us, "Don't talk like educated folks, misses, or you will give yourselves away. And, Miss Susan, I noticed you often have a sour face on you. If a white person sees it, you will be thrashed. Miss Ellen, you have got to act haughty to make people believe in this mummery." He'd addressed himself to Margaret last: "Child, try not to fuss and call attention to yourself." I do believe he never realized that Margaret was a grown woman.

At the ticket window, I nearly lost my nerve.

"Don't you have any baggage?" asked the purser.

"No, sir." Instantly, I regretted having shown him deference. I was masquerading as a fine lady, though a northern one.

"Not even a 'carpetbag'?" he asked, smirking.

"I do not." I tried to look down my nose at him, but my eyes crossed.

"Why's that?" he asked suspiciously.

"Our trunks were stolen," I blurted.

"Plenty of thieving niggers hereabouts."

Fortunately, the purser had not even glanced at "my negroes," who were unworthy of his notice. I doubted if their disguises or Margaret's subterfuge could have withstood his scrutiny. But then again, most of us see according to our expectations. He lectured a knot of sympathetic listeners who had gathered behind us on the innate depravity of the negro. Having emptied his duct of bile, he turned to me and said in a perfunctory voice, "That'll be four-fifty." Opening my purse, I was dismayed to find that my federal money had changed into Confederate notes. Their worthlessness notwithstanding, he stuffed them into his cash box.

We went below, locked ourselves in our cabin, and prepared to wait for six o'clock.

"It was all I could do to hold my tongue and not rip his

out of his rotten mouth!" said Susan, furious at the treatment we'd received from "a puffed-up specimen of meanness, worse than the worst plug ugly."

"He never so much as looked at me!" said Elizabeth in like temper.

"General Thumb would never have stood for it!" said Margaret, her green eyes moist with remembrance. "He would have stuck him with his sword stick."

While the women continued to air their resentment, I fell into that loveliest of phrases—a "brown study."

Questions of right and wrong are better left to parsons and judges, who are paid to answer them; however, I feel obliged to mention one question that clamored for an answer as I lay on my bunk with the baby in my arms. (Strange, that he was so well behaved! You might have thought him a cloth poppet.)

Should I keep the child, or find a decent black family to raise him?

I shook off my torpor and listened to the black-faced suffragists talk of trivial matters. Even noble minds will sometimes stoop to folly under nervous strain. I glimpsed my face in the mirror on the cabin wall and was heartened to see Ellen Finch looking back at me.

"It's nearly time for the boat to be getting under way," said Elizabeth, having glanced at her watch. "By 'time,' I mean what ordinary people experience going about their lives and not the fitful, skittish time we've been keeping ever since we left Grand Central."

Life, for me, had been governed by a very different

clock since my nightmare on the train from Sing Sing, the strange events at Dobbs Ferry, and the encounter with Alma Bridwell White in Zarephath. For me, time was neither straightforward nor dependable.

"I'm feeling peckish," said Susan. "What about you, Margaret?"

"I could eat a horse!"

The shrill voice of the *Rufus J. Lackland*'s steam whistle announced her departure. The cabin floor shook as the stern paddles chewed water that had first begun to flow from Lake Itasca ages before a regretful God scuttled His creation, all save an ark of refugees, who would prove to be no better than their ancestors. The instant before the paddles took purchase and the steamer lurched forward, possibility held sway over all the universe. The Mississippi River could have reversed its course, ceased to flow, or dried up in its bed. The boat could have taken wing and flown to the antipodes or to Missouri, where people are said to be skeptical. Martin II could have turned white, and I become a Chinese or a Cherokee. But nothing out of the ordinary occurred except that the packet, as ponderous as a hippopotamus, turned inelegantly in the channel and headed for its first stop, Napoléon, Arkansas, at eighteen knots. Soon the river's reaches would turn copper and tarnish into dusk. Late on the following night, we'd arrive in cosmopolitan New Orleans, where we would have less reason to be afraid.

We went up on the main deck, where supper was being served, and ate our fill of ham and oysters, rice and green beans, followed by ice cream and peach cobbler. I sipped a mint julep because it was expected of me, while Margaret drank lemonade and our two reluctant servants water. The male passengers nipped Kentucky bourbon, save for a traveler in Bibles, who took gin "because of its purity." Had Gallagher been there, his red face would have inched ever closer to his plate until it rested on the remains of his supper, with only an imbiber's snore to signify the presence of life or the absence of death, however one chooses to view the matter. As the boat steamed south, the sun was falling over Arkansas. Soon Tennessee would be overthrown by darkness. The Father of Waters would shine like quicksilver before it was quenched.

After supper, we yielded to the drowsiness that can steal over passengers on a riverboat, especially at night, when the day's rude noise has faded and the stern wheel's threshing and the water's lapping on the hull produce an unearthly calm. Passengers become subdued, as if in the presence of something that could be called "holy" but is usually mistaken for the workings of digestion. Drunk with love on such a night, Solomon sang to his beloved, whose belly was "like an heap of wheat set about with lilies," and Marc Antony, the Roman, became enamored of his Egypt as she floated down the Cydnus River, "her barge like a burnished throne."

On such a night, Lincoln rode through the streets of Washington to Ford's Theatre, happy that, at long last, peace was in the April air. On such a night at war's end, the grossly overloaded Steamship *Sultana* sank off Memphis, and 1,200 Union soldiers liberated from Andersonville

Prison drowned. They'd been packed into a boat meant to carry eighty-five passengers and crew. What Confederate captain Henry Wirz, the only officer, north or south, to be hanged for war crimes, had failed to accomplish, abetted by starvation, dysentery, and typhus, the Mississippi's icy runoff, the prisoners' enfeeblement, and the greed of Union officers Hatch and Mason did. (They were promised five dollars, COD, for every soldier delivered from captivity.) Time is often fragrant with desire, but more often, it is pregnant with disaster and stinks of death.

The lamps were lighted in the *Lackland*'s dining room. A blacked-up quartet sang "Old Aunt Jemima." Believing the song ridiculed negroes, the white passengers joined in gleefully, unaware that Billy Kersand, a black minstrel, had written the lyrics to make fun of the crackers, who'd have gone to any lengths to keep their negroes in perpetual servitude. "God damn 'Ape' Lincoln and his blue bellies!"

> My old missus promise me,
> Old Aunt Jemima, oh! oh! oh!
> When she died she'd set me free,
> Old Aunt Jemima, oh! oh! oh!
> She lived so long her head got bald,
> Old Aunt Jemima, oh! oh! oh!
> She swore she would not die at all,
> Old Aunt Jemima, oh! oh! oh!

Next, the *Lackland*'s lord of the revels introduced a troupe of "Ethiopian delineators," who portrayed three negroes in fancy dress, arguing over a watermelon during a performance of *La Dame blanche*.

When he pointed his baton at Elizabeth and Susan, they gasped in unison, fearing they'd been found out in spite of having enhanced Brister's charcoal daubing with greasepaint purloined from the Ethiopians' dressing room.

"Ladies and gentlemen," began the showman as urbanely as a cotillion caller. "It has come to my attention that two sophisticates of the art of minstrelsy are here with us tonight. I refer to those comedic sisters in blackface who have performed humorous sketches of colored life for audiences throughout the South—Lizzie and Sue! Maybe they can be persuaded to regale us with one of their famous delineations."

Uplifted by a tide of applause, Elizabeth and Susan were swept up and deposited onto the stage. By some mischievous wiggle of fate (as might be read by Madame Singleton), two white suffragists masquerading as black maids had turned into a pair of white minstrels in blackface.

"Ladies, be seated," said the master of minstrelsy in a sequined voice as he assumed the role of a straight-faced Interlocutor flanked by Tambo and Mr. Bones. Helpless to do otherwise, Elizabeth and Susan sat in the "end men's" chairs. "We will commence with the overture!" he announced as he tapped his baton on a jug of white lightning.

A fiddler, a trombonist, and a banjo player went to work on a ludicrous air until, at a sign from Mr. Interlocutor, it squeaked and wheezed to a stop.

"Esteemed passengers of the *Rufus J. Lackland*, it's time for some monkeyshines!"

> MR. INTERLOCUTOR: How are you this fine evening, Sister Bones? *(No reply)* Why, what's wrong, Sister? You look down in the mouth.
>
> SISTER BONES *(Susan)*: I sorry.
>
> MR. INTERLOCUTOR: What about?
>
> SISTER BONES: I sorry I was born a slave in America.

Elizabeth, in the role of Sister Tambo, rattled a tambourine against her knee.

> MR. INTERLOCUTOR: Why, didn't you hear the news?
>
> SISTER BONES: What news might dat be?
>
> MR. INTERLOCUTOR: Mr. Lincoln emancipated the slaves!
>
> SISTER TAMBO: He sure did! The massa hisself read the Emasculation Proclamation over da heads of da colored men. Then dey all lined up in da yard and got demselves emasculated.
>
> SISTER BONES: I don' know nothin' 'bout dat. *Our* massa read us the Maceration Proclamation, and den we all got ourselves macerated.
>
> SISTER TAMBO: I never heard 'bout no Maceration Proclamation befo'.
>
> MR. INTERLOCUTOR *(Ignoring Sister Tambo)*: So you were macerated.
>
> SISTER BONES: Right down to da bones!

Susan clacked a bone castanet.

MR. INTERLOCUTOR: What did he do with all those macerated bones?

SISTER BONES: He carved little Nativity figures outta dem to set under his Christmas tree.

MR. INTERLOCUTOR: Your master must be a Christian gentleman.

SISTER BONES: He whips da Devil outta us for our souls' sake.

SISTER TAMBO: What your massa do wid all da leftover dark meat?

SISTER BONES: He boiled it up with some greens and ate it.

SISTER TAMBO: Dass a awful way to treat colored folk!

SISTER BONES: Pshaw! He saved us da most nourishin' part.

MR. INTERLOCUTOR: And what might the most nourishing part of a darky be, Sister Bones?

SISTER BONES: OUR HATRED!

Elizabeth rattled the tambourine and laughed hysterically while Susan clacked.

No one in the dining room could decide whether he'd been mocked or treated to a sophisticated "coon show" such as people saw in the big cities. Although nobody clapped, neither did anyone hiss, and the supper plates weren't shied in remonstrance at the two smart aleck ladies in blackface.

Martin slept through the entire evening. To this day, I believe he was under a spell.

The next day, we were ignored by the other passengers, who glanced suspiciously at Susan and Elizabeth, who had rid their faces of greasepaint. The *Lackland* steamed toward Vicksburg, having stopped in the early-morning hours at Greenville, whose tolling bells had not disturbed our sleep. The Lower Mississippi offered a myriad of picturesque scenes, but we took no notice of them. We were like traveling salesmen for whom novelty had faded and, with it, curiosity. My interest—and the story's—lay elsewhere. I will mention, however, the gentleman we met on the last day aboard the *Lackland*.

He was gaunt, his face drawn and of an unhealthy color. It was plain to see that he was gravely ill. He wore a woolen skullcap. I didn't recognize him as the man whose photograph I'd seen in history books and, recently, on the wall of the Spottswood jailhouse, desecrated by brown spittle. Southerners despised him because during Reconstruction he had enforced the Fourteenth and Fifteenth amendments and scourged the Ku Klux Klan with federal troops.

"Ladies," he said politely, although he did not rise from the deck chair on which he sat. He held a book of poetry in his gnarled hands. Despite the day's heat, he wore a shawl around his frail shoulders. Had it not been for the beard, I would have mistaken him for a pinched and aged spinster. Squinting because of the glare on the water behind us, he looked at Elizabeth and Susan. "I heard about your performance. It took guts. Had I a proper hat on, it would be off to you both."

"Thank you, sir," said Susan. Although shrunken, the

man had a gravity that could have made my womb wander. Acknowledging his authority, Susan bent her stiff back in a curtsy—perhaps the first and only one in her long, unyielding life.

"It's kind of you to say so," said Elizabeth. And then astonishment registered on her face. "Why, you're President Grant!"

He smiled wanly. "The president—and also the man—that was. I've nearly finished both my terms. Forgive me if I don't stand. I'm not up to snuff today."

We called to a steward to bring three additional chairs. Margaret had stayed in our cabin, along with Martin. The steward's having ignored our request, we dragged chairs across the deck ourselves and arranged them about the former president.

"I've been reading Herman Melville's *Battle-Pieces and Aspects of the War*. He gave it to me last year, signed in his own hand. It's not a book I enjoy, any more than I do Mathew Brady's pictures. It was a bloody business! Sometimes I wish I had stayed home in Galena." The general read a stanza from the book:

> And horror the sodden valley fills,
>   And the spire falls crashing in the town,
> I muse upon my country's ills—
> The tempest bursting from the waste of Time . . .

"A most bloody, barbarous business—necessary though it was. Not like the Mexican War or the war against the

Mormons or the war that's coming against Spain. America seems helpless not to engage in lunatic adventures."

"Most of the horrors are still to come," said Susan, eyes clouded like an oracle's. "Thank God we won't live to see them."

"You look tired, Mr. President," said Elizabeth maternally.

"I am worn to the bone, Mrs. Stanton. "Ladies, I have been picked clean. If not for Sam Clemens, I would draw my last breath in the poorhouse."

"You know our true identities?" asked Susan, surprised.

"I would know your famous red shawl anywhere, Miss Anthony."

He shut his eyes, and his breathing became labored.

"Can I get you anything?" I asked, for the man looked half-dead.

"No thank you, my dear. In a minute, I'll be right as rain—unless the Massa comes and takes my breath away."

"What has brought you here?" asked Susan gently.

"I want to see Vicksburg again," rasped Grant in a voice ruined by too many cigars. "Once upon a time, I had plenty to do there."

In 1863, Major General Grant laid siege to Vicksburg with a bombardment that lasted forty-eight days. His batteries shelled the town from across the Mississippi until hardly a house or building was left standing. Thirty-three thousand Confederate gray backs were encircled by 77,000 blue bellies. The townspeople lived in caves dug out of the hills' soft yellow clay and ate rat meat after they had run out of cats and dogs.

"They sat in caves and ate boiled shoes served by slaves on linen tablecloths," said Grant, eyes glazed in reverie. "We blasted Vicksburg all to Hell. Three thousand rebels died of scurvy, malaria, dysentery, and starvation." The general shook his head, and we saw disbelief shadow his ravaged face. "People are beyond understanding. I expect not even the Almighty can make head or tails of us. We are His folly—His greatest one."

"The Greatest Show on Earth!" I had the uncanny sensation that someone had spoken through me like a ventriloquist throwing his voice through a dummy.

The two women looked at me askance, but the general concurred: "You are right, young woman. We are performers in a spectacle." He brooded a moment and then asked sadly, "Is it likely that our enemies will ever love us? In any case, I shall see Vicksburg again before I die."

"What do you expect to find?" I asked. I spoke to this old man with a sincerity I had not felt since my child was taken from me. I don't know why that should have been the case, unless I sensed that we two had been granted the dispensation sometimes given to the sick that allows them to see clearly.

"Something I lost, maybe," he replied with a contemplative air. "Or something I might find that would make me less afraid."

"What're you afraid of?" asked Susan, trying to conceal a pity that would have offended him.

"The future, of course."

"Yours?" asked Elizabeth.

Grant laughed painfully because of his throat. "Mine is all used up, or nearly so. You must excuse me, but I'm tired, and my voice is about to give out."

"Forgive us," I said, like an inquisitor to a man stretched on the rack, which the general's deck chair did, in fact, resemble.

"Good-bye, ladies."

We didn't see him get off the boat at Vicksburg. We were below, in our cabin, when night fell across the Delta.

The Commodore

WE BELIEVED THAT WE'D BE SAFE in a city more interested in commerce than the lunacy of racist hooligans dressed in sheets. But we hadn't counted on the fury unleashed at Memphis or the confederacy of dunces up and down the river, nor could we have known that the Spottswood sheriff had choked the truth out of his wife and denounced her to the Grand Cyclops. Brister Warwick had also given us away moments before the ghouls lynched and burned him at French Fort. Brister was no more to blame for our trouble in New Orleans than the rope around his neck was for his death or the match for his immolation.

No sooner had the *Lackland* lowered her gangway than Elizabeth and Susan were seized by three cigar-chewing zealots who had sworn before the Grand Turk and the Grand Cyclops to lynch the suffragists who had defiled the sacred regalia of the Klan, upset its secret conventicle, and stolen its child sacrifice. Keeping to the shadows, I followed them while Margaret hid little Martin inside a custom's shed. The Klansmen soon found a beam on which to hoist the objects of their enmity. Excited by the prospect of seeing two loudmouthed northern women strung up, a crowd of wharf rats gathered and ignited a row of smudge pots, which cast a lurid light upon the scene. Eyes bright with malice, they sang:

> Wheel about, and turn about, and do just so;
> Every time I wheel about, I jump Jim Crow.

Bound hand and foot and their necks in nooses, my friends were invited to speak their last words. I couldn't help thinking of Mary Surratt on the scaffold, whose own valediction had been "Don't let me fall."

Elizabeth might have been on a lecture platform, facing an audience of reasonable men and women, so calm did she seem as she addressed the jeering mob:

> We declare our faith in the principles of self-government; our full equality with man in natural rights; that woman was made first for her own happiness, with the absolute right to herself—to all the opportunities and advantages life affords, for her complete development; and we deny that dogma of the centuries, incorporated in the codes of all nations—that woman was made for man.

She had neither begged for mercy nor protested against the indefensible act to which she herself was about to fall victim. I wept in admiration, forgiving her for the small acts of vainglory that had annoyed me.

Susan concluded the declaration, her stern voice like a hatchet: "We ask of our rulers, at this hour, no special favors, no special privileges, no special legislation. We ask justice, we ask equality, we ask that all the civil and political rights that belong to citizens of the United States, be guaranteed to us and our daughters forever." She'd spoken above the heads of the crowd she scorned to the men in Washington who even now, in 1904, have not unpacked their ears of chaff or their hearts of rubbish.

A Klansman replied, "Ladies, we mean to hang you the same way we would a man—with a rope. So you can't complain of being treated unfairly."

The crowd sniggered and then shrieked in enmity, "Hang the bitches! Hang the bitches! Hang the bitches!" I was amazed to hear the women shout as loudly against their sisters as did the men.

Offered filthy handkerchiefs, my two suffragists declined to be blindfolded.

"To Hell with you both!" snarled a man who, by his clothes, could have been a clerk in a law office or a minor customs official. He was ordinary—someone you could picture tipping his hat to a lady in the street more readily than knotting a noose for her neck.

"If we should find ourselves in Hell, we'll wave our handkerchiefs as the devils drag you, kicking and screaming, to its most infernal region," said Susan, visibly pleased by her remark.

"If in Heaven, we'll pity you, since not a damned one of you fiends will make it past the gates," said Elizabeth unflappably.

"Speak for yourself, Lizzie!" countered Susan with her usual acerbity. "I would not waste a tear to pity or a gob of spit to quench the thirst of these polecats!"

From my covert behind a stack of cotton bales, I shivered in fear for my two friends.

"Ladies and gentlemen, we will commence with the overture," said a man who resembled the master of ceremonies on board the *Lackland*. In answer, a fiddler, a trombonist, and a banjo player lurched into the snide tune I'd heard on the river two nights before. The overture having concluded, he sat on a barrel head and resumed the role of Mr. Interlocutor.

> MR. INTERLOCUTOR: Without further ado, Sister Bones, I wish you adieu. May you macerate eternally.

He put a noose around Susan's neck and tightened it.

"We shall go up or down together," she managed to say before rising into the night air (an intoxicating mix of jasmine, musk, and tar), her feet kicking in her high-buttoned shoes.

> Possum up a Gum-Tree,
> Up she go, up she go!

The voice that had vexed and stung congressmen, nabobs, and the remonstrants of her own sex may have gone silent, but the red shawl set at defiance the rampant beast that is a mob.

MR. INTERLOCUTOR: Without further aside, Sister Tambo, I bid you good-bye. May you choke on your words eternally.

Elizabeth inched upward as a man hauled on the rope. Two others from the mob lent a hand, and she was quickly lofted.

Pully hawl, pully hawl,
Scream and bawl, scream and bawl!

In the glow of the smudge pots, Elizabeth was gloriously illumined. Gilded by the light, her face showed her contempt and her triumph. Had Elijah's fiery chariot descended from the heavens and carried her off to the Rapture, I would not have been surprised. Lincoln, Frederick Douglass, John Brown—you are one of them, my dear Mrs. Cady Stanton! You and Miss Susan!

"*Non Silba Sed Anthar*!" proclaimed the Klansmen in the pig Latin of their childish and murderous cult.

I was about to fling myself on the mob and cut down the dangling suffragists with Brister's shears, when a noise like rain on a tin roof scattered the rats. Cautiously raising my head like a turkey at a turkey shoot, I peeked and saw a submarine lying against the pier, its Gatling gun raking the wharf with grapeshot. In an instant, I'd cut the hangmen's ropes. Like two fish gasping in asphyxia, Elizabeth and Susan drew a rattling breath in unison and opened their eyes on the star-spangled sky of a Mississippi Delta night.

"How do you feel, Lizzie?" asked Susan.

"My neck feels longer!" she replied querulously, fingering it as a bassoonist would the keys of her instrument.

We were joined by Margaret and the child, and together we hurried to the submarine half-hidden in a cloud of steam.

"Quick, ladies!" urged a sailor leaning over the iron deck to hand us on board. "We must not give them time to drop their nets." He helped us through an open hatch. Elizabeth caused an anxious moment, but with a final effort, she wriggled though the iron collar, tearing her sateen dress on the rivets. While the sailor screwed down the hatch cover, we descended a ladder into a gaslit interior. Was I surprised by this novelty? I'd lost the capacity for astonishment, not all at once, as a woman loses her virginity, but gradually, as she grows tired of her husband or her life.

Elizabeth called to a fine-looking sailor, "Young man, I am feeling peckish."

"I'll have a word with the cook, ma'am." He doffed his white cap and smiled, his mouth full of handsome teeth.

"A hunger of the mind can only be appeased by a well-nourished brain," she explained.

A gentleman wearing a Vandyke and gold epaulets on

his blue flannel escorted us to a commodious stateroom decorated in a circus motif.

"Why, it's Mr. Barnum!" cried Susan.

"Welcome to the *Fiji Mermaid*! Except for my stateroom, it resembles Nemo's *Nautilus* to a tee. And please address me as 'Commodore' until we're ashore again. Hello, my dear!" he said, kissing Margaret's dainty hand. "Your friends send their love."

"We're happy to see you, Commodore!" exclaimed Susan, who once had been scornful of his vulgarity.

"How on earth did you know we were in New Orleans?" asked Elizabeth.

He laid his finger aside his nose. "Never underestimate Madame Singleton. She saw your plight." With the same finger, he tapped his forehead. "You must look beyond the requisite tawdriness of her stock-in-trade. She's a gifted medium. Until its demise, she was an honorary member of the British National Association of Spiritualists. The eminent 'Poughkeepsie Seer,' Andrew Jackson Davis, paid her homage in his book *The Fountain with Jets of New Meanings*."

"What about the Fox sisters?"

"I was suckered."

"Where are the clowns?" I asked.

"You can shoot a clown from a cannon, but you can't entrust him with a submarine. The crew is comprised of eminent yachtsmen whose only weakness is a fondness for grog. The bottle will be passed at eight bells." He glanced sharply at the suffragists. "Remember, you two, this is not a temperance hall."

Barnum shot the cuffs of his uniform, cut by the son of the tailor who had sewn Cornelius Vanderbilt's nautical attire when he had been known as the Commodore. The tycoon had owned a splendid yacht in his day, but he couldn't take it with him onto the waters above the firmament or the lake of fire far below it. In the opinion of many, the ruthless skinflint deserved an eternity of brimstone and castor oil.

The underwater boat slipped toward the Gulf. Its steam boiler burbled like a teapot, the crankshaft thumped, the miraculously restored Prince Albert shaving mug trembled as the screw churned the water into froth, scattering the little fishes.

A fish that must have been prodigious rubbed against the *Fiji Mermaid*'s hull.

"What in the world was that?" asked Elizabeth, helping Susan to her feet.

"Moby Dick, I expect." He gazed at the brass-bezeled instruments. His voice was tinged with sadness. "Melville, also, is smitten by phantoms."

Barnum escorted us through his cigar-shaped domain. The decks, cabins, and passages appeared to multiply impossibly, and I was reminded of Bellevue Hospital after my encounter with a maniac. I mentioned it to the impresario.

"The architecture of the madhouse and the circus are quite similar."

His answer startled me. "Is this a circus?" My glance took in a table heaped with charts showing the location of the world's forgotten chimeras, monsters, and beasts.

"One or the other, or both."

"Commodore, was the Voice that routed the Invisible Empire yours?"

"Yes." I saw that the admission gave him pleasure. "A nice effect, don't you think? It was produced by an augmenter. Edison ginned it up for me. It will be a tremendous addition to the Traveling Museum, Menagerie, Caravan and Hippodrome."

"It was *you* I saw getting on the caboose at Grand Central!"

"Barnum, like God, is ubiquitous."

In the wardroom where we assembled for dinner, Elizabeth inquired, "Commodore, how long will it take to reach New York?"

He smiled indulgently. "Who can say how long a dream lasts? But I must be in the city in time to lead the elephants across the New York and Brooklyn Bridge to assure the public of its integrity. That of the moral sort, I leave to theologians and philosophers. I promised those two great cities a parade, and the newspaper scribblers will turn out in droves to witness this latest coup de théâtre of Phineas T. Barnum and . . ." He looked me in the eye while he finished his boast: "the Greatest Show on Earth!" I had uttered those five words to President Grant on the deck of the *Rufus J. Lackland*. Barnum winked, as if we two were conspirators in a plot whose purpose would be forever unknown to me.

He wiped his lips on a napkin embroidered with the word *Excelsior* and said, "A terrible waste of life that could have been avoided if the mayors had let me test the bridge before it was opened to the public."

He was referring to the stampede on Decoration Day, 1883; two opposing juggernauts of pedestrians in their thousands met midway on the span. Twelve people were trampled to death, and many others injured in the panic incited by a woman who screamed, "The bridge is falling down!"

Barnum rang his crystal goblet with a gold spoon smeared with sherbet and invited us to toast America. "The woebegone and the small-minded say that America is nearly finished; her imperial days are fast coming to an end. We had our moment, and the moment has passed. In the future, it will be said of us that we were alive in the age of America's greatness and fortunate to have been so, for that age and that greatness are like a book closed forever and shrouded in dust.

"My reply to the skeptics and cynics, the defeatists and naysayers, is that America is only beginning, that a continent is waiting for us to conquer and bestride. Do you believe that the frontier is closed because a few scholars say that it is so—men who have ventured no farther than the margins of their books? Do you believe that the American character will content itself with land north of the Río Grande, when the whole of Mexico remains an unplucked fruit? We will take Mexico, and hardly stopping for breath, we will take all the territory south of it that is worth having. The more we take, the larger our appetite will become, until the land beyond the Great Lakes is absorbed into the nation's growing body. Natural science tells us that the more massive an object, the more powerful is its sway over lesser objects. America will possess that massiveness, and she will exert a force far stronger than that of any foreign power. We will take Cuba. We will take the Philippines. We will take Hawaii and the other islands of the Pacific and the South Atlantic. We will take Japan and China. America is destined to be the Greatest Show on Earth. Our borders will be boundless, our wealth incalculable; and our end will come only when the Earth itself has perished. Ladies, I give you America!"

I could tell that Elizabeth and Susan were reluctant to drink to the health of a country so much at variance with their principles. Susan opened her mouth, no doubt to ask Barnum what place women would occupy in the glorious epoch, but she said nothing. I wish I could say that we refused to toast the America that Barnum, in his megalomania, foresaw. We were weary of argument. I wanted to take Martin home to Maiden Lane and wait for news of Franklin. I hoped he was on his way from San Francisco with the promise of a job and not in Sing Sing, taking an icy shower as punishment for a violent act of anarchy, or on a cold mortuary table in the Dead House on First Avenue. We emptied our glasses but forbore to break them against the bulkhead in emulation of the showman's bravado. At that moment, our nerves would've given way at the sound of shattering glass.

Leaning back in the captain's chair, Barnum confided in us his grand ambition: "I dream of a circus without tents or high wires, elephants or chariots, scientific fencers or contortionists, bareback riders or trombonists, peanuts or eccentrics—all but *mon petit chou* Margaret, who is indispensable to Barnum." She nodded her head in acknowledgment. "A circus that originates in the brain of Barnum, whose thoughts Madame Singleton and Eugenia Roux would transmit to impressionable minds throughout the universe. Barnum would sit in his Moorish palace, which exists, though it was reduced to ashes almost thirty years ago, and astonish the world with a spectacle beyond the wildest dreams of Manius Valerius Maximus or Tarquin the Proud. The Rape of the Sabine Women at Circus Maximus was small potatoes compared to what Barnum can conceive."

"Women have made little progress since the Romans lorded it over the ancient world," said Elizabeth with something akin to dejection in her voice, rare for one of the great optimists of the age.

"Ah, but Barnum adores women, and in his dreams, he will exalt them!"

At the heart of the submarine, the great engine spun a silver thread of sound into a radiant cocoon bathed in Pythagoras's music of the spheres. I closed my eyes and opened them. Had the ravaged oyster shells and the puddles of lemon sherbet in the spoons not been replaced by ham and eggs, I could've sworn that I had merely blinked. We women sat and rubbed our eyes and gazed in wonder at the table set for breakfast.

"I must have fallen asleep," said Susan groggily.

"My watch stopped," said Elizabeth, winding the stem.

"You were saying," said Barnum, his head turned to Margaret.

"What news of my friends?"

He put down his fork. "Mrs. Stoner has a new snake. Miss Etta has a new trick. Poor Mattie Elliott dislocated her hip. Eugenia Roux's cold is no better. Mr. Dode is in Bellevue, suffering from delusions."

"And Gallagher?" asked Susan, showing her teeth.

"Sacked."

"Good!" said Susan.

"He was overzealous in his duties."

A boatswain's whistle shrilled.

"We've arrived in New York Bay. Shall we go up on desk?"

We stood in the bow, grateful to breathe fresh air. I licked my lip and tasted brine. How delicious! I thought. We steamed past Castle Garden, where emigrants waited with their trunks to be admitted to a much greater and graver circus than any hippodrome, one that will require them to jump through hoops of fire, snatch a living with their teeth, and walk a tightrope high above the most desperate straits.

We disembarked at Canal Street and were free to take

up our lives once more (as free as women could be, which was hardly at all). We had one last duty to perform for our benefactor: to ride in his parade across the Brooklyn Bridge. He'd saved us, and we couldn't well refuse him. I remembered his prophecy of the American century to come as a dream that dissolved on the morning air.

On Saturday, May 17, 1884, P. T. Barnum, having exchanged his commodore's uniform for that of a ring-master, kept his promise to his public and led a menag-erie from Manhattan to Brooklyn. Jumbo, together with twenty lesser elephants, and a caravan of camels sauntered across the Roeblings' magnificent bridge, followed by Robinson's Celebrated Band. Elizabeth, Susan, Margaret, and I sat regally on the backs of four Indian elephants. Elizabeth had bought a turban and commissioned a pair of Turkish pants for the occasion. From on high, she nod-ded graciously to the spectators, who cheered her lustily, as if, for more than thirty years, she had not been the object of their scorn. Less flamboyant, Susan wore her gray dress and scowled at the multitude from the shadow of her coal-scuttle bonnet. Draped over the side of her elephant, a red banner demanded VOTES FOR WOMEN. Having shown great courage, my suffragists had a right to their eccentric-ities. Sober-sided Emerson had enjoyed pulling pranks, and in his day, clodhopper Thoreau would dance like a man visited by a fit of ecstasy.

Midway across the prodigious span of steel and stone, I seemed to see Herman Melville and Mr. James standing arm in arm.

As we crossed into Brooklyn, Edison photographed the spectacle from the roof of the old ferry house. Look closely at the picture, and you'll see four women perched on lumbering pachyderms. Elizabeth Cady Stanton is singing the women's anthem "Daughters of Freedom," Susan B. Anthony is pretending to be displeased by Barnum's folly, Margaret Fuller Hardesty is blowing kisses to the crowd, and Ellen Finch is gazing at little Martin asleep in the crook of his father's arm.

One Last Shuffle & Good Night

MAY 2, 1904, THE PRESIDIO, SAN FRANCISCO

Doctors are gentlemen,
and gentlemen's hands are clean.

—Dr. Charles Meigs, obstetrician,
Jefferson Medical College,
at Philadelphia, Pennsylvania

TWENTY YEARS AGO, I LOST MY WITS to childbed fever, much less common now that the nabobs of medicine have acknowledged Pasteur's discovery that pullulating matter and not miasma spreads infection. At the time of my lying-in, obstetricians delivered one baby on the heels of the next, their hands unwashed and their frock coats stiff with gore. Women might have been laboring in a sty instead of a hospital. In one, I was delivered of my own small vitality, squalling with pent-up rage against the assumption of an existence that was doomed to end. I expelled my child into a pair of gentleman's hands rudely tugging at my womb, a violence that caused it to wander into hysteria and madness. (I never mentioned my wandering womb to Mr. James, who would have bullied me into describing every nuance of sensation that I had experienced, for the sake of his literary ambition.)

This recounting I have undertaken, like the agony attendant on creation, with its elements of shame and folly, is for my lost son. Martin, I never saw you! For all I know—or care!—you were a mulatto babe gotten on me by one of God's black angels. All this long time, I have been yearning for you. The cards are against us, shuffle them as we will! I have been apostrophizing a ghost.

I look out the window onto Golden Gate Park. Beyond its green sward and eucalyptus trees, the ocean wets the Orient's ragged hem and our own. Its contrary motions are regulated by the moon, which is said to be feminine. The resolution of contrarieties in nature comforts me.

I hear your father at the door. With an ink-stained hand, he will take one of mine and quietly—he is a silent man—wait with me by the window for the coming of the night.

A Note to Readers

I DO NOT CLAIM TO HAVE WRITTEN A NOVEL about Elizabeth Cady Stanton and Susan B. Anthony, great and necessary American women as they continue to be. Although they are alive in every page of the book, they are no more its subject than Henry James, P. T. Barnum, Herman Melville, Jacob Riis, or Alma Bridwell White, figures in Ellen Finch's dream of late-nineteenth-century America. I wrote of the nightmare that was, and is, America for the disenfranchised and powerless. How better to describe it than from inside a febrile mind? Ellen saw through a glass darkly and knew it to be the truth. How better to portray race relations in America in her day and ours than as a minstrel show? The section headings "Overture," "Cakewalk," "Intermission," "Olio," and "One Last Shuffle & Good Night" are intended to suggest that detestable, but hugely popular, theatrical form of the nineteenth century and early twentieth, which did much to engrain racial stereotypes in the national consciousness.

I ask the pardon of students of, and activists in, the American woman's movement for sometimes finding comedy where none was to be found. One of my purposes in writing the books of the American Novels series (*American Follies* is the seventh) is to humanize those who have left the turbulence of public and private life behind them and gone into the silence where great women and men can become mere reputations, legends, and sacred emblems. Humankind is best served by human beings—glorious and inglorious.

I have taken a novelist's liberties with the biographer's truth. For example, at the time of my story, Mrs. Stanton and Miss Anthony were not in America. Also, while they worked on the early volumes of the *History of Woman Suffrage* (aided by the radical suffragists Matilda Joslyn Gage and Ida Husted), they stayed at Mrs. Stanton's home in Tenafly, New Jersey, and not in Murray Hill. I quoted from Stanton and Gage's incendiary *Woman's Bible*, which was not published until 1895 and resulted in the former's being disavowed by many of her allies, who viewed the book as either a sacrilege or a distraction from the immediate business of obtaining rights for women. I allowed the two suffragists of my story greater familiarity than was the case; in public and even in their correspondence, Susan referred to Elizabeth as "Mrs. Stanton." Frequently, I treated them as if their views on how the cause could be advanced were interchangeable; they were not.

Although I have occasionally brought forward or pushed back events in Mrs. Stanton's and Miss Anthony's lives, to my knowledge I have not referenced historical events that occurred after 1904, the year of Ellen Finch's narration. There are two exceptions: The Klan did not adopt the white robe and hood until the second decade of the twentieth century, when D. W. Griffith's infamous

Birth of a Nation and the advent of mail-order catalogues standardized the image that has come down to the present day. (While writing the Memphis section, I had in mind Philip Guston's Klansmen paintings.) As for the second exception, Alma Bridwell White, founder and bishop of the Pillar of Fire Church in Zarephath, New Jersey, was a zealot of the Klan during the 1920s and 1930s. (At that time, New Jersey had sixty thousand Klan members, more than Louisiana, Alabama, or Tennessee.)

In its telling, Ellen Finch's story smacks more of Barnum and Mark Twain than Stanton and Anthony. Both of those men found a truth about our kind in the grotesque and the absurd. Ellen stumbled on it as the result of a postpartum infection following the birth of her son, Martin. (Whether he was stillborn or is a figment of Ellen's imagination, I leave to the reader to decide.) Delirium is only another lens through which to view the world. What is seen and heard under its influence may have a dreadful significance—and truth—all its own.

In "The Solitude of Self," the farewell address to the movement she helped to found, Mrs. Stanton posed this question: "Who, I ask you, can take, dare take on himself the rights, the duties, the responsibilities of another human soul?" Although it was meant to admonish men to respect woman's sovereignty, we can, from our vantage, reply that Elizabeth Cady Stanton and Susan B. Anthony dared to take responsibility for disadvantaged human beings. We can only admire their courage and compassion.

Acknowledgments

I RELIED ON LORI D. GINZBERG's fair-minded and fascinating biography *Elizabeth Cady Stanton: An American Life* for information concerning significant events in the American woman's rights movement and, in particular, its two celebrities, Elizabeth Cady Stanton and Susan B. Anthony, whose complex personalities I have attempted to capture despite the exaggerations of a satirical novel. The words spoken in the novel by Stanton and Anthony are largely of my own invention. Stanton's invidious comparison of women's non-existent right to vote with the rights of black, "lunatic," and "idiot" males of the time is borrowed from one of her many writings on the subject. The second and third paragraphs of her otherwise-fictional letter to Julia Ward Howe were drawn from Stanton's *The Woman's Bible*. The passage beginning "If a woman finds it hard to bear the oppressive laws of a few Saxon Fathers" is also hers. So, too, are her interrogatories to the New York State legislature concerning infanticide. Stanton's and Anthony's "last words" in New Orleans were taken from the former's "Declaration of Rights of the Women of the United States." Students of the woman's movement may recognize—and pardon—other instances of my "appropriation," which are on behalf of the continuing and universal struggle for equality.

In addition, I consulted Laurie Robertson-Lorant's *Melville* and David McCullough's *The Great Bridge*. For the structure and vocabulary of a minstrel show, I referred to Brander Matthew's *A Book About the Theatre*, published in 1916.

I credit Emily Holmes Coleman's extraordinary novel *The Shutter of Snow* (1930) with having made me aware of the complex delusional world created by puerperal fever and, because of her brave mining of her own temporary insanity, its literary and comic possibilities. (That remark would have infuriated Mrs. Stanton and Miss Anthony, were they still among us, and may well incense every living woman who has born a child. Having made it, I am no better than Henry James, who was curious about Ellen's wandering womb!)

I remain indebted to Bellevue Literary Press, especially to Erika Goldman, its publisher and editorial director, for having given a home to my American novels. My thanks, as well, to Jerome Lowenstein, M.D., founding publisher; Elana Rosenthal, former associate editor; Molly Mikolowski, publicist; Joe Gannon, production and design consultant; and Carol Edwards, my perspicacious copyeditor. My gratitude to my wife, Helen, is as constant as her support during the past fifty years.

ABOUT THE AUTHOR

Norman Lock is the award–winning author of novels, short fiction, and poetry, as well as stage, radio, and screenplays. His most recent books are the short story collection *Love Among the Particles* and six previous books in The American Novels series: *The Boy in His Winter*, a reenvisioning of Mark Twain's classic *The Adventures of Huckleberry Finn*, which Scott Simon of NPR *Weekend Edition* said, "make[s] Huck and Jim so real you expect to get messages from them on your iPhone"; *American Meteor*, an homage to Walt Whitman named a Firecracker Award finalist and *Publishers Weekly* Best Book of the Year; *The Port-Wine Stain*, featuring Edgar Allan Poe, which was also a Firecracker Award finalist; *A Fugitive in Walden Woods*, a tale that introduced readers to Henry David Thoreau in a book Barnes & Noble selected as a "Must-Read Indie Novel"; *The Wreckage of Eden*, a story evoking the life and artistry of Emily Dickinson; and *Feast Day of the Cannibals*, featuring Herman Melville in a dark tale of ambition and the secrets of the heart.

Lock has won The Dactyl Foundation Literary Fiction Award, *The Paris Review* Aga Khan Prize for Fiction, and has been longlisted for the Simpson/Joyce Carol Oates Prize. He has also received writing fellowships from the New Jersey State Council on the Arts, the Pennsylvania Council on the Arts, and the National Endowment for the Arts. He lives in Aberdeen, New Jersey, where he is at work on the next books of The American Novels series.

BELLEVUE LITERARY PRESS is devoted to publishing
literary fiction and nonfiction at the intersection of
the arts and sciences because we believe that science and the
humanities are natural companions for understanding the
human experience. With each book we publish, our goal is to
foster a rich, interdisciplinary dialogue that will forge new tools
for thinking and engaging with the world.

To support our press and its mission, and for our full catalogue
of published titles, please visit us at blpress.org.

BELLEVUE LITERARY PRESS

New York